The Amoveo Legend

UNCLAIMED

SARA HUMPHREYS

Cover design by Jamie Warren
Photography by Jon Zychowski
Model: Steve Moriarty

Published by Sourcebooks Casablanca, an imprint of Sourcebooks, Inc.
P. O. Box 4410, Naperville, Illinois 60567-4410
(630) 961-3900
Fax: (630) 961-2168
www.sourcebooks.com

Printed and bound in the United States of America
VP 10 9 8 7 6 5 4 3 2 1

"I can no other answer make, but, thanks, and thanks."

—William Shakespeare

For my readers.

Chapter 1

"OKAY, PAL," TATIANA SAID EVENLY AS SHE STROKED the puppy's coat and carried him to the exam room. "I know you're not going to like this, but you need some stitches."

Bumping the door open with her backside, she placed the puppy on the table. He lay quietly and timidly, watching her with those soulful brown eyes as she gathered the supplies she needed.

Tatiana found the poor thing on the side of the road, but she'd felt his energy signature—red with pain and anguish—before she ever saw him. The only good thing about being half Amoveo was her ability to connect with animals on a psychic level. It made her an extremely effective veterinarian and had her patients' owners calling her an animal whisperer.

It wasn't that she actually spoke to them or that she could hear them speak with words—it was more like the ability to feel what the animals were feeling. Tatiana was able to sense their emotions and in turn could send the animal soothing energy waves. It allowed her to connect with them on a deeper level, which made the animals more willing to let her treat them.

Tatiana made quick work of cleaning up the little beagle as he responded to her calming energy, lying perfectly still while she sutured and dressed his wound. He licked her hand as she finished, and though she sensed gratitude in his energy waves, she also saw it in those gorgeous eyes.

She could connect with all animals but had an affinity for dogs, which was probably from being part of the Timber Wolf Clan. Sometimes she wondered if the animals knew she could shapeshift into a wolf.

"You're just a big flirt, aren't you?" she asked as she scooped him up and placed a kiss on his head. "Made me fall in love with you with one look from that sweet face. So you know what? I'm going to keep you."

Tatiana leaned back to get a better look at him and smiled.

"Yup," Tatiana said through a smile. "You're a heartbreaker, alright. So what do you think about the name Casanova?"

The puppy answered with a face full of warm licks and a nibble on her ear.

"Alright," Tatiana giggled. "Casanova it is, but I think we'll go with Cass for short."

Satisfied with his new moniker, he snuggled against her chest and lay still as her sister's voice floated into Tatiana's head. *Hey, sis*. Layla's familiar sound filled her mind. *Are you alone, or is Matt with you? I need to see you right away*.

I'm alone, Layla.

Tatiana grinned. Matt was her assistant and only friend outside of her siblings. Like her, he never knew his parents, but instead of being raised on a farm by a loving aunt like she had been, he grew up in foster homes and had no family to speak of.

Tatiana and her twin brother, Raife, may not have

known their parents, but at least they had each other and their aunt Rosie. They were adopted and moved in when they were twelve, but they couldn't have been closer to Rosie than if they were actual blood relatives.

Matt always said he and Tatiana were like two peas in a pod. Tatiana felt a bit sorry for him because he really didn't have anyone other than her. He showed up looking for a job about a year ago, and they'd been thick as thieves ever since. However, as close as they were, he was still unaware of her unique heritage.

I'm in the exam room, but meet me in the waiting room, okay?

Tatiana held Cass a bit tighter as she made her way to the front office. Within seconds, the air-conditioned space filled with static electricity, and the air shimmered. Layla materialized in the center of the room. Her unruly red curls flowed wildly around her, and her brilliant green eyes sparkled brightly as she made quick work of kissing her sister on the cheek.

"I'll never get used to that," Tatiana said quietly as she hugged Cass for some much-needed reassurance, and to her surprise, the puppy snuggled closer and licked her neck. "Can all of them do that?"

"You mean all of *us*?" Layla said playfully as she let the puppy sniff her hand. "Yeah. The pure-blood Amoveo can do it, and the hybrids like us can do it." She lifted one shoulder and scratched Cass behind the ears. "At least, the few that I've met so far. Once you find your mate, you'll be able to do it too."

"No thanks, sis. I'll stick to regular forms of human travel *and* human dating, for that matter. So what's up?" Tatiana asked, changing the subject. She sat on the edge of the reception desk and watched her sister carefully. "You don't usually *pop in* like this."

"Hardee har har," Layla said with a roll of her eyes.

"Sorry," Tatiana said. "I couldn't help myself."

The smile faded from Layla's eyes, and Tatiana sensed the tension in her energy waves as they swirled faster through the room. It was something akin to a breeze that only another Amoveo could feel.

"We need your help."

"We?" Dread crawled up Tatiana's back.

"Richard, the Prince of the Amoveo, asked me to come here to see if you'd be willing to help him. He has about a dozen Arabian horses that have all come down with something. And before you ask, *no*. Richard doesn't want to use the vet he usually hires because he's concerned the animals might have been poisoned, and if that were the case, then the vet would want to get the police involved. He suspects it was either a Purist, or possibly, part of the recent Caedo activity. Either way, we obviously can't involve the human community."

"No way."

"Hear me out." Layla put her hand up to stop the inevitable protest, and Tatiana snapped her mouth closed.

Tatiana made no secret about her feelings regarding the Amoveo. Purist Amoveo killed her father for mating with her human mother. After their mother died, none of *them* came looking for her or her twin brother, Raife. The two felt as though they'd been completely abandoned. Therefore, she had no love for the Amoveo or their world.

Tatiana's mouth set in a tight line as she waited for her sister to continue.

"Thank you." Layla let out a slow breath. "Now, listen. I know you aren't jazzed about getting involved with the Amoveo. Believe me. I get it. You know that until I met William, I was on the same train as you. I thought they *all* hated hybrids—hated *us*—but it's simply not true. Yes. There are *some* Amoveo—the Purists—who would sooner see us dead than sullying their bloodlines with human blood, but most Amoveo aren't like that." Her jaw tilted determinedly. "William isn't," she said, referring to her new husband. "He's a Loyalist, just like the prince."

"I know," Tatiana said in a gentler tone. "I met William only a couple of times, but it's obvious he's crazy about you. I mean, he hovers around you and is more protective of you than Raife has ever been of either of us. I'm happy that you found someone who makes you so happy." Tatiana's face twisted with confusion, and she paused for a minute. "Wait a minute. Back up. Who or what is a Caedo?"

"The Caedo are a human family who know about us and hate us," Layla said with a casual shrug as she sat on the sofa. "Apparently, they were the big bad enemy until the Purists got their panties in a bunch about us hybrids."

"That's a lovely little tidbit—hard to believe you've been keeping that to yourself," Tatiana said sarcastically. "So there are two different groups that want to kill us. Awesome."

"Richard and the others thought the Caedo were a nonissue, but it seems they started acting up again. They got wind of the little civil war we had with the Purists and decided to exploit the rift. Anyway, you wouldn't have to worry about that. All you have to do is come to the ranch and check out the horses. When you're done, you can split."

"You're killing me, you know that? Today was supposed to be my first day of vacation in the three years since I opened this place."

"Perfect." Layla smiled brightly. "You can vacation in Montana at the ranch. It's gorgeous in the summer. Actually, it reminds me of the farm where we grew up."

Tatiana glanced down at the sleeping puppy in her arms.

"You can bring the dog."

"Thanks." Tatiana chuckled. "Actually, he seems to be an empathetic little soul. I have a hunch he'd be a great therapy dog." She locked eyes with her sister as an idea bloomed. "I'm bringing more than the dog. I'm bringing Matt too."

"Shit." Layla laid her head back on the sofa and tapped her jean-clad legs with her trimmed fingernails. "Bringing a human to the ranch is not going to go over well with anyone, especially not with the Guardians. Dominic in particular—he's a big one for rules and tradition."

"Sorry, sis," Tatiana said all too sweetly. "That is a deal-breaker. No Matt, no doc. Whoever this Dominic guy is, well, he'll just have to like it or lump it."

Tatiana meant it. She wanted to help her sister, but she needed a security blanket, a way to be sure she wasn't going to get schooled by the Amoveo twenty-four-seven—a bunch of shifters trying to talk her into this mate nonsense. If she brought a human with her, then the Amoveo would have to be on their best behavior. Otherwise, they would risk letting the proverbial cat out of the bag.

"Fine. I'll run it by Richard and Salinda. If that's the only way we can get you to help, then I'm sure they'll be okay with it." Layla stood up. "So you'll come to the ranch and help us find out what's making the horses sick. Right?"

"Yes." Tatiana rose from her spot on the desk and met her sister at the center of the room. "I'll book Matt and me a flight and be there in a couple of days."

"Right." Layla nodded. "I'll pick you up at the airport."

"No," Tatiana added quickly. "I'll rent a car and drive there myself. Really, it's fine."

Layla let out sigh of frustration as she hugged her sister vigorously, which elicited a whine from Cass.

"It's okay, little buddy." Layla rubbed his ears and looked fondly at Tatiana. "I'm sorry as hell that the horses are sick, but I can't say I'm disappointed to have you visit." Her smile brightened. "Hey, you never know, maybe you'll find your mate, or at least get a visit from him in the dream realm."

"No thanks." Tatiana laughed and shook her head vehemently. "When love finds me, it will be the old-fashioned way. No dreams. No weird shit. Just good, old-fashioned, true love and romance. We *are* half human, in case you've forgotten."

"I guess that means that you and Matt aren't…"

"Nah." She made a face. "I think he'd like more, but we're better as friends. No sparks. Y'know? I want a guy who will knock me out and have my head spinning."

"Oh, I know exactly what you're talking about." Layla's face turned as red as her hair, and she stuffed her hands in her pockets. "Actually, until I met William, I didn't really know what sparks were, and *believe me*, when you find your mate, you'll know what *I'm* talking about."

"When I find the love of my life, there will be plenty of sparks." Tatiana winked. "See you in a couple of days."

Tatiana watched as Layla's image wavered as though she were underwater, and as static crackled in the air, she vanished in a blink. As quiet settled, guilt swamped her.

She lied to her sister.

Tatiana already found her mate, or more to the point, her mate found her. She watched him time and again from the shadows of the dream realm as he hunted and stalked her in his tiger form. She had no idea what his name was or what he looked like as a human, but she *did* know he was dangerous. A predator. Yet for all his searching, she managed to stay hidden, and if she had anything to say about it, she would keep it that way.

"I'd have killed him twice if I could've," Dominic growled, his voice bouncing through the sterile medical facility.

"Easy there, tiger," Steven teased as he inspected the injury on his face. "You may be a badass from the Tiger Clan, but you're still my patient, so sit still or you won't get a lollipop."

Steven's teasing did nothing to improve Dominic's mood. He was itching to get back outside and patrol the property, but the doctor was taking his sweet time. Steven, a member of the Coyote Clan and an excellent healer, was known for his use of humor to put his patients at ease, but right now, the last thing Dominic wanted to do was laugh. He was surprised Steven even had a sense of humor left given the suffering he had endured over the past year.

Dominic's sense of humor, on the other hand, was nowhere to be found. There was nothing funny about what had transpired in the past week. Two Caedo assassins, members of the one human family who knew of the Amoveo's existence, snuck onto the ranch and attempted to murder the prince. Dominic killed one, but another shot Eric, the other Guardian, and escaped into the surrounding mountains.

Dominic sat unmoving on the hospital bed as Steven inspected the almost-healed injury, which ran down the left side of his face. Hands balled into fists in his lap, he stared past the healer to the blank wall behind him and concentrated on keeping his fury in check. Getting pissed at Steven wouldn't help anything.

"The stitches have dissolved, and the wound is beginning to fade. You'll have a scar, but from what I hear, chicks dig scars." Steven removed the latex gloves and tossed them in the trash. "I have to be honest. I'm surprised you healed this quickly, especially considering you haven't found your mate yet. Most fully mated Amoveo take longer to heal from a laceration as severe as this one."

Steven picked up the tablet on his desk and entered information as he continued speaking.

"I guess you Tiger Clan boys are as tough as they say you are. Some say the tigers are the fiercest of all ten clans, and after treating you, I'd have to agree. However, you can't avoid the inevitable outcome if you don't connect with your mate."

Frustration flared, and despite Dominic's best efforts,

his sharp brown eyes flickered and shifted into the glowing amber eyes of his tiger. He breathed deeply as he struggled for self-control and willed them back to their human state.

"A mate is irrelevant," Dominic said evenly. "As Guardian, my loyalties and responsibilities lie with the prince and his family. Wounded or not, I will continue as Guardian and keep our prince, and everyone else on the ranch, safe."

"Right." Steven ran a hand through his shaggy blond hair and shook his head. "I get it, dude. You are not one to fuck with. You more than proved it when you killed that Caedo assassin and ripped his head off like he was made of tissue paper."

"I would've done the same with the other one if I'd found him, but Eric's wound looked severe and—"

"And you did what anyone would do. You stopped to help your friend and fellow Guardian. Eric healed as quickly as you did, by the way. It's too bad we can't figure out what's making the horses sick, but from what I hear, they've got someone in mind to help."

"Yes." Dominic's mouth set in a tight line. "One mare died this morning, and given the recent Caedo activity and the continued animosity with lingering Purists, Richard is reluctant to bring in the local veterinarian."

"You're pretty good at changing the subject, Dominic."

Dominic swore and hopped off the bed. He snatched his black T-shirt off the chair before quickly pulling it on. "Why do you feel the need to bring up the issue of a mate, or more to the point, my lack of one?"

Dominic knew he sounded like a defensive asshole, but he couldn't help it. Steven was right. He still hadn't found his mate, and if he didn't find her soon, his Amoveo abilities would vanish, leaving him to live the rest of his existence as a human.

That was the fate of any Amoveo who didn't bond with a life mate by the age of thirty, and it wasn't one he was interested in participating in. However, with his thirtieth birthday just a year away, he knew the reality of what awaited him.

No shapeshifting, minimal strength, no powers of visualization.

How would he effectively serve as Guardian if he was void of his Amoveo abilities? Dominic shoved the dark thoughts from his mind, refusing to believe that it was actually a possibility. His military training brought him to this place, and he would be damned if some bullshit legend of fated mates would take that away. Mate or no mate, he would stay the course and fulfill his duties.

Even if it meant dying in the process.

"Hey, man." Steven raised his hands in surrender. "I'm just stating a fact, and it's only out of concern for you as a healer and a friend."

Dominic nodded and tucked his dog tags beneath his shirt. Even though he hadn't been in the human military for four years, it was still a part of who he was, and he'd feel naked without that cool stainless steel pressing against his skin. It was where he learned his combat skills and intense focus, both of which were crucial to his position.

"Have you connected with her at all?" he asked. "Any sign of her in the dream realm?"

"Not exactly," Dominic bit out, unable to look Steven in the eye.

All Amoveo connected with their mates in the dream

realm before the physical plane. It was a crucial part of the mating process and one he hadn't experienced yet.

"I don't see her, but sometimes I can feel her there in the shadows and mists. I can sense her energy signature, and just when I think I have it, it slips away. It's frustrating as hell, and if I didn't know better, I'd think she was intentionally avoiding me."

"I see." Steven went to his desk and connected the tablet to his computer.

"And vanilla." Dominic crossed his arms over his broad chest and breathed deeply as the memory of the scent filled his head. "Sometimes I catch the scent of vanilla and cherries."

"Interesting." Steven shucked his white lab coat and draped it over the back of the desk chair, revealing an Iron Maiden T-shirt and torn jeans. Without his lab coat he looked more like a roadie than a doctor. "I never saw Courtney in the dream realm either, not clearly at least, and if I hadn't stumbled on her at that blasted Purist compound, I may never have found her. Don't use us as an example though, our mating has been… unorthodox."

"How do you mean?"

"Never mind." Steven waved him off. "As far as your mate avoiding you, that is certainly a possibility, and if you're concerned, I would suggest having a chat with my boy, Willie."

"Layla avoided him?" Dominic's brow knit in confusion. "That doesn't make any sense. Why would our mates avoid us?"

"Dude, are you serious?" Steven smiled and punched a few buttons on his computer before looking back at

Dominic. "If she's a hybrid and has been raised away from our people, God only knows what she *knows* or *doesn't know* about us. *If* she knows what she is, she may think all Amoveo are like the Purists and want her dead for being a hybrid. *Maybe* she thinks we're all a bunch of chauvinistic pigs looking to drag our women into servitude. Hell, she may be a human and not even *know* that the Amoveo exist."

Dominic was quiet as Steven's words settled over him, and he felt like a dope for not thinking of these things sooner. This whole mate business was far more complicated than anyone ever let on.

"Or—" Steven sighed. "She could think you're butt-ass ugly and be running in the other direction."

Dominic cracked a smile in spite of himself and ran a hand over his cropped black hair.

"My point is," Steven said solemnly, "avoiding your mate or ignoring it isn't doing you any good, my friend. Your mate is out there somewhere, and if you don't find her soon, then you'll have to face the music one way or another."

Dominic clenched his jaw and strapped the leather weapons belt securely around his waist. He pulled the massive hunting knife from its sheath and briefly inspected it. Seeing that shiny blade instantly put his anxious heart at ease, but the reality of what Steven said still weighed heavily.

"I appreciate your concern, but I can assure you that finding, or not finding my mate, will not impact my ability to protect the prince. I would give my life to protect our people from anyone who threatens our existence."

"Yeah, I'm getting that," Steven said through a

laugh. "Listen, I don't want to sound like an ungrateful ass. Courtney and I live here too, so your quick actions with those Caedo assassins protected her and the baby. She's already been through so much and still isn't fully recovered emotionally. The pregnancy is making it so much worse."

Steven's face darkened at the memories. Dominic heard about what some of the women were put through as involuntary participants in the Purist breeding program. He couldn't imagine the helplessness and rage that Steven must have felt knowing his mate had suffered. Whatever it was, it must've been bad, because he never talked about it.

"It's good to know that you and Eric have our backs." Steven stuck his hand out, and Dominic promptly accepted. "Thank you."

Dominic shook his hand quickly and gave him a brief nod of understanding before opening the door.

"Hey," Steven called. "Catch."

Dominic turned around and caught a lollipop as it came flying in his direction. He gave Steven a friendly smile as he stuck the lollipop in the pocket of his camo pants and headed out the door.

It's not that he didn't appreciate Steven's gratitude, but it made him uncomfortable to be thanked for doing his job. Hell. He hadn't even done it that well. One assassin got away, and as far as Dominic was concerned, that was a failure.

However, it was not one that would be repeated.

As Dominic headed up the steps from the medical facility to the main floor of the house, he couldn't stop thinking about what Steven had said. Perhaps he was right. What if his mate had been avoiding him all along out of fear or ignorance?

Dominic swung the door open at the top of the stairs and instantly sensed familiar energy signatures, the spiritual fingerprints made by all Amoveo. Then an unfamiliar ripple in the air sent his protective instincts on high alert. He detected fear and apprehension flickering through the enormous house, and it was coming from an unknown Amoveo… and a human.

Caedo? That was all he could think. Another Caedo assassin or a Purist had infiltrated the property.

Dominic cut through the grand entry hall and in a blur of speed, he went immediately to the lavish living room to the left of the main hall. The scent of vanilla swamped him as he came to a halt in the doorway, ready for battle with glowing eyes and his knife drawn. The room was empty, but movement to his left captured his attention.

Without thinking, moving only on gut instinct, he spun to the left and grabbed the intruder, throwing them to the ground. In a matter of seconds, he straddled the small body and pinned the stranger easily beneath him. His knees held struggling arms to the floor, one hand curled over a slim shoulder, as the other held his knife poised high in the air, ready to strike.

As the haze of rage receded and the imminent danger was stifled, Dominic found himself staring into a pair of beautiful, furious golden eyes. A stunning hybrid Amoveo woman who smelled of cherries and vanilla glared at him, and if looks could kill, he'd be toast.

Shoulder-length dark hair framed a heart-shaped face stamped with anger, but through it all he detected a hauntingly familiar energy signature. It was the same one that slipped in and out of the dream realm and eluded him night after night.

Layla's voice drifted over his shoulder.

"Do you think you could get off my sister?"

Sister? Dominic blinked in surprise and sheathed his knife as he stared at the woman still trapped beneath him. Her eyes burned brightly in their clan form as her intoxicating scent filled his head.

As he remembered those nights in the dream realm, his body tightened and responded to her on an instinctual level. She wiggled, attempting to get out from under him, but he kept her there as the pieces fell into place.

Mate. That one word ran through his head over and over like an ancient mantra. This woman, the one he just tackled, as if she were a Caedo or Purist assassin, was his mate. *Son of a bitch*.

Chapter 2

THE WEIGHT OF HIS BODY HELD HER TO THE FLOOR, BUT it was the predatory look in his eyes that kept her from moving. Tatiana didn't notice the knife at first. She couldn't think. All she could do was feel.

The pressure of his hard, male body and the heat of his gaze were frightening and intriguing. Her heart hammered in her chest as she wrestled for calm amid the storm of emotions that battered her. If it had been any other stranger, she would have cried out for help, but this man wasn't exactly a stranger.

Tatiana knew those eyes.

They were the same amber eyes she hid from night after night. This man, whoever he was, was the one who stalked her in the dream realm. Although this was the first time she had seen him in his human form, there was no mistaking him. Between the intense, piercing stare and the vivid energy signature, she knew exactly who he was.

This was her Amoveo mate.

The man had been powerful and intimidating in his tiger form. As a human, he was equally formidable and had a penetrating gaze that sent her body into overdrive.

Sparks flickered over her skin, and her heart thumped uncontrollably in her chest. What was it she said to Layla? She wanted to get knocked on her ass by sparks? Apparently, the universe was listening and had a sense of humor.

Jet-black hair cut short in a military style and dark eyebrows framed fierce glowing eyes. He was ruggedly handsome with a well-chiseled face that was marred only by a jagged scar running down his left cheek. Instead of making him seem macabre or scary, it made him dangerously sexy.

Tatiana resisted the crazy urge to reach out and touch it, to soothe the raw-looking flesh with tender strokes. In spite of the bizarre situation, every cell of her body lit up beneath his touch and intent observation. Her stomach fluttered with a heady combination of nerves and lust, making her cringe at her body's ridiculous response.

This guy had tackled her for God's sake. The last thing in the world she should have felt was *turned on*, but that didn't change the fact that she was.

Gritting her teeth, she glared back at him, meeting his challenge. The man embodied danger. He was relentless, aggressive, and intense. The thought of denying him was both empowering and terrifying. Somewhere through the haze of sensations she heard Layla's voice drift in between them.

A smile curved his lips, and the spell was broken. Fingers, which were curled around her shoulder, loosened and brushed over her skin as he immediately stood up and offered her a hand.

Tatiana shot him a look of contempt and hopped to her feet without help. He studied her quietly, and she did her best not to squirm under his inspection, praying all the while he didn't suspect the same thing she did.

Perhaps he didn't recognize her? Maybe her efforts to hide from him had worked. However, as his eyes twinkled wickedly, she knew she was out of luck. *Damn it.*

"Charming." She sighed as she brushed off the back of her shorts and adjusted her tank top. "Well, you get points for the most original greeting I've ever gotten, and considering I've been tackled by animals twice your size, although markedly more civilized, that's saying something."

The smile faded from his lips. The man actually looked contrite, and it gave her hope that perhaps, beneath all that aggression, there was a *person* willing to overlook the fated mate nonsense. Sparks or no sparks, she would not be told whom she could love or spend her life with, and she had zero interest in being dragged into the crazy Amoveo world.

"Apologies," he said tightly with a tilt of his head. He held his hands behind his back and stood at attention before casting an accusing glance to Layla. "I was unprepared for visitors this morning. I didn't think our guests were arriving until later this afternoon."

"Sorry, Dominic. I forgot to tell you they caught an earlier flight," Layla said with a short laugh. She brushed past him and quickly grabbed Tatiana in a warm hug. "It's so good to have you here, Tati. Don't mind Dominic, he's a little quick on the draw ever since those Caedo guys started acting up."

Tatiana hugged her sister, and they giggled like children. She pulled back and tugged one of Layla's long red curls.

"I'll be sure to announce my presence before I enter a room." Tatiana gave Dominic a sidelong glance. "I wouldn't want to get tackled again."

"Sorry." Dominic shrugged as he held her gaze. "Your energy signature wasn't *entirely* familiar."

"Right." Tatiana looked away and ran a hand through her dark hair. He did recognize her, or at least he sensed something. Shit. "Well, now it is."

"So you talk to animals?" He cocked his head to one side as he looked her up and down. "Like Dr. Dolittle?"

"Not exactly." Tatiana lifted one shoulder and adjusted her top as she tried not to notice the way his eyes lingered on her body. "I don't hear them speak with words. I read their energy signatures and feel their emotions. I sense things. That's all."

"I sense things too. Like a human," Dominic said quietly. "I can smell one all over you."

"Oh really? Well, that would be my vet tech, Matt, *or* it could be any human I was on a plane with today."

"Oh man." Layla laughed and walked to the picture window. "You made him wait in the car?" Dominic flicked a glance toward the window but didn't move from his spot as Tatiana continued. "Hell, it could even be *me* because in case you haven't noticed, I'm half human."

Tatiana shot him a look of annoyance and folded her arms over her breasts. He referred to it as though it was the worst odor he'd ever had the displeasure of experiencing.

"So, tell me, Dominic. Are you one of those Purist Amoveo assholes that I've heard about? If that's the case, then I'll get back in my car and go home."

"What?" His features darkened, and his stubble-covered jaw clenched. "I am not a Purist." Dominic's dark eyes locked on her, and though Tatiana's heart raced faster, she refused to give an inch. "I am a *Guardian,* and it's my business to know who is here on the ranch."

Dominic stepped closer as he spoke, but she held her ground and looked him in the eye.

"Two *human* assassins snuck onto the property recently and attempted to kill the prince and his family." His tone grew gentler as did his expression. "I *do not* hate humans. I do, however, have a bone to pick with anyone who would harm the people I care about. That includes humans *or* Amoveo."

Heat spread over her skin as she held his stare, and Tatiana's breath caught in her throat. She hoped like hell she could get a hold over her out-of-control hormones before she embarrassed herself and let her eyes shift. That only happened when she got really mad, or turned on, or in this case, both.

Dominic stilled and arched one eyebrow. "Did Layla say there's a human waiting in your car?" His voice dropped low. "You brought a human to this ranch?"

"Yes." Tatiana stepped to the side and picked up the backpack she'd tossed on the couch when she came in. "If you hadn't been so busy lecturing me and telling me how badly I stink, you might've realized it sooner. In fact, now I'm the one who's being rude, because he's been out there for a while."

"*He?*" His eyes flickered and snapped to their clan form as his hands balled into fists at his side. "You traveled here with a man? Alone?"

Holy crap. He was jealous.

Tatiana suppressed a smile as she realized the tide had turned in her favor. Matt's presence would not only keep the Amoveo at bay, but he could also keep Dominic at arm's length. How could he pursue her and claim her as his mate if she was already spoken for?

"Yes." Tatiana threw her backpack over one shoulder casually. "Matt's my vet tech *and* my boyfriend."

"What?" Dominic and Layla said in unison.

Before Layla could call her out on her big fat lie, two of the most beautiful people Tatiana had ever seen swept into the room. The woman had a little girl about eight or nine months old in her arms. They radiated power, and based on the strength of their energy, they had to be the royal couple.

Her heart pounded as they moved toward her. She had never been around this many pure-blood Amoveo in her life. Long-held fears flooded her, and she gripped the strap of the backpack, praying for the strength to at least *look* like she wasn't terrified. She was relatively certain that her energy signature revealed her for the coward she was. It practically screamed *get me the hell out of here*.

"Outstanding," the prince said as he entered the room with his wife at his side. "We're glad to see you've arrived safely."

Dominic stepped aside but didn't take his intense gaze off her. Tatiana tried not to notice the way he looked at her, but it was unavoidable. *He* was unavoidable. She did her best to ignore him and focused her attention on the prince and his wife.

Richard had long, shoulder-length black hair and light blue eyes. Dressed in jeans and a tailored shirt, he radiated casual confidence and approached Tatiana with an extended hand. The two of them didn't look a day over thirty-five, but according to Layla, they were over three hundred years old.

Maybe that mating thing wasn't *all* bad?

"I am Richard Muldavi, Prince of the Amoveo. This is my mate, Salinda, and our daughter, Jessica. Welcome to the ranch, Tatiana. We are immensely grateful that you agreed to treat our horses."

"We can't tell you how much we appreciate this," Salinda said as she leaned into her husband's embrace and gave him a loving look. Jessica gurgled and smiled at her parents as she grabbed a lock of her mother's long, dark hair. "Richard was worried you wouldn't be willing to do it, but Layla assured him you would rise to the challenge."

"I'd do anything for my sister." Tatiana smiled tightly and stuck her hand in the pocket of her shorts. "Even come to a ranch full of Amoveo."

"What is that supposed to mean?" Dominic interrupted. Everyone looked at him in surprise, and Layla moved across the room. She stood protectively at Tatiana's side and sent her comforting waves of reassuring energy. "You are Amoveo, a hybrid from the Wolf Clan—Timber Wolf Clan, if I'm not mistaken—so why are you reluctant to be among your own people?"

"Dominic—" Layla began.

"No, Layla. I am the Head Guardian of this property," Dominic continued. "It is my duty to protect everyone here from *any* threat. Purist. Caedo." He leveled a deadly glare at Tatiana. "*Anyone* who is a threat to our people will not be tolerated, so I think we deserve an answer to my question."

A heavy silence filled the room, and just when Tatiana thought she'd scream with frustration, the baby laughed and reached toward Dominic. The sound of Jessica's gurgling immediately broke the tension, and without missing a beat, Salinda passed the baby to Dominic.

The transformation from beast to man was instantaneous and rendered Tatiana speechless.

"It seems your girlfriend is vying for your attention again, Dominic," Salinda said with a laugh. "She adores him."

Tatiana watched in stunned silence as the hulking brute of a man was reduced to jelly by the chubby little baby in his arms. Dominic grinned at Jessica as her pudgy fingers found the chain around his neck. He pulled a set of dog tags from beneath his T-shirt and gave them to the baby, who promptly drooled all over them.

"The feeling's mutual," Dominic said as he glanced at Tatiana.

Tatiana's gaze met his briefly, and even that momentary connection made her stomach flutter. What was it about the sight of a man holding a baby that could make a woman swoon? A couple of minutes ago, Tatiana would never have suspected that he was capable of anything other than caveman-like behavior, and yet here he was, wrapped around the finger of an adorable little girl.

"Dominic," Richard said. "Tatiana is our guest, and she has come here, after much convincing by her sister, to help us." Richard faced Tatiana as he placed his arm over Salinda's shoulders. "She is not only a hybrid, but also a talented veterinarian, and if Layla trusts her, then we will as well."

"I'm sure that before long, the trust will flow both ways," Salinda said warmly. "We have set up one of the guest cabins on the property for you. I hope you will be comfortable there. I can assure you that your privacy will be respected, and Dominic and Eric will do their best to keep all of us safe."

"Yes, well, I heard about the incident you had here recently. How can you be certain something like that won't happen again?" Tatiana asked the question as though she wasn't totally unnerved by the entire situation. She glanced at Dominic and the baby, and when the cherub-faced little girl smiled back, some of her nervousness eased. She turned her attention to Richard. "Are you concerned about other surprise visits?"

"We've taken a few extra safety measures. I've placed a shield around the property, which should alert us if any other Amoveo visualize themselves here." Richard smiled at his daughter who reached out to him with chubby little arms. He took her from Dominic and placed a kiss on the child's head. "The people I care most about in the world are here on this ranch, Tatiana. The last thing I want is violence taking place at my home and around my daughter. I won't lie to you. Ever since Artimus and his followers declared war on the rest of our people, we have all been in danger."

"Artimus?" Tatiana looked at Layla for answers.

"He was the leader of the Purist rebellion. A real bastard," Layla said. "The kind of charismatic psycho who gets people to follow his lead, and then by the time they figure out what a crazy asshole he is, they're too terrified to stop him."

"Great." Tatiana gave her sister a look. "Where is he now?"

"Dead," Dominic said with a shrug.

"At any rate," Richard said. "While *I can't* promise

you no one will try anything, *I can* promise you we will do everything we can to keep you safe."

"Thank you," Tatiana said without sparing so much as a glance at Dominic. "But there is one other thing. The friend that I have with me, my *boyfriend*, is human and doesn't know about the Amoveo or my *unusual* background. I realize that might make some of you uncomfortable, so we can stay at the motel in town instead. I already reserved a room."

"Can't be much of a boyfriend if he doesn't know who you really are," Dominic said evenly.

The beast was back. Great.

Tatiana opened her mouth to retort, but snapped it shut immediately because he was right. If she did have a boyfriend, someone she loved and trusted, the last thing Tatiana would do is keep such a special part of herself a secret. She didn't know what was more annoying. The fact that he was right, or that she didn't have a retort.

"Don't be silly." Salinda shot Dominic a look of reproach before he could make more remarks. "You are doing us a favor and have left your home and your business to come help us. Layla tells me that you even changed your vacation plans, so I'm sure we can control ourselves while your friend is here. I'll simply let the others know to avoid shifting and so forth in front of—"

"Matt," Tatiana said with a brief glance to Dominic. "His name is Matt."

Dominic folded his lean, muscular arms over his chest, and Tatiana watched his jaw flicker with tension… and then she heard him.

A human? They're going to let some human they've never met stay on the property, and a human male no less?

Tatiana froze as Dominic's deep baritone brushed the edges of her mind, and all the breath rushed from her lungs as the surprising effect from the intimate mental connection washed through her. The only people she ever telepathed with were her siblings, Raife and Layla, but it *never* felt like this.

Warmth rippled over her skin, her breasts tingled, and the most feminine part of her tightened. Dominic's eyes narrowed and flickered to their clan form as the mental link solidified. *Another man will not share your bed. Not a fucking chance.*

Tatiana's lips parted as another rush of heat flared through her, and before she could stop it, her eyes tingled and snapped into the glowing eyes of her wolf.

The room fell silent as the others looked from Dominic to Tatiana.

Dominic's lips lifted at the corners as his voice touched her mind on a growl. *I see you... mate.*

Tatiana sucked in a deep breath and willed her eyes to shift back to their human state. Dominic's, however, glowed brightly and remained locked on her.

"No," she said out loud.

Nobody moved, and you could cut the tension in the air with a freaking knife. Tatiana steeled her resolve and kept her voice calm, hoping her energy signature would follow suit.

"I may be half Amoveo, but I'm also half human, and if you ask Layla, she'd probably say mostly human. I have zero interest in this fated mate stuff."

Flicking an apologetic look to Richard and his wife, she continued.

"I'm sorry. I know all of you feel differently, including

Layla. I've seen how happy she is with William, and I've heard about others like us who found their mates, but that's just not part of my plan. I hope I'm not embarrassing anyone by addressing this publicly, but I'd rather nip it in the bud, so to speak." She was babbling and seemed unable to stop. "As I mentioned, I have a boyfriend, and I'm already spoken for. I'm here only to help the horses, and then Matt and I will go back to Oregon."

Tatiana looked at the others and, to her relief, saw nothing but curiosity, from her sister in particular. *Liar, liar pants on fire.* Layla's teasing voice touched her mind with comforting familiarity, instantly quelling her nerves. *You told me he wasn't your boyfriend. No sparks, remember? Based on the combustible energy waves flowing between you and Dominic, I'd say you found sparks… and then some.*

Tatiana elbowed Layla but said nothing, and she didn't miss the knowing look that passed between Richard and Salinda. Wonderful.

"Not a problem." Dominic's calm, even voice broke the silence. "My priority is protecting this ranch." To her surprise, he turned his attention to the prince. "Speaking of which, I should get back to it." Dominic smiled at baby Jessica and tapped her nose with one finger. "See ya later, kid."

The baby gave him a drool-filled grin as he left, and Tatiana tried not to notice that he looked as good from the back as he did from the front. The black T-shirt molded perfectly to his broad muscular back, and the camo pants certainly didn't camouflage that rock-solid ass.

The man didn't seem to have an ounce of body fat anywhere.

Just as that thought whisked through her mind, Dominic paused in the archway and turned to face her. Tatiana's face burned with embarrassment as he caught her staring at his backside.

"Oh, and for the record, I have no interest in a woman who isn't interested in me." His eyes crinkled at the corners, and the muscles in his chest flexed beneath the black T-shirt. "But we both know," he said with a wink, "you're interested."

Before she could respond and tell him what an arrogant, presumptuous jerk he was, Dominic left. Tatiana snapped her mouth shut and prayed her face wasn't bright red, but based on Layla's smile, she was red like a tomato.

As the front door closed, his deep baritone drifted into her mind.

Let the games begin.

The smile fell from Dominic's face the second he stepped out onto the front porch of the sprawling colonial house. The telepathic connection with Tatiana was unexpected, and Dominic was not a huge fan of surprises. He'd never telepathed with anyone unintentionally, and based on the look on her face, neither had she. It's not that he wasn't happy about the instant contact, he was simply unprepared, and Dominic was never unprepared for battle.

He shook his head as a smile bloomed. Getting that pixie of a woman to agree to be his mate would probably be the toughest fight of his life. She was beautiful and sexy in an understated way. She had a toned, well-shaped body that fit perfectly with his, but it was her enormous dark eyes that had him spinning.

Aside from her physical beauty, she possessed a steely inner strength that he admired. She was stubborn and determined, two qualities he found desirable in a woman. Dominic knew some guys liked women who needed rescuing, but not him. He wanted a woman who would challenge him and keep him on his toes. Something told him that Tatiana Winters fit the bill. Nothing in the preliminary report he'd received could have prepared him for the swarm of sensations he just experienced.

One look. Damn it all. She turned him inside out with one look.

Sun glinting off the blue rental car in the driveway, along with the faint energy wave from the human sitting in it, captured his attention. He detected the man's weak signature, and even though he knew he should walk on by and patrol the property again, he didn't. Dominic trotted down the steps and made his way to the car, barely noticing the heat of the summer sun as it beat down.

Gravel crunched under the soles of his shoes as he studied the human with each step he took. The passenger door swung open as Dominic approached, and a young man, perhaps mid-twenties, stepped out. He had a grin on his face and a puppy in his arms. He may have been around the same age as Dominic, younger by a year or two, but he gave the impression of someone more youthful.

The dog whined and sniffed at Dominic as he approached, which was not unexpected. Dogs seemed more in tune with the animal side of Amoveo, and this little mutt was no different. The guy, on the other hand, remained as clueless to Dominic's true nature as most humans were.

Matt's energy signature was typical for a human, and he had an open, innocent look in his eyes. Dominic suspected Tatiana was lying about Matt being her boyfriend, and now that he met him, he was relatively certain it was bullshit. This kid was no match for the feisty, no-nonsense woman he had just met.

Matt was all of five foot nine with a slim, wiry build. Hell, he was no match for anyone. Even the puppy could kick his ass.

"Hi, I'm Matt," he said as he placed the dog on the ground, allowing him to explore. "I'm Tatiana's assistant and, at the moment, dog walker."

"Dominic." He shook Matt's hand briefly before folding his arms over his chest and staring the kid down. "Head of security here at the ranch."

"Security?" Matt laughed and ran a hand over his messy brown hair as he looked at the sprawling property with the backdrop of looming mountains. He stretched his arms over his head and arched his back, working out the kinks from traveling. "What does a place out here in the middle of nowhere need security for?"

"Never can tell," Dominic said quietly. "Things aren't always what they seem to be."

"Right." Matt stuffed his hands in his pockets awkwardly and turned his attention to the dog currently sniffing around Dominic's feet. He was clearly intimidated by Dominic and visibly nervous. "Maybe I should put Cass on a leash?"

"So," Dominic asked, "how long have you and Tatiana been together?"

"We've been working together for about a year. She's incredible," Matt said enthusiastically, his demeanor immediately changing at the mention of Tatiana. "I've never met anyone who has the kind of connection with animals that she does. It's uncanny, man, and if I didn't know better, I'd think she could actually talk to them."

"She's a regular Dr. Dolittle, huh?" Dominic said as he squatted down and scratched the dog's floppy ears.

Dominic had heard that hybrid Amoveo possessed unique abilities, and it sounded like Tatiana was no different. Communicating with animals was an interesting power. He'd never met another Amoveo with that particular ability, and it made Tatiana even more intriguing.

Glancing over his shoulder toward the house, he caught a glimpse of her in the window as he rose to his feet. She didn't look happy that Dominic was chatting with her *boyfriend*.

"Tell me, Matt," Dominic said quietly. "Are you and Tatiana involved on more than a professional level?"

"What?" Matt's blue eyes grew round, and his face went bright red. "No. I mean, sure we're friends, and we work together." He stuffed his hands in the pockets of his jeans and looked down at the dog again, avoiding Dominic's stare. "She's too busy with her practice to date *anyone*."

Matt shot him a quick look of disapproval as he fiddled with the change in his pockets. Dominic suppressed a victorious smile. *Bingo*. Matt wasn't Tatiana's boyfriend, but he'd probably give up his paycheck for the chance.

Silence stretched awkwardly as Dominic studied Matt. He seemed harmless enough, but in Dominic's experience, sometimes those were the ones you had to watch. Dominic, better than anyone, knew looks could be deceiving.

Hell, Dominic's own sister had been a traitor, and her betrayal stung as badly as the fact that he didn't see it coming. He'd never been more humiliated in all his life and, after everything settled down, Dominic even offered to relinquish his role as Guardian, but Richard and Salinda wouldn't hear of it.

The Muldavis may not have held him responsible for his sister's actions, but Dominic sure as hell did. Mistakes were unacceptable for a Guardian because people could get killed.

Dominic stuffed down the uncomfortable memories and prevented his eyes from shifting. Poor Matt would probably piss himself, and even though the idea was amusing, he refrained from breaking the rules. Besides, he wasn't a bully.

"I wonder how much longer Tatiana is going to be?" Matt said while keeping his eye on the puppy and off Dominic.

"I have a feeling she'll be along in a minute."

Dominic sensed her agitated energy from all the way outside and suppressed a grin as he touched her mind with his. *I'm having a nice chat with your boyfriend, Tatiana.*

The connection was severed as quickly as it had been made, and a dark void swiftly replaced the vibrant telepathic contact. Dominic's smile faded as he realized she had closed her mind to him and for all intents and purposes, slammed the door in his face.

About five seconds later, he heard Tatiana and Layla coming down the porch steps, and the now familiar humming of Tatiana's energy signature filled the air. She didn't respond when he tried to reconnect. Try as she might, Tatiana couldn't completely hide from him. A warm gust of wind preempted her arrival and announced her presence with a whiff of cherries and vanilla.

"Hey," Matt said with a wave. A smile of relief washed over his face as he spotted Tatiana, and he quickly cut a wide path around Dominic.

"Hey, yourself," she said sweetly.

Dominic turned around just in time to see Tatiana plant a big kiss on Matt's cheek before taking the puppy from him.

"Cass," she said as she patted the dog's head. "Are you being a good boy?"

The look of surprise on Layla's face was only matched by Dominic's. *Son of a bitch.* A low growl rumbled in his chest, and it took herculean strength not to let his eyes shift as he loomed large behind Matt. *I suggest you stop doing that, or we're going to have problems. And by we, I mean you and this kid who almost fainted when you kissed him.*

You were the one who wanted to play games. Tatiana's sweet voice touched his mind as she peered at him over the puppy's head before turning her attention back to Matt.

"Sorry I kept you waiting so long, but we had to get a few things straightened out," she said, flicking her eyes briefly to Dominic. "Just needed to lay the ground rules for the duration of our stay."

"N-no problem," Matt sputtered happily and gave a victorious glance over his shoulder at Dominic. He hooked his thumbs in the back pocket of his jeans and nodded toward the house. "Are we staying at the motel in town, or should I bring our bags inside?"

"Neither," Layla said. She bit her lip, as though she was trying to stop herself from laughing. "You two are staying in one of the guesthouses here on the ranch, next door to Dominic's, in fact," she said with a big smile. "But Tatiana wanted to look at the horses first."

"Matt, grab my medical bag from the backseat. Would you?" Tatiana followed Layla to the massive red and white barn to the right of the house. "We'll get some vitals on them and see where to go from there. No point in wasting time," she said over her shoulder with a pointed look to Dominic. "We're here to help the horses, so let's get to it."

"You got it." Matt turned around and almost ran face-first into Dominic's chest. "Whoa, sorry."

Unmoving, Dominic kept his eyes on Tatiana as she disappeared through the barn doors. Matt ran bag in hand to catch up to her, wasting no time in putting distance between him and Dominic.

What was he doing? Why the hell was he letting some woman he barely knew get under his skin? So what if she was his mate? He never in his life forced himself on a woman, and he sure as shit wasn't starting now—mate or not—no matter how intriguing, sexy, or enticing she was. Dominic swore, and his eyes shifted with a tingling snap.

There's a human on the ranch. Eric's urgent voice interrupted his thoughts. *Dominic, do you see him? Is it a Caedo?*

It's fine, Eric. Dominic responded tightly. *It's the vet's assistant.*

Seconds later, static electricity filled the air as Eric materialized next to his fellow Guardian, looking no less irritated by the situation. Eric was as tall as Dominic but with a leaner build, typical for men of the Panther Clan. He was a fierce fighter and adept at slipping in and out of situations undetected.

Eric's eyes glowed yellow, and his nostrils flared as he stared at the open door of the barn. "Layla's sister brought a human to the ranch?" His eyes flickered back to their human state. "What the hell is she thinking?"

"He's her shield." Dominic stood stone-still and fought to keep his energy signature from betraying his irritation. "She's using him. At least, that's what I suspect."

"Shield?" Eric adjusted the dagger he had tucked in his belt. "What are you talking about?"

"Tatiana's using his presence to shield *herself* from all of us." Dominic flicked a brief glance at Eric. "Remember what William and Layla said? She agreed to come here only as a favor to her sister. She's not interested in our world, and by having this human along for the ride, she knows the rest of us will have to play along."

"So, this human isn't part of the Vasullus family?" Eric asked, referring to the select few humans who knew of the Amoveo's existence and helped if needed.

"Nope." Dominic turned on his heels and strode away from the barn as Eric followed. "Has no idea what we are."

They walked in silence for a few moments, and Dominic debated telling Eric the most important part. Up until today, both were without their mates and had practically given up hope of finding one. He wondered if Eric would be happy for him or feel betrayed.

"She's not trying to keep all the Amoveo away," he murmured. "Tatiana is my mate."

"Hold up." Eric grabbed his arm and stopped dead in his tracks. "Say again?"

"Tatiana is my mate." Dominic flicked a brief glance at Eric, and his mouth set in a tight line. "She's a hybrid from the Timber Wolf Clan."

"I don't get it." Eric's brow furrowed in confusion, and the smile at his lips faltered. "Why aren't you doing a fucking backflip right now? Shit, man," he said through a laugh. "You should grab that girl and get busy. Now you'll have no trouble staying on as Guardian."

"It's not that simple." He put his hands on his hips and let out a slow breath, struggling to hang onto his patience. "She tried to get me to believe that Matt, this human, is not only her assistant, but also her boyfriend. She basically told me to fuck off, and I have a feeling that it'll be a cold day in hell before she mates with me."

"Bullshit." Eric clapped him on the shoulder. "She's your mate. You're hers. End of story."

"It's not that cut and dry." Dominic shook his head and walked toward the open field with the mountains looming large. Now, more than ever, he could use a run in his tiger form, but that wasn't in the cards until he was deep into the mountains. "She is not the least bit interested in mating. I don't care how desperate I am to keep my full strength, there's no goddamn way I'm forcing her to hook up with me."

Eric started to protest, but Dominic held up his hand, preventing further conversation. "They'll be leaving soon enough, but while they're here we have to be careful about when and where we use our abilities."

"Shit." Eric matched his stride and groaned as he wiped sweat from his brow with the back of his hand. "Damn it all! If it were winter, the guy would be less likely to roam outside."

"Matt seems harmless enough, but I'd like you to keep an extra eye on him. He and Tatiana are staying in the empty cabin by mine, and since I don't know him, I don't trust him. Run a background check. Layla should have his information. I'll speak to William and see what he knows."

"You're the boss," Eric replied. "I'll take care of it this afternoon. Do you want me to take the night shift?"

Dominic nodded as he scanned the area. "Let's keep a rotation of twelve-hour shifts while our guests are here. We'll patrol in our human form on the main grounds and limit our clan form to the wooded-mountain areas. We can't risk Matt seeing more than he should. I've imprinted on Tatiana's energy signature, so I'll be able to find her if and when necessary." He let out a sigh.

"We get to play human twenty-four-seven?" Eric grumbled. "I don't know about you, Dom, but I'm not much for playing games."

"Me either," Dominic said on a growl. "But if I'm going to play, you can bet your ass I'm going to win."

Chapter 3

The encounter with Dominic had Tatiana all twisted up and made her brain feel muddled and off kilter, not to mention her body. He was here. The very man she'd tried like hell to avoid was on this ranch in living color and possessed all the arrogance she would expect from an Amoveo man.

The image of Dominic holding the baby flashed into her mind, and she smiled in spite of herself. He dressed like a soldier and acted like a beast, but apparently, inside he was mush. It would be easier to deny her attraction if he was one hundred percent beast.

No such luck.

Cass whined and licked her face, offering comfort.

"Thanks, buddy." Tatiana smiled and kissed the top of his head. "You always know when I need a little extra snuggle."

"Hey, let me have him for a minute." Layla took the puppy from her sister gently and eyed her warily. "Are you okay?"

"I'm fine," Tatiana said. She avoided her sister's gaze as they walked the length of the stable. She knew Layla wanted to address the situation with Dominic, but that was the last thing she wanted to think about or discuss. "I want to get to work."

It was an impressive setup, with ten stalls down each side, and high ceilings with exposed beams. The front sections of the walls were lined with high-quality grooming equipment, and there was a tack shed around the corner, which made it abundantly clear that the prince spared no expense on these animals. The horses were spectacularly beautiful Arabian purebreds worth a small fortune.

Her thoughts were interrupted by images of Dominic, and within seconds, his distinctly male scent filled her nostrils. *Damn it*. It was as though he'd crawled under her skin and mingled his essence with hers in that one brief encounter. Tatiana shook her head and sucked in a deep breath, praying she could clear her mind. She had to focus on work, and she couldn't do that with a six-foot-three-inch man plastered all over her psyche.

"Are these all of them?" she asked Layla as scattered bits of hay crunched beneath her hiking boots. Sandals were more appropriate for summer, unless you were about to work with horses. One misplaced hoof could get you several broken toes. "I know you said one died."

Tatiana felt more at ease as the familiar scent of the animals filled her head. Her sense of smell was heightened, thanks to her Wolf Clan heritage, and she could detect each unique scent within the massive space. Hay, manure, horse, water, and leftover apple and carrot rounded out the plethora of smells.

However, the usual odors of a barn weren't the only thing she sensed. The long, cavernous structure was filled with anxiety, fear, and pain—all coming from the horses as they shuffled their hooves nervously. The Arabians approached the doors of their stalls as she walked slowly down the center aisle. They lifted their heads and let out snuffling breaths.

It appeared they sensed her as easily as she did them.

She breathed deeply, closed her eyes, and focused on connecting with the animals and their energy signatures. Tatiana could read emotions of animals big or small, and she preferred it to reading humans. The air around her hummed, and her body tensed as she solidified the connections. Tentacles of energy touched hers like invisible tethers, linking them together.

"There are ten left," Layla said quietly as she stood to the side and let Tatiana work. "Eight mares and two stallions."

"Several of them are sick," Tatiana whispered. "But there's more to it than that. They're scared."

Eyes closed, she held her arms out wide, allowing the buzzing flickers of power to wash over her, flashing around her bare arms and rippling up her back swiftly and silently. She turned her palms toward the animals and sent them calming energy in return, hoping to put them at ease and reassure them that she meant no harm. Sweat broke out on her forehead as she concentrated and absorbed their energy, allowing it to mingle with her own.

"They're definitely frightened," she whispered. "But not by me or you."

"I've got the bag, Tatiana." Matt's eager voice cut through the room, bringing a sudden end to her focused connection.

Tatiana dropped her hands abruptly and forced a smile as she took the bag from Matt, who gave her a quizzical look. The leather handles, cool and smooth in her hands, rooted her to reality and helped pull her back from the foggy place of reading the horses, but nothing, it seemed, could get Dominic out of her head. The image of his fierce gaze fluttered around her mind like a buzzing fly.

Placing the bag on a weathered wooden table by the doors of the stable, she made quick work of getting the items they needed. Over the next hour or so, they took basic bio readings on all ten horses with Matt recording the information on her tablet. Layla watched quietly as they tended to each of the massive creatures.

Even Cass got in on the action. When Layla put him down, Tatiana thought he would shy away from the much larger animals, but he did the opposite. In fact, after investigating the length of the stable, he parked himself outside the stall of the sickest of the horses—a beautiful white mare.

"Three of them have slightly elevated temperatures of one hundred and two." Tatiana removed the latex gloves and nodded toward the first stall. "This white mare is in the worst shape." She smiled down at Cass. "But you knew that already, didn't you?"

"Oh man," Layla said, approaching the mare's stall. "That's Salinda's horse. Her name is Spirit."

"Well, in addition to the fever, she's got diarrhea. The other two are only exhibiting fevers at the moment, but I imagine it's only a matter of time before they show other symptoms."

"What do you think it is?" Layla picked Cass up, and the puppy instantly began to chew on her long, curly hair. "Is it poisoning, like Steven suspected?"

"Who's Steven?" Matt asked as he packed the bag and cleaned up the medical waste. "Your usual vet?"

"Um, no." Layla flicked her gaze to Tatiana. "He's a people doctor and the Muldavi's personal physician.

He and his wife, Courtney, live here on the ranch. He had a look at the horses because our local vet is… out of town."

Yeah, right. Tatiana thought. *Not exactly a people doctor, more like a shapeshifting Amoveo healer.* Tatiana squashed her gut instinct to scoff aloud and continued.

"Based on the symptoms of these three and what you told me about the one that died, I have a feeling it's poisoning. Selenium maybe. I doubt it's viral, since they aren't exposed to other horses." Tatiana pushed sweaty strands of hair off her forehead. "I'm going to run a couple of tests to be certain, and I'll need to check the feed as well."

Without even having to ask, Matt handed her a specimen cup.

"Matt, would you get a sample from each of the feed containers and water buckets and mark them accordingly. If it is poisoning, then food or water is likely contaminated. I'll look around the areas they graze and see if there are any plants that could've contributed to the problem. Selenium is an important part of their diet, but too much or too little causes problems. If someone wanted to make the poisoning look like an accident, using too much selenium would be a good way to do it."

"Sure," Layla said as she placed Cass on the ground. He immediately sat in front of Spirit's stall again. "Steven has a pretty extensive lab, and it's at your disposal while you're here. I'll take you there after we're done here."

"Right." She nodded and gave Layla a tight smile.

Tatiana fought the growing feeling of claustrophobia,

the sense of being surrounded with no way out. Hunted. As soon as she'd arrived on the ranch, the overwhelming sensation of being stalked swamped her. At first she thought it was coming from Dominic. After all, he did tackle her to the floor, but after connecting with the horses, she suspected it had more to do with them.

Tatiana gently lifted the latch on Spirit's stall door and cautiously stepped inside. Cass tried to follow, but stopped when Tatiana sent him a gentle push of energy. Her heart went out to the elegant mare, who stood watching her through large dark eyes. Although she sensed apprehension, the big horse didn't move or attempt to avoid her.

"Hey, girl," she said in hushed tones. "It's okay, and I promise I won't hurt you."

Tatiana closed her eyes and stroked the slight bulge on Spirit's forehead that was specific to the Arabian breed—a *jibbah*. Spirit's energy waves hummed as Tatiana created a psychic connection, and the horse's energy fluttered over her like butterfly wings.

In seconds, it went from cool and nervous to warm and content as the horse relaxed, growing accustomed to the link. The animal let out a huffing breath and rested her head in Tatiana's hand.

Tatiana smiled and gently touched the horse's mind with hers, expecting the usual wave of nausea as the link was made, but none came. They joined smoothly and easily, and while she recognized the pain Spirit suffered, something different happened.

For the first time, Tatiana heard the whisper of an animal's inner voice with a single word.

Hunter.

Tatiana's body jolted and buzzed with newfound energy. The specimen cup fell from her fingers, bouncing noiselessly on the carpet of hay and dirt as she struggled to get her bearings amid the unfamiliar sensation. Somewhere through the fog of the connection, she heard Matt and Layla calling her, but it was no use. She was consumed by the driving need to hear that voice again.

Eyes shut she tilted her body and moved in close, pressing her cheek against the elegant arch of Spirit's neck as she ran her other hand along the coarse hair of her mane. Tatiana's body shook with concentration, and her breathing quickened as she focused and stretched her mind further than ever before.

Then through the warm blanket of silence and a haze of red and orange, she heard it again, a whisper along the edges of her mind that rattled with the unmistakable waver of fear. *Hunter killer*.

Tatiana's heart thundered in her chest as Spirit's energy waves undulated violently in the air and tore through her body in teeth-chattering waves. One last word rasped through her mind… *Traitor*.

A lightning bolt of power passed through her as Spirit reared back and sent Tatiana flying into the door of the stall. Her back hit the wooden planks, knocking all the wind out of her, and as the world around her went dark, the growl of a big cat filled her mind.

Tatiana moaned as the darkness receded. Her head throbbed, and her back ached from where she hit the stall, but all of it eased as she found herself cradled in warmth. Instinctively, she snuggled deeper into the comforting embrace lulled by the strong, steady sound of a heartbeat thrumming beneath her cheek. She felt safe. Cherished. As her awareness came back, she realized she was sitting in someone's lap. *Matt?*

Not likely. Dominic's oddly familiar baritone flickered through her mind.

Tatiana's heart beat like a rabbit's, and her fingers curled against the muscles of his chest. *Dominic?*

Tatiana's eyes fluttered open, and she found herself staring into a pair of familiar, pale brown eyes edged with worry. Dominic's inky black brows furrowed, and his mouth set in a tight line as his arms held her tighter against his muscular frame.

"What the hell were you doing?" he said through clenched teeth. "You, better than anyone, should know how to act around horses. I thought you grew up on a farm? She almost took your damn head off."

"I'm fine," she seethed as she pushed at him, trying to release herself from his ironclad grip, but it was an effort in futility. "Let me go, you big ape. I got the wind knocked out of me, but unlike you, the horse didn't do it on purpose."

"You should sit still, Tatiana," Layla said.

She was standing next to Matt who looked worried.

"Seriously." Matt flicked a wary look to Dominic. "You're lucky. Spirit probably would've trampled you if Dominic hadn't shown up." He moved his feet back and forth nervously. "That was some crazy Bruce Lee shit. I know you said you're security and everything, but you move like some kind of ninja."

"Let me up." Nausea surged, and Tatiana grabbed the

back of her head instinctively. She let out a slow breath and battled the feeling back. "Let. Go."

"No." The muscles of Dominic's jaw clenched beneath the beard stubble, and he held her tighter. "You're not going anywhere until Steven has a look at that lump on your head." His voice dropped low. "You're acting like the pigheaded woman I pegged you for. I'm not going to let you run off so you can pass out and hit your head again."

Before Tatiana could protest, he rose from the hay-strewn floor with her firmly in his grasp. Carrying her as if she weighed nothing, he walked through the open stall door. She folded her arms over her chest and shot a furious look at Layla as they brushed past. Casanova whined and went to follow, but Layla picked him up.

"This is ridiculous," Tatiana huffed. "Layla, tell him I can take care of myself. You're my sister, and you should be taking my side."

"Just give it a rest, Tatiana." Layla's freckled face twisted with concern. "You really took a tumble. Matt's right. If Dominic hadn't shown up when he did, Spirit might've trampled you when she ran out. Something spooked the hell out of her."

"Yeah." Matt looked wide-eyed from Tatiana to Layla as he clutched specimen bottles in both hands and stepped back, giving Dominic plenty of room to pass. "M-maybe you should let the doc have a look at you, Tatiana."

"Listen to that." Dominic spared her a glance as he strode through the stable doors toward the house. "Even your *boyfriend* thinks I'm right."

The man was infuriating. He knew that Matt wasn't

her boyfriend, and now he was gloating because he'd figured out her ruse.

"I'll be fine, Matt," Tatiana shouted while glaring at Dominic as he walked across the lawn. "Just get the samples, and help Layla get Spirit back in her stall. She's sick and shouldn't be wandering around."

"See," Dominic said in a teasing tone. "You should follow your own advice. Although the horse has more sense than you do." He jerked his head to the right. "She's dying to get inside and rest."

Tatiana saw Spirit standing by the edge of the barn waiting to go back inside. A smile curved her lips, and she let out a short laugh. Pain shot through her head and down her back.

"Shit," she said in a rush. "That hurts."

"What?" Dominic asked as he carried her across the property. "The bump on your head or the fact that I'm right."

"Both."

Silence stretched for a beat or two and, with only the feel of his body occupying her every thought, Tatiana had to talk about something to distract herself.

"How did you know I grew up on a farm?" Tatiana asked.

"I did a little research before you showed up here, as I do with anyone coming to the ranch." Dominic flicked his eyes to her briefly. "In addition to Layla, your adopted sister, you have a twin brother named Raife. Purists murdered your Amoveo father from the Timber Wolf Clan, and your human mother died when you were a toddler. You and Raife were raised by your Aunt Rosie in Maryland, and you're stubborn as hell."

"You got all of that from your research?"

"Well, everything but the stubborn part," Dominic said through a chuckle as they approached the house. "I found that out the minute I met you."

Tatiana rolled her eyes, which only made him laugh again.

"So you talk to animals, huh?" Dominic smirked as he climbed the steps of the porch. "Why didn't she tell you to get out of the way?"

"Very funny."

Dominic stopped at the front door and tightened his hold on Tatiana as he peered at her intently. He held her gaze as his thumb brushed along her bare thigh beneath the edge of her shorts. She tried not to notice the way the muscles of his chest moved temptingly against her arm or the warmth of his hands as they pressed against her flesh, but it was no use.

Dominic surrounded her in every way a person could be surrounded.

Tatiana's breath caught in her throat, and even though she wanted to look away, she couldn't. That penetrating stare held her captive and studied her, as if he could peer directly into her soul. Perhaps he could?

"I'm sorry," he said quietly. "I don't want to see you get hurt anymore than you already are. You're too important."

Tatiana's eyes widened as panic welled. She knew what he meant. She was his mate, and he needed her so he could keep his abilities. Resentment flared as she remembered what Layla told her. If Amoveo didn't find their mates, then they would lose their powers and age like humans. She was merely a means to an end.

"I am?" Her voice shook with fear and uncertainty.

"Yes." His mouth set in a tight line as he abruptly looked away. "Richard and Salinda need you to figure out what's wrong with their horses. They are Salinda's most prized possessions. Well, more like family, really. Especially Spirit."

Tatiana's mouth snapped shut with surprise. She'd been ready to rail him with a scathing response about how she was not going to be part of this whole you-complete-me mate crap.

"Right." She nodded and looked away, unsure of what was happening. Maybe she misjudged him. Perhaps he wasn't going to try and convince her to mate with him? Maybe Dominic was as annoyed by the prospect of having a life-mate as she was.

The front door swung open, and a young blonde woman with a shy smile and large green eyes greeted them. Tatiana sensed she was from the Coyote Clan. She looked about seven months pregnant, but her expression switched to concern when she saw that Tatiana was hurt.

"Oh my goodness," the young woman said quickly, stepping aside as she rubbed a hand over her round belly. "What on earth happened, Dominic? Hurry, take her downstairs to the medical suite."

"She got a bump on the head and the wind knocked out of her when one of the horses got spooked. By the way, aren't you supposed to be resting, Courtney?"

"I'm fine, Dominic. What is it with you Amoveo men?" She smiled and gave Tatiana a knowing look. "I'm Courtney, by the way," she said as they crossed the spacious front hall to a door leading to a set of steps. "Steven's mate." She looked away and opened the door for them.

Tatiana noticed a subtle change in her energy signature when she identified herself as Steven's mate, and it gave Tatiana pause. It was like a hiccup in a steady stream of energy, as if she momentarily let down her guard. Perhaps Tatiana wasn't the only one who didn't embrace the whole fated mate idea?

"Be careful with her, Dominic." Courtney smiled at Tatiana and led the way down the steps.

"Believe me, I will be," Dominic said. "She's the careless one, not me."

Tatiana made a sound of frustration and bit her lip to keep from telling Dominic off. Besides, with her luck, he'd probably enjoy it.

"Nice to meet you, Courtney." Tatiana kept her arms folded over her chest and her eyes straight ahead as Dominic carried her down the steps into a long, well-lit hallway. "I'd shake your hand, but I'm afraid Dominic will think that's too strenuous," she muttered.

"Keep joking, but *you* are the veterinarian who got clobbered by her patient. Not me." His brow knit together as Courtney scooted past and opened a door marked *Exam Room* on the right side of the hall. "What got Spirit so riled up, anyway? The horses are examined on a regular basis and are used to shifters, hybrid and pure-blood, so what happened?"

"Steven is finishing up in the lab," Courtney said with a faint smile. "He said that he'd be here in a minute."

Dominic carried Tatiana in and placed her gently on the cushioned exam table. She glanced at him briefly as he stepped back, and she tried not to notice how swiftly her skin cooled when she left the shelter of his embrace. There was no denying that her body responded to his, and it reminded her of the imprinting that some animals do when they find their mates.

Tatiana couldn't help but wonder if that's what this was—a genetic, imprinted response—but if that were true, it actually gave her hope. If this intense attraction between them was merely biological, then she could choose not to participate.

"Thanks," she said as she gingerly adjusted her position. Tatiana arched her back, trying to work out the kinks, but stopped as another sharp pain shot into her head. "Damn, she got me good. I'm not usually careless."

"I didn't think so," Dominic said darkly. "What happened?"

The truth was that she wasn't quite sure. She had never connected with an animal so clearly before. Staring into Dominic's eyes, she had a sinking suspicion of what caused the sudden boost in her abilities. Before she could answer, a tall, handsome man with shaggy blond hair, wearing a lab coat and a warm smile, came into the room.

"I've been looking forward to meeting you, Tatiana," Steven said with a friendly grin as he shut the door behind him. "I have to admit I hoped it would be at dinner tonight and not in the exam room."

"Hey, babe." He placed a quick kiss on Courtney's cheek. "Aren't you supposed to be resting?"

"I'm fine, Steven." Courtney lifted one shoulder, and a look of embarrassment passed over her face as she glanced at Tatiana. "I wanted to make sure Tatiana was alright, but I'll go back to our cabin and lie down if that will make you happy."

"It would," he said with a wink. Steven squatted down so that his face was directly in front of her large belly. "Tell your mother she needs to rest."

"Fine," Courtney sighed. "You men are so bossy."

"Thank you." He kissed her tummy and stood up. "And we're not bossy, just concerned."

Courtney opened the door and looked back at Tatiana before she left. "I know what it's like to be new around here and surrounded by a bunch of overprotective alpha males."

"Hey." Steven put his hand to his chest, feigning injury.

"When you're feeling up to it," she said through a short laugh, "I'd be happy to take a walk with you and show you around the property. The cabin you're staying in is across the way from ours. I know you have your sister here, but a girl can never have too many female friends."

"I'd like that," Tatiana said through a smile. "Thank you."

Courtney waved as she left, but for all her pleasantries, Tatiana couldn't shake the feeling she was hiding something. It was the way she interacted with Steven. She didn't appear to share the seamless bond with him that the other women shared with their mates. They lacked the comfort level and innate intimacy she'd witnessed with the others.

"What happened?" Steven asked.

"Huh?" Tatiana's face burned when she realized that Steven had been talking to her, and she didn't even hear him. "I'm sorry, what did you ask me?"

Dominic grumbled something under his breath but didn't move from his protective stance by the door.

Tatiana shot him a look of disapproval before turning her attention back to Steven.

"How did you end up in a fight with the stall door and lose?" Steven stood in front of her and checked her vital signs as they spoke while Dominic kept tracking every move. "It's my understanding that you have the ability to communicate with animals—read their energies. I have to admit, that's a pretty radical power, and I would bet it makes you a kick-ass vet."

Steven removed the blood pressure cuff and hung it on a hook behind her.

"What did you see? Was it the same thing that spooked the horse?"

"I'm not sure," Tatiana said as she recalled the incident. "It was probably a fluke."

"What was a fluke?" Dominic's voice, low and dangerous, cut into the conversation. He stepped closer but didn't take his focus off of her. "What the hell happened in that barn?"

"I heard her," Tatiana whispered. "I actually heard her *speak*."

Tatiana looked from Dominic to Steven, who stared with curiosity and concern. The words poured out of her mouth as the excitement about this new development registered.

"That's *never* happened," she said excitedly. "I mean, I've always been able to read an animal's emotions. It's hard to explain, but I usually see colors in their energy waves, and if I want, I can connect with their signatures, much like we can with other Amoveo, but this was much more. I heard her *voice* in my mind like I hear Layla, but it was further away, like a bad connection on a telephone."

"Interesting." Steven turned her upper body so he could inspect the back of her head. "So, before coming to the ranch, you didn't have this particular layer to your abilities? Correct?"

"That's right," Tatiana said slowly. She locked eyes with Dominic as Steven finished examining her, and a knot gathered in her belly. "Why?"

Tatiana didn't have to ask the question, because she already knew the answer. It was Dominic, or more to the point, her and Dominic. He didn't flinch but continued to stare with those intense brown eyes. Dominic knew it as well as she did, but to his credit, he didn't say a word.

"Could be a couple of explanations," Steven said with a knowing look at Dominic. "We may just have to wait and see." He went to the sink and washed his hands. "I suppose you could try it with another horse and see if you get a similar reaction, but give yourself more distance next time so you don't end up with hooves in your face."

"Got it. So, am I free to go, or will I be carried around all day?"

Tatiana winced at the way that came out. It sounded as if she was hoping for that, and she totally wasn't. *Yeah, right*. She rubbed her hands over her face, wishing she could rub away how out of sorts she felt.

"You'll be fine. You're already beginning to heal, and the soreness should be gone in a few hours." He smirked and glanced at Dominic while he dried his hands. "As for being carried around by Dom, here… I suppose that's between the two of you."

"I think I can walk just fine." Tatiana's face heated with embarrassment, and she let out a nervous laugh. "I have to get back up there. Matt is probably worried, and besides, he's got the samples."

"Matt can wait a good goddamn minute." Dominic's eyes narrowed, and he moved toward her. "I want to know what she said." His voice, strong and steady, filled the room. "Spirit—what did she say?"

Dominic inched closer. Heat wafted off him and drifted over her in erotic waves, and it took a second for her to realize she was holding her breath.

"I only heard a few words." Tatiana's back stiffened, and she gripped the edge of the table, fighting against the insane urge to reach up and stroke that scar on his face. Her tongue flicked out and moistened her lower lip, and she brushed the hair off her forehead as she met his challenge. "The first two were: *hunter killer*."

"Shit." Dominic stuffed his hands in his pockets and turned to Steven, breaking the spell. "I knew it. Someone messed with the horses, and I'd bet anything it was those fuckin' Caedo assassins we snagged here on the property. They probably put something in the food."

"It's possible. Based on the symptoms, I'm betting on poisoning, but I have to run some tests to be sure." Tatiana took a deep breath and looked between the two men. "Where are the men you caught? I'm sure you questioned them already, but—"

"I killed one," Dominic said evenly, as if killing people was commonplace. "But the other got away after he shot Eric."

"You killed him?" Tatiana's voice was barely audible. "You just go around killing people?"

"Only the ones who try to kill me," Dominic said in a matter-of-fact tone. "Or the people I care about."

Tatiana stared at him, trying to wrap her brain around what he said. A chill rippled up her back, and a knot of fear twisted in her belly. This was exactly why she didn't want to get mixed up with the Amoveo or their topsy-turvy world. They operated under their own rules, and so far, she didn't really care for them.

"Well," she said in a far shakier voice than she'd intended. "I'll be sure to keep that in mind, and if nothing else, you've given me one hell of a good reason to finish my job and go home."

Tatiana hopped easily off the exam table, but when her feet hit the floor, pain shimmied up her back. Though she did her best to hide it, she could tell by the look of disapproval on Dominic's face, he didn't miss it.

You're not being completely honest. Dominic's voice shot into her mind with his now-familiar bossy tone. *There's more. I can feel it.*

"Steven?" Tatiana did her best to ignore Dominic. "Layla mentioned you have some lab equipment here. Would it be alright if Matt and I use it to run a few tests?"

"You bet." He shucked his lab coat, revealing a rock-n-roll T-shirt, and she couldn't help but smile. Steven may be an Amoveo, but she could tell he was a down-to-earth guy. "It's just down the hall. *Mi casa es su casa.* I'll see you two kids later. I'm going back to the cabin to check on Courtney."

Steven whispered the ancient language, static filled the room, and seconds later, he vanished.

"That shit still freaks me out." Tatiana shook her head and blinked. "Count me out for that particular gift."

Turning around, she walked face-first into Dominic's

broad chest. He linked his hands around her biceps and held her firmly against him. His dark eyebrows furrowed as he peered down at her through serious eyes. She licked her lips nervously, trying not to notice the firm muscles of his pecs beneath her fingers. Yup. No fat anywhere.

"What is it that you're not telling me, Tatiana?" His voice dropped to low seductive tones as his fingers relaxed and brushed the skin of her arms. "You can trust me. I—I would never hurt you."

Tatiana should have been put off by the fact that he invaded her space, but *that* would be operating under the assumption she could think clearly. All she could do was feel—feel his fingers as they melded against the flesh of her arms or his heartbeat as it thundered steadily in his chest beneath the soft cotton T-shirt.

Before she could stop herself, Tatiana reached up and ran her fingers down the scar on the side of his face. The strip of marred flesh felt surprisingly smooth beneath her fingertips, and something inside her ached to ease the pain he must have felt. A growl rumbled in Dominic's chest, reverberating through her as he held her close, and his eyes shifted to glowing amber orbs.

Tatiana swallowed hard but held his gaze as her fingers trailed down to his stubble-covered jaw. His eyes reminded her of a wildfire, like the ones she'd seen out west that burned bright and out of control.

That's what she was feeling—completely out of control. No say over her emotions or her body. Everything burned. Heat flashed over her skin, and her eyes shifted into the bright yellow-gold orbs of her wolf.

"Mate," he growled.

In a blur, Dominic leaned down and covered her mouth with his as the rumbling in his chest grew louder. Tatiana moaned and opened to him. Her arms slipped around his neck, and everything else fell away. In that moment, she let go of whatever semblance of control she had and tumbled blindly into the abyss.

Tatiana had been kissed before, but *never* like this.

Dominic devoured her, like wildfire consuming everything in its path. He suckled and drank from her as though his existence depended on it. He held her head in his strong hands, angling and allowing him better access. His tongue tangled with hers as she threaded her fingers through his short hair and hung on for dear life.

Through the rage of desire, she heard his voice scrape along the edges of her mind… *mate*.

What the hell was she doing?

Tatiana dropped her hands to his chest as he trailed hot, wet kisses along her jaw and down the sensitive skin along her neck. This wasn't just *some guy* she was plastered all over. This was *the* guy. The one she'd been desperately trying to avoid, and here she was making out with him like some horny kid. Fear, panic, and an overwhelming sense of danger swamped her as reality came crashing back into focus.

Tatiana abruptly shoved herself out of his grasp and swiped the back of her hand over her mouth. They stood there for a moment, breathing heavily, glowing eyes locked on one another. Dominic's fingers curled at his side as Tatiana held up both hands in a peace offering.

"I'm sorry," she said through heavy breaths, her lips still tingling from his touch. "We can't do this, or more to the point, *I* can't do this."

Tatiana expected him to argue or protest, but neither happened. His eyes shifted to their human state, and he gave a curt nod of agreement. "Agreed."

"Good," she said hesitantly. "Why aren't you fighting with me about this?"

"I like to pick my battles." Dominic's mouth tilted into a lopsided grin. "For example, why don't you tell me what else you heard in the barn?"

Tatiana blinked with surprise. She'd forgotten that's what they'd been talking about before he kissed her senseless.

"What's the matter, doc?" His grin broadened. "Did I kiss it right out of you?"

"You would think that." Her eyes narrowed, and she felt her face color again. Good God, she'd blushed more in the past twelve hours than she had in her entire life. "Fine. I'll tell you," she huffed and moved toward him with her hands placed firmly on her hips. "Just before I blacked out, I did hear something else."

Tatiana got right in his face, daring him to retreat, but he held his ground.

"*Traitor*," she whispered.

Dominic's face darkened, and she didn't need to read his energy signature to know how upset he was. "Purists?"

Tatiana nodded slowly and turned on her heels to the door, but paused as she opened it. "That's not what scared Spirit though." She tilted her chin and delivered a challenging glare in his direction.

"Oh really, Dr. Dolittle? Then what did?"

"Very funny." She rolled her eyes. "It seems Spirit isn't fond of big cats."

"That doesn't make sense." Dominic gave her a confused look. "They're used to us and our clan forms."

"Be that as it may. I heard the growl of a big cat as I passed out." She blew the hair off her forehead and looked away, embarrassed to bring up the fact that she'd gotten knocked on her ass. "When she reared up, that was the last thing I heard."

Dominic moved toward her slowly, with the easy, fluid motions of a cat and that feral, predatory look in his eye. Tatiana gripped the doorknob for dear life as he approached. Her feet felt like they were nailed to the floor, and even though her gut instinct was to run, she held fast as he stopped inches from her.

"That growl you heard?" he asked as he leaned closer, his lips a breath away from hers. "That was me, Doc. Your energy signature has been tangling with mine from the second my body touched yours, and you know what? I'm not a fan."

"What?" Tatiana's eyes widened. She didn't know whether to be insulted or relieved. Maybe she was a bit of both.

"I can't get you out of my head." Dominic stepped back, giving them distance. "I'm Guardian of this property. It's up to me to keep a clear head and a sharp mind. People depend on me to protect them."

"Dominic, I—"

"No." He held up one hand to stop her. "Let me finish."

"Fine." Tatiana folded her arms over her breasts and waited.

"I'll admit, before I met you I was worried as hell about not finding a mate and losing my powers, but now I'm not so sure." His voice was barely above a whisper. "How the hell am I supposed to do my job if all I can do is think about you and keeping you safe? So, if you don't want to mate with me, well, that's just fine. You do your job, and I'll do mine. When we're done, we go our separate ways." Dominic stuck his hand out to her. "Deal?"

Tatiana looked at his outstretched hand and then to his serious, masculine face. "Deal," she said quietly.

They shook hands briefly, neither wanting to linger. As she followed him out of the room, one issue nagged at her.

Tatiana got what she wanted. Her Amoveo mate agreed to let her off the hook and not follow through with the whole life-mate deal. She should be on top of the world and completely relieved… but just the opposite was true. *Damn it.*

Chapter 4

A THICK SUMMER BREEZE WHISKED PAST DOMINIC AS A flock of birds swooped overhead and landed in a tall pine tree. As he strode along the dirt road, he scanned the area for unusual energy patterns, but so far, all was well. When he reached the top of the hill, three log cabins came into view, one of which was his.

Richard and Salinda built several cabins when the Purists began making trouble last year. They knew any hybrids they found might need a safe haven, and the Muldavi Ranch always provided exactly that. Dominic had been living here for two years, and a few months ago, Steven and William moved in with their mates.

The place had turned into a full-on compound, and when he made the occasional trip into town, he didn't miss the funny looks from people who were convinced Richard and Salinda ran a cult. Dominic scoffed under his breath at the ridiculous notion as he approached his destination.

Steven and Courtney's cabin was down the road to the left, across from his. When they'd first moved in, it took some getting used to because he'd enjoyed the solitude, but now, he'd gotten accustomed to them.

Dominic sensed both of their energy signatures flowing from inside the cozy cabin and couldn't help but smile. The two had been through hell in the last year, and while Steven bounced back quickly, Courtney seemed unsteady and ready to bolt. He'd asked Steven about it, but he brushed it off, blaming it on her pregnancy.

Sweat trickled down his back, and even though he itched to shift into his tiger, he refrained. The ranch was over three hundred acres, and distances like that were easier to travel in his animal form. Ever since the Caedo attack, he and Eric had been sticking closer to the main part of the property. So as much as he wanted to, he didn't. Tatiana and Matt would be coming by this way any minute to settle into their cabin, and the kid might freak out if he saw a Bengal tiger loping along the path.

Their cabin.

A low growl rumbled in his chest, and his eyes shifted harshly at the very thought of Tatiana sharing anything with another man. The image of her heart-shaped face drifted into his mind, and his body hardened at the memory of her softness. Dominic wanted her. There was no denying it.

Dominic's body reacted to her on a primal, animalistic level. However, that's not what set him on edge. If he'd only been attracted physically, it would be a hell of a lot easier to distance himself from Tatiana. It was the flood of unexpected emotions that had him all fucked up.

Hell, after that kiss, he knew she wanted him just as badly. Her body said *yes* to everything, but her head screamed *hell no*. He couldn't blame her because he wasn't feeling all that different. He didn't have the time or the luxury to wade through his feelings. Dominic cursed under his breath and kicked a stone out of his path, glowering at it as it tumbled into the tall grasses along the edge of the road.

Dominic knew he'd shown all the self-control of a goddamn dog when he jumped her bones back in the medical lab. It was like something or someone took control over him. It didn't matter that she told him she didn't want to be his mate. All that mattered was tasting, licking, and nibbling those sweet, cherry lips until he couldn't breathe.

There was no thought or concern for consequences. He didn't think, he merely acted on impulse, and *that* was unacceptable. He let his emotions cloud his judgment, and it was those emotional blinders that could get people killed. His sister, Daniella, had been a Purist traitor, and he didn't see it until it was too late.

Dominic clenched his teeth and fought the urge to shift as the energy rippled over his muscles. The animal inside strained to be released. No. He would not allow his feelings to blind him anymore. He would keep his distance from Tatiana, do his job as Guardian, and let her go home to Oregon.

It would mean eventually losing his powers, but what good would they be if he ended up with a woman who loathed him? Better he lose his abilities and live his life as a human, rather than force Tatiana to be with him.

Nothing would make him forget the look on her face when he told her he'd killed that Caedo assassin. It was a mixture of horror and fear. Dominic had plenty of people look at him fearfully, and it never bothered him. On the contrary, it made him feel like he was doing his job. But when Tatiana looked at him like that, it was a kick in the gut, as if he'd somehow let her down.

Bullshit.

Dominic straightened his back. He didn't owe her an

explanation. He would never apologize for doing his job no matter how many disapproving looks she gave, but as he walked up the flagstone path to Tatiana's cabin, he knew that was a full-fledged lie. If she looked at him like that again, he might fall to his knees and beg for forgiveness.

"Jesus," he muttered as he took the key from his pocket and unlocked the door. "I'm acting pussy-whipped already."

Just as he stepped into the cabin, he heard tires crunching along the dirt road, and Tatiana's now-familiar energy signature whisked over him on a warm breeze. He breathed deeply and willed his eyes not to shift as he stood on the porch and watched them pull up. Tatiana wore a pair of dark sunglasses, but he could tell she was tracking his every move.

"Hey, Dom," Layla said, stepping out of the passenger seat. "Thanks for dropping off the keys."

Tatiana and Matt emerged and gathered their bags. They'd been running tests all afternoon in the lab, and Dominic was glad to see they were finished because having that human in the main house made him uncomfortable.

Layla let Cass down, and the puppy quickly began to claim the area as his by peeing on one of the stones lining the path.

"Hope Cass isn't going to mark up the inside too," Dominic muttered as the puppy bounded enthusiastically along the path and attacked various pieces of grass on the way.

"He's claiming his territory," Tatiana said with a grin as she watched Cass tumble along.

"You know how male animals are," Matt chimed in. "They want the world to know what belongs to them. Tatiana and I see it all the time in the practice. Don't we?"

Dominic grit his teeth and fought the urge to say something. He hated that this guy knew things about Tatiana and shared things with her that he didn't. It was dumb as dirt to be jealous of this scrawny kid, especially because Tatiana clearly wasn't interested in him, but it didn't make it less true.

"Mm-hmmm." Tatiana nodded but didn't look at either of them as she continued up the steps. *Careful.* The teasing lilt of her voice floated into his mind. *Your alpha male Amoveo is showing.* Her sweet scent filled his nostrils, and combined with the telepathic connection, it made his dick twitch.

"I suppose I can't say as I blame them." Dominic breathed her in as she brushed past him and murmured in a low voice, "Marking their territory is embedded in their DNA." He touched her mind with his. *But I promise you, when I stake claim to my territory…I'll choose a far more pleasant method.*

Tatiana stumbled and almost fell, but Dominic grabbed her arm and kept her on her feet. "Careful," he murmured. He gave her a knowing look. "You've already taken one tumble today."

"Thank you." She pulled her arm from his grasp and gave him a tight smile. "I think I can manage."

Cass bounded up the steps between them, breaking the spell. They all watched as he went sliding across the smooth wood floors and landed butt first into the back of the couch.

Tatiana let out a whistle as she looked around the

surprisingly roomy cabin. The first floor had an open layout with a large living and dining area to the left and a spacious kitchen to the right. Windows surrounded much of the first level, giving it the feeling of being far larger than it was.

"Just wanted to be sure you got settled. Did everything go well in the lab? Is it poisoning like you suspected?" Dominic asked as he closed the door behind him.

"Yeah," Matt said with awe. "I've never seen such a cool setup. This Richard guy must be freakin' loaded to have a med lab like that."

Dominic ignored the kid and kept his attention on Tatiana.

"Yes. Someone tainted their feed supply, but the water came up negative." Tatiana looked around the kitchen as she spoke, carefully avoiding him and his gaze. "We emptied and disinfected the feed buckets, so we'll have to go out tomorrow to get clean food. They should be fine once it works its way out of their systems, but someone definitely messed with them. Although, I'm a bit worried about Spirit. I hope we got to her in time."

"Yeah," Matt chimed in. He scrunched his face up and ran a hand through his messy hair. "I don't get it. Who would anyone mess with this guy's horses?"

"He's not just some guy," Dominic said evenly. "He's—"

"The horses are worth a fortune," Layla interrupted and shot Dominic a look that screamed *shut up*. "Who knows why crazy people do crazy things? Anyway, Dominic and Eric will obviously have their hands full and are stepping up security. Right, Dominic?"

"It's really none of our concern, Matt," Tatiana added quickly. She smiled and lifted one shoulder. "We were hired to figure out what was going on, and we did. As soon as they're all on the mend, you and I will be on our way."

"So, what?" Dominic walked to the granite island and leaned both hands on it as he turned his full attention to Tatiana. "That's it? You're leaving?"

"Not yet." She held his stare, meeting his challenge. "We'll stay for a few more days to make sure their symptoms dissipate… and then we'll go."

"Aw, man," Layla huffed. She leaned both elbows on the end of the island and looked at her sister. "I was hoping you'd stay longer."

"Oh please." Tatiana laughed. "You'll be sick of me by tomorrow."

"Well," she said slowly, as if she was afraid to say more. "I won't be here tomorrow or the rest of the week actually."

"What?" Tatiana's eyes widened, and she flicked them briefly to Dominic before narrowing them at her sister. "You're *leaving*?"

Tatiana's energy waves fluttered with panic and a touch of fear, making Dominic surprisingly uncomfortable. Was she afraid of him? Of being alone with him? He pushed himself away from the granite counter and walked over to the window, pretending to be interested in something outside.

"I'm sorry, sis. I got a call from *National Geographic* this morning for a photo shoot, and it's too good a gig to pass up. William and I are leaving tomorrow afternoon. I'm surprised he didn't give me a hard time about going, but I think the latest assassination attempt has him on edge. Listen, if you're pissed at me, just take heart in knowing that I'll have my husband doing his overprotective macho stuff during my entire trip. I've never taken him on a shoot, so I have no idea how this is going to go, and it could turn into a cluster-fuck of epic proportions."

Dominic glanced over his shoulder and caught sight of Tatiana. Her arms were folded over her breasts, and she was biting her thumbnail. The woman had turned into a bundle of nerves in a matter of minutes, and he knew full well it was because of him. The puppy seemed aware of it too because he whimpered at her feet and rubbed against her legs.

"When will you be back?" Tatiana asked quietly. She let out a slow breath as she reached down and petted the dog.

"Saturday—a week from today—and I *promise* we'll have some serious sister time, but I really can't pass up this opportunity."

"I know," Tatiana said on a sigh of frustration. "I just… well, I guess this means we can finish up and head out as soon as possible. There really isn't any other reason for me to stay. You and William should visit my place in Oregon when you're finished with your gig."

Dominic fought the urge to grab her, throw her over his shoulder, and tell her she wasn't going anywhere without him ever again. However, he suspected a move like that would go over like a fart in church.

"Well," Dominic interrupted. "However long you're going to be here, you'll need keys to the cabin. Here they are." He placed them on the small table by the front door, trying not to sound like a possessive dickhead. He faced her again. "Not that anyone ever locks their doors around here."

"First time for everything," Matt said from his spot on the large leather sectional. Dominic had almost forgotten he was there. "Wouldn't want any unwelcome visitors in the middle of the night."

"Right." Dominic sliced a look in his direction before turning his attention back to Tatiana. "There are two bedrooms upstairs, each equipped with their own bathroom. So you'll have plenty of privacy." He leveled a stare back to Matt. "There are locks on those doors too," he said pointedly.

Matt shrugged awkwardly and picked up a magazine from the coffee table.

"The kitchen has been fully stocked, but if there's anything you need, I'm sure you can find it in town. Although," Dominic said with a smile as he put his hands in his pockets, "it's pretty limited as far as shopping options are concerned. If you blinked on your way here, you may have missed it."

"Yeah." Tatiana looked at him and laughed softly.

Dominic tried not to notice that the knot in his stomach eased with the sound of her laugh.

"It did go by quickly." Tatiana smiled. "Not exactly a bustling metropolis, but that's fine by me."

"Tatiana I are used to rural towns," Matt chimed in.

Dominic turned and gave the kid a bored look.

"Come on." Layla chuckled. She grabbed one of the bags off the couch and gave Matt a friendly pat on the shoulder. "I'll show you where the bedrooms are."

"I call whichever room has a view of that," Tatiana said, pointing to the back windows of the house. "I miss

Oregon, but I've got to admit, those mountains make for one breathtaking skyline," she said on a sigh.

Tatiana strode toward the back of the cabin and tugged open the glass sliders. She stepped out onto the small deck and leaned on the railing. Dominic's gaze skimmed up her well-shaped legs, which were bronzed from the summer sun, then wandered along the curve of her hip and up her toned arms.

Images of her naked body curled around his flooded his mind…

"Can we swim in that pond?" She looked at him over her shoulder and smirked as she caught him checking her out.

"What?" He blinked and shook his head, but those images of her still wandered through his imagination. "I'm sorry. What?"

"Dominic?" Smiling, she looked back out to the mirrorlike body of water in the distance. "That pond? Can we swim in it?"

"It's not a pond, actually. It's a swimming pool." He moved closer so he stood next to her, but not close enough to accidentally touch her. "It's a freshwater swimming pool complete with heat in the winter and lights at night. Salinda had it designed to look like a pond so it wouldn't ruin the natural landscape."

Heat radiated from her body, and even amid the thick summer air, he could feel it rippling over him like a siren song. Calling him. Daring him to touch her again. Tempting him to break the stupid deal he made with her, throw her on the ground, and kiss her silly.

Why did he make that deal? That was the dumbest fucking move ever.

Dominic tightened his grip on the railing and squared his shoulders against the all-consuming urge to stroke that gorgeous skin. Instead, he focused on the setting sun and grit his teeth against the driving, physical need to connect with her.

"Are you alright?" Tatiana's voice, soft and delicate, drifted over him with the breeze.

"No," he said, his voice tight with restraint. Dominic looked down into those huge brown eyes, and he knew he was a goner. "I'm not alright. Not at all."

Without thinking he brushed a lock of dark hair off her forehead, and as her warm skin rushed beneath his fingertips, a wave of static electricity rippled up his arm and shot through his body. Her eyes widened, and those red lips that tasted like cherries parted temptingly as she sucked in a slow, quivering breath.

"I'm doing my best to be a gentleman and keep my word," he whispered as he trailed one finger along her jawline. Her body wavered closer, her eyes searched his for answers, but none came as the ripples of nerve-tingling electricity slowed. "I have a feeling I'm going to renege on our deal."

"I think we should try to stay clear of each other," Tatiana murmured. She nodded slowly. Her tongued darted out, moistening her plump lower lip.

"It's really the best way to handle this situation. Neither of us wants a mate, so the smart thing to do would be to forget it. We still have free will. Don't we?"

Tatiana inched nearer in spite of what she was saying. Her hand brushed his as it curled along the weathered wood railing, and that same zapping sensation fired through his body. An odd buzzing filled Dominic's head as their energy signatures whipped through the air like an invisible tornado, dancing around them like a whirling dervish. The buzzing reached a crescendo, and with one final pass, their energy waves merged with a jolt.

Tatiana cried out in surprise and stepped back, but Dominic linked one arm around her waist and pulled her up against him. Her hands gripped his shoulders, and although she didn't push him away, she gaped at him like a deer in the headlights.

"Wha—what was that?" she asked breathlessly, her voice edged with fear. "I don't think I can handle this."

"I'm not entirely sure, but I think our energy signatures merged, and we've imprinted on each other. There is one thing I *am* sure of." Dominic kissed the corner of her mouth and murmured against her cheek. "The only woman I'm looking to *handle*... is you."

Tatiana's fingers dug into his shoulders, and her body trembled against his as she leaned into him. He knew she wanted him. Her energy waves, now clearly joined with his, were thick with lust but wavered with fear. She was afraid of him, his people, and their way of life.

"Man, this place is freaking awesome," Matt said, but the smile fell from his face when he saw the two of them. Dominic stepped back, abruptly releasing her. "Sorry to interrupt," Matt said tightly.

Dominic put his hands in his pockets and leveled a glare at Matt, who gave him his best dirty look right back.

"Don't be silly," Tatiana said, waving off Matt's comment. She glanced briefly at Dominic before turning to face the mountains. "We were admiring the view."

"Is that what they're calling it these days?" Layla said in a teasing tone as she sidled up next to her sister.

Tatiana elbowed her sister and shot her a look.

"I'll be on my way." Dominic strode past them without sparing a glance at anyone and trotted down the steps.

"Good night, Dominic." Tatiana's tentative voice was edged with a promise to continue what they both knew had already started.

"Yeah. It's a real shame you have to go, but I guess you have security stuff to do." Matt moved in on the other side of Tatiana. "Bye."

"I won't be far away." Dominic stopped and turned to face them. He jutted a thumb toward the cabin next door. "I live right over there."

"That's awesome," Matt mumbled under his breath before going into the house. "This place has like a million acres, and his cabin is right next door."

"Thanks for your help today, Dom," Layla said. "And I, for one, am glad my sister has you nearby. A girl can never have too much security, especially *this* girl. If I know her, she's gonna stumble out here in the middle of the night to take a midnight dip in the pool."

"No, I won't," Tatiana said. She gave Layla a playful smack on the butt as her sister brushed past and went inside. "I have to be up early to check on the horses."

"Then you better get some sleep." Dominic winked before heading toward his cabin. As he strode through the tall grass, he touched her mind easily. *Sweet dreams, Doc.*

The fog of the dream realm rolled gently around Tatiana in billowy gray and lavender clouds flickering with light. She had dream-walked many times over the years, though most of them had been spent avoiding Dominic—but not tonight.

Tonight she would face him head on.

There was no denying she was attracted to him. She rolled her eyes at the enormous understatement. Attracted. Right. That didn't cover the half of it. It was like her body was genetically programmed to respond to his, and Dominic had become an itch she had to scratch. So she would—but only if he agreed that's all it would be.

Just sex.

Sex with no strings attached.

It was possible. Layla told her about the binding rite. Amoveo weren't really mated until those words were spoken. So why not go ahead and scratch the itch, as long as neither of them said those words?

That was her plan. Find him in the dream realm and offer him a new deal. Based on the way the two of them couldn't keep their hands off each other, they needed one quick.

Tatiana steeled her resolve, closed her eyes, and reached out to him. She followed the path of their merged energy signatures, and moments later a humming sound blanketed the realm. Light flashed behind her eyes as a low, rumbling growl filled her mind, growing louder with each passing second, until it sounded as though it came from right in front of her.

Dominic. *She said his name on a whisper, and when she opened her eyes, the clouds were gone and Dominic stood before her in his tiger form.* Whoa.

He was big and gorgeous, and his striped, furry body hummed with pure power. His amber eyes glowed brightly, and a low growl continued to rumble in his throat.

For all his strength, his fur looked silky soft, and before she could stop herself, she ran one quivering hand along the top of his head. Her suspicions were correct. The fur whispered soft and warm beneath her flesh as she trailed one finger down his snout before abruptly dropping her hand.

It took a second to realize his growl had turned into a purr. She folded her arms over her chest quickly worried she might rub him behind his ears.

I wasn't sure if you would come. *Her voice echoed around them, giving Tatiana the sense that they were the only two people who existed in the universe.* I have a new deal to propose. So thank you for meeting me here.

Static filled the air, and he shimmered as though he were underwater as he shifted into his human form. Dominic towered over her now, wearing the same black T-shirt and camo pants she'd seen him in earlier. He looked more sexy—and dangerous—than ever before.

Sharp, dark eyes fixed on her with that familiar predatory look, and she suddenly became self-conscious as Dominic looked her up and down. She tugged the edge of her nightshirt down with one hand, but it didn't do much good. The summery T-shirt she wore was barely long enough to cover her backside and left little to the imagination.

Actually, Doc, you came to me. *He gave her a lopsided grin and waved one hand out.* This is one of my favorite places in the world.

Tatiana gave him a puzzled look. What are you talking

about? I didn't—*She gasped, covering her mouth with both hands, when she saw where they were.*

It was stunning. They were standing on top of a volcano looking out over one of the most spectacular views she'd ever laid eyes on. Lush, thick foliage rolled down the mountain until it met a sparkling, azure ocean. It was rich green and blue for as far as the eye could see. She'd been so captivated by him that she didn't notice where they were.

Dominic. *She dropped her hands and gave him a wide smile.* This place is gorgeous. Where are we?

It's a volcano in Hawaii. I was stationed here for a while when I was in the military, and it was the most beautiful place I'd ever been. So I come back in the dream realm whenever I can. *He took her hand in his. Warm and strong, it curled easily around hers, sending every coherent thought out of her head. His thumb brushed the top of her hand, sending shivers up her back.* I'd love to visit again in person, especially if I had a traveling companion.

Military. That made sense, Tatiana thought as she gave him a sidelong glance. Dominic was stealthy, attuned to everything and poised for battle at a moment's notice. He was ruggedly handsome and had an ever-present five o'clock shadow.

The scar that ran down the side of his face made him even sexier, probably because he seemed blissfully unaware of it. His self-possessed confidence was as much of a turn-on as his smile. It was wicked and edged with promises of lust-filled nights.

To be honest, until you showed up today, I hadn't been able to visit here in a long time.

I see. *Tatiana swallowed the lump in her throat and fought the inevitable wave of panic*. Your powers were fading because we hadn't connected?

That's part of it, yes. *Dominic turned those gorgeous, fiery eyes to her*. The real reason is because I've spent most nights looking for you. *He smirked and wagged a finger at her playfully*. You were there too, weren't you? But you were hiding from me.

Maybe. *She lifted one shoulder and looked back out at the ocean, but her hand remained linked with his*. I'm not hiding anymore, Dominic.

Hey. *He placed his hands on her shoulders and gently turned her to face him*. I'm not going to force you into anything, and believe it or not, I'd like to get to know you. *He trailed his index finger along her jawline and tilted her chin, making her look him in the eye. His brow furrowed, and his mouth set in a firm line*. I would never hurt you.

Eyes wide, her skin on fire, all she could do was nod as her body took on a life of its own. He ran the back of his fingers down the sensitive skin of her throat, along the curve of her shoulder.

On the contrary, I want to give you pleasure, *he murmured. He cradled one hand around the back of her neck and kissed her cheek before blazing a trail down her throat*. In fact, all I can think about is pleasuring you.

Tatiana moaned, closed her eyes, and sank into the delicious sensation of his lips, moist and hot against her skin. She linked her arms around his waist and held him to her, wanting him closer. His hard, distinctly male body pressed against hers, hot and needy. It would be so easy to just…

Wait! *She grabbed his head with both hands and pulled him back. Breathless, they remained like that. Eyes glowing, bodies locked in an embrace that held promise of more to come, she wrestled to find the right words in her lust-muddled brain.*

What's wrong*? Dominic's fingers dug into her hips, and his erection pressed against her belly, daring her to make a move, but she held her ground.*

We need a new deal. *The words tumbled carelessly from her mouth.*

A new deal, huh? I suppose we do, especially since we just broke the last one. *He looked at her quizzically, and a smile played at his lips. One hand drifted down and rested on her ass, pressing her harder against him, and his voice dropped to a seductive tone*. What did you have in mind?

Sex with no strings. *He gave her a wary look, but she continued*. Look, this attraction, *she said, waving a hand between what little distance was between them*. It has a crazy hold on us, right?

Agreed, *he said slowly.*

And as far as I understand it, the bonding rite must be said during sex in order for the mating to be finalized. So I don't think there's any reason we can't have sex as long as we don't say the mating rite. *She leaned closer, popped on her toes, and kissed his throat*. See? Sex with no strings.

Is that what you want? *The winds of the realm picked up and blew briskly around them as Dominic peered down at her through those eyes of wildfire*. Are you sure that's all you want?

I want you, Dominic. *Tatiana pulled back and looked*

at him through the glowing eyes of her clan. She did want him. That wasn't a lie, but as he studied her intently, a little voice inside of her disagreed. She'd never been a one-night-stand girl. In fact, she'd only had two lovers—both of whom she'd been in relationships with. However, as her body burned against his, the fire consumed her doubts. We're consenting adults with the will to choose what we want. So do we have a new deal?

Thank God, *he groaned.* You bet your sweet ass, we do. *In one fluid motion, Dominic swept her into his arms as the winds blew harder. His mouth crashed down, and as his lips tangled with hers, all she could do was think about getting more. Hands linked around his neck, she kissed him back desperately and reveled in the feel of his arms wrapped around her.*

The winds whistled past as he laid her down on a soft bed of grass and covered her body with his. Straddling her on his knees, he broke the embrace long enough to take off his shirt, and Tatiana let out a gasp when she saw the multitude of scars that marred his muscled chest.

Tatiana sat up and ran her hands over the battle scars that marked him, and her throat tightened with emotion. Where on earth did you get these? *She looked into his face as a tear rolled down her cheek.* You really do put your life on the line for the Amoveo, don't you? It's not some macho badge you wear or something you say… you would die for them.

I would do anything to protect my people, Tatiana, and that includes you. *He pushed her back gently and covered her small frame easily as the weight of him settled between her legs. He brushed the hair from her face with his fingers and kissed the tip of her nose.* Mating ceremony or not.

A tsunami of emotions battered her. This man she barely knew was telling her he would lay his life down for hers, protect her at all cost. Tatiana remembered how gentle he was with the baby and the concern he expressed for Courtney. The man was fiercely devoted, and it was evident he loved the people he protected, though she doubted he would admit as much.

Running her hands over his back, she felt the unmistakable ridges of scarred skin. He had experienced more pain in his life than anyone she'd ever encountered, and looking into those fiery eyes, all she wanted to do now was to give him pleasure. Afford him an escape from the weight of his responsibility.

Tatiana pulled him to her, and just as his lips met hers, the haunting sound of a woman crying filled the realm. Dominic's body tensed. He jumped to his feet and pulled her up with him. Holding her in the shelter of his body, he scanned the realm, which had become unrecognizable.

Tatiana had been so wrapped up in Dominic that she hadn't even noticed the change to the environment—neither of them had. The sky was awash in angry, gray storm clouds, and the winds, once warm and inviting, were now cold and damp, as the woman's wailing grew louder.

Who's there? *Dominic's voice, deep and commanding, thundered through the unsettled dreamscape.* Show yourself.

Dominic. *Tatiana huddled deeper into his embrace and looked around the unstable new world.* What's going on?

Someone has invaded our dream. *His jaw clenched, and he held her tighter against his taut frame.* We have to leave. Come on. *He took her hand and started climbing up the hill.* Picture some place safe, *he shouted above the wind.*

Like where? *She put her hand up to block the rain that stung her face and blinded her. Tatiana stumbled, and Dominic's hand slipped from hers as she dropped to her knees and slid in the muddy ground.* Dominic?

Tatiana! *One strong hand encircled her arm and pulled her to her feet.* We have to wake up.

I'm not as good at this as you are, *she shouted over the thunder.*

The sound of weeping grew louder still. Tatiana strained to listen more closely, and then she heard it… Liar.

Did you hear that? *Tatiana shouted.*

Before he could answer her, a clap of thunder blared overhead, and lightning cracked across the black sky as the crying welled and throbbed, like a spirit lost in the night.

The haunting wail came again… Betrayer.

There it is again. *She looked around, but couldn't see anything through the sheets of rain.*

We have to go, Tatiana, *he yelled over the thunder.* Right now. *Tatiana shook with fear as Dominic grabbed her hand and ran. Blindly, she followed him through the pelting rain, and they stopped suddenly at the edge of a cliff. Tatiana screamed and grabbed onto Dominic for dear life as mud and rocks skidded off the edge into the roiling sea below.*

Do you trust me? *He yelled as he stuck his hand out.*

The crying grew louder and swirled around them in the storm. Traitor, *the voice wailed.*

Fear gripped Tatiana's heart, and it felt as though it would beat out of her chest, but looking into those orbs of fire, Tatiana knew she could trust him. She glanced at his outstretched hand, slick with rain and mud, and nodded.

I trust you. *Tatiana placed her hand in his, and as a black tornado approached, they leapt off the cliff and into the crashing sea below.*

Chapter 5

Tatiana shot out of bed, tumbled over the side, and landed on the floor with a butt-bruising thud. Her sweat-soaked sheets were tangled around her legs, and it took her a moment to get her bearings. Her breath came in quick gasps as she looked furiously around the bedroom of the guest cabin and was greeted by a series of warm licks on her arm from Cass.

"I'm okay, buddy." She rubbed his head reassuringly and whispered to him soothingly, knowing it wasn't just for his benefit. However, the little dog was a rather empathetic little creature. "It's going to be alright."

Pressing a hand to her chest, she let out a slow breath and squeezed her eyes shut as a sense of calm flooded her, and the effects of the dream faded. Still shaking, she unfurled the sheet from her ankles and tossed it onto the bed as she stood on unsteady legs. Casanova trotted over to the pile of pillows where he'd been sleeping and settled back in, but kept a watchful eye on Tatiana.

Seconds later, static electricity filled the room, and Dominic materialized next to her in his half-naked, shirtless glory. His face was etched with concern, and his glowing amber eyes shone brightly in the dimly lit room.

Without saying a word, he gathered her in his arms, and within seconds she could feel his heart beating in rapid time with hers. She should protest, or at the very least, admonish him for coming into her bedroom uninvited, but as her cheek pressed against the smooth, warm skin of his chest every coherent thought was driven from her.

"I'm so sorry," he whispered.

One hand rested on Tatiana's hip with tender strength as he kissed the top of her head and sat with her on the edge of the bed. He leaned back, looking at her intently. Holding her face in his hands, he tenderly brushed his thumb along her cheek. It was the same look that made her stomach flutter and her heart race, but this time it wasn't from panic or fear—it was lust.

White-hot-pin-me-to-the-wall-and-make-me-scream kind of lust.

"Are you alright?" He let out a deep breath, and the dog tags he wore glinted. "I know it can be a little rough getting torn out of the dream realm like that."

She nodded and held his hand against her cheek but couldn't bring herself to say anything. Tears fell, and she sniffled as she wiped them away quickly, feeling embarrassed for getting so upset. The truth was she wasn't sure if she was upset about the frightening end to the dream or her reaction to him.

Everything was spinning out of control, and she didn't know what was real. Was she truly feeling something, or was it some stupid legend? Was it hormones or was there something more?

"It's okay." He leaned his forehead against hers and threaded his fingers through her short hair. "That freaked me out too."

Tatiana allowed herself to float in the comforting warmth of his touch. Their combined energy signature surrounded her like a blanket, and one word came to mind—*safe*. Dominic, against all odds and contrary to everything she thought she would feel, made her feel safe.

That was a first. She'd never felt safe before. Even growing up on the farm with Rosie, Raife, and Layla, she lived as though she was waiting for the other shoe to drop. Once Layla found William and they knew more about the Amoveo, she thought she'd feel better, but she didn't. She still lived with the unknown… until now.

Tatiana opened her mouth to tell him how she felt, but when her gaze locked with his, her eyes tingled and shifted intensely into the golden eyes of her wolf. A low, barely audible growl filled her head. Her grip on his hand tightened, and as Tatiana leaned in and brushed his lips with hers, she realized the growl was her own.

"That's it, Tatiana," Dominic whispered. "Show me all of you."

In one swift movement, he flipped her onto her back and devoured her mouth with his. Tatiana moaned as he settled his weight over her, and heat pressed against heat. She wrapped her legs around his waist and held him to her as she licked and nibbled at his firm lips. Her hands wandered over the broad expanse of his back and down to the perfect curve of his rock-hard ass.

Tatiana slipped her fingers beneath the waistband of his gym shorts and pressed him harder against her as he kissed his way down her neck. She let out a soft cry of pleasure as he tugged the top of her nightshirt aside and flicked her nipple with his tongue. He peered at her over the curve of her breast as he ground himself against her, eliciting another gasp of pleasure from her.

"You're gorgeous," he whispered. Dominic squeezed

her other breast and ran his thumb over the sensitive nipple. "I can't decide which part of your beautiful body I want to feast on first."

Sliding off the edge of the bed onto his knees, he pulled her toward him, which sent her short nightie up to her waist, leaving her covered only by skimpy purple underwear.

"So many options," he murmured. Dominic tugged her closer still and placed warm, wet kisses on her quivering belly, while his hands paid thorough attention to her breasts. "Like here." His hot tongue flicked along her belly button. "Or here."

Pleasure washed over her as he rolled her nipples between his fingers and kissed his way down to her hip.

"But I love this spot, right here," he said, licking a trail along the edge of her hip. He grabbed her underwear in his teeth and started to pull.

"Not yet," Tatiana said as she pushed herself onto her elbows and met his wicked grin with her own. "I want to kiss you some more."

Sitting up, she grabbed his face with both hands and kissed him deeply, enjoying the primal, carnal reaction her body had. There was something liberating about this experience, throwing caution to the wind and acting on instinct, but through it all she reminded herself that this was purely physical.

Tatiana's heart, life, and freedom weren't at stake—only her celibate streak was at risk of being broken. Even as she repeated it to herself over and over, she knew it was a lie.

Dominic pulled her off the bed and into his lap, so she straddled him on the floor. She explored the hot cavern of his mouth and curled her body around his, moaning as his erection pressed against her most sensitive spot, sending shuddering waves of pleasure through her.

Dominic grabbed the hem of her nightie and whipped it off her in one swoop. She groaned and suckled his lips as flesh met flesh, and her breasts crushed deliciously against his chest. He dragged his fingertips down her back and slipped them beneath the top of her panties, cupping her bottom.

"You feel so good," she whispered against his lips. "Maybe the universe is on to something."

Tatiana arched back, allowing him access to the sensitive skin of her throat. She held his head to her and floated in the exquisite pleasure of his skin melding with hers. They fit together in a frighteningly familiar way, but she shoved that thought aside, allowing herself to focus only on the physical.

Sex with no strings, she reminded herself. Its *just* sex.

That's what Tatiana wanted to believe, yet she couldn't escape that sensation of feeling safe… and cherished.

A rap at the door cut through the hot haze of lust, and both of them froze. The room had brightened considerably as rays of early morning sunlight streamed in through the window, picking up bronze highlights in Dominic's hair. He lifted his head and locked eyes with her just as Matt's muffled voice came through the door.

"Hey, Tatiana?" Cass jumped up and ran to the door, sniffing it furiously. "I'm going to make breakfast before we head to the barn to check on the horses. Do you want anything?"

Dominic's grip tightened, and his eyes glowed brightly with unmistakable possessiveness. He shook his head slowly, making it clear he didn't want her going anywhere with Matt.

Anger crept up her back at his territorial response. Matt may not have been her boyfriend, but he was her friend, and she'd be damned if anyone was going to tell her who she could have breakfast with.

"No," she shouted without looking away from Dominic. "I'll grab something when I come downstairs. Don't worry about me, Matt… I can take care of myself. Why don't you head to the barn and check on Spirit and the others."

"Oh—okay."

Matt's footsteps faded as he went to the kitchen, and Dominic pulled her in for a kiss, but she placed her hands on his shoulders, stopping him. Tatiana extricated herself from his lap, grabbing her discarded nightshirt along the way.

"Hey." Dominic linked his hand around her ankle, preventing her from walking away. She gave him an exasperated sigh and peered at him over her shoulder. "What's your hurry?" he asked with a wicked grin.

"I have to get ready for work," she said quietly as she tugged her leg from his grasp. She turned her back and pulled her shirt on. "I imagine you do too."

"Yeah," he said as he rose to his feet. "Right now, I'm concerned about why you went from hot to cold in record time. Seriously, what gives? You're acting like I'm the one who knocked on the door and interrupted."

"Like I said. I have to work." Tatiana turned around and folded her arms over her chest. "That's why I'm here. Remember? I came to the ranch to help with the animals, not to help you get your rocks off. We had fun, but the moment is over." Her chin tilted defiantly. "Please leave so I can get dressed."

Dominic moved toward her, the muscles in his chest flexing, his hands balled into fists at his side. Eyes glowing, he inched closer so his body brushed hers, but Tatiana held her ground, refusing to back down.

"You're right about one thing." His jaw flickered, and his voice dropped low. "It was fun." With a devilish smile, he leaned closer, and his hot breath puffed enticingly against her cheek as he whispered in her ear. "But you're dead wrong about something else… this is far from over."

Tatiana opened her mouth to tell him off, but before he could say a word, he swept her into a knee-buckling kiss that stole her breath. Kissing her, he pushed her up against the wall, grabbed her wrists, and pinned them above her head. Her back arched, pressing her breasts against his chest, and Tatiana groaned as he suckled her bottom lip.

Breathless, she stared as she struggled to form a coherent sentence, but she couldn't. Everything burned. Inside and out, she was on fire.

"In fact, Doc," he murmured against her lips and pressed his taut body harder against hers. "We're just getting started."

Dominic uttered the ancient language, "*Verto*."

A rush of static filled the room, along with a blast of heat, and he was gone. Shaking with lust that remained unsatisfied, Tatiana slid down the wall and landed on her butt. She pulled her knees up and hugged them to her chest, wishing she could get control over her raging hormones. Cass immediately came over to comfort her, and she gathered him into her arms, giving him the affection he sought.

As the effects of Dominic's touch coursed through her body, she knew what he said was true—things were just getting started.

Would she survive or be consumed by the flames?

By the time Tatiana got downstairs with Cass at her heels, Matt had already eaten and left. When she saw the car was gone, she couldn't help but laugh. He wasn't a big fan of exercise and avoided it at all costs. Yet he ate like a horse and still weighed all of a hundred and sixty pounds.

Grabbing an apple from the bowl on the kitchen island, she headed out with Cass leading the way. As they walked along the path, the door from the cabin across the road opened, and Courtney, the pregnant woman she'd met yesterday, came outside. She gave Tatiana a friendly smile and wave as she carefully made her way down the steps.

"You're up early," Tatiana said. "I would think you'd be getting all the sleep you can before the baby arrives. I don't have kids, but if human babies are anything like animal babies, you're gonna be up at all hours feeding it."

"I haven't been sleeping well lately." She sighed as she met Tatiana on the dirt road. She ran her hands over her rounded stomach and shrugged. "Plus I have to pee every five minutes, so sleeping for long intervals hasn't been happening."

"Gee—" Tatiana laughed. "You're making pregnancy

sound really appealing." Her smile faded as she saw the dark circles under Courtney's eyes. "It's got to be almost a quarter mile to the main house. Are you sure you're up to walking? I got the feeling that Steven's worried about you and the baby."

"I'll be fine." She waved it off and started walking. "Steven's a little overprotective. Can't really blame him though. Our mating hasn't exactly been *normal*."

"How do you mean?" Tatiana tried to keep the question casual, but her curiosity was at an all-time high. She suspected there was something different about Courtney and Steven's relationship. "As far as I can tell, there's not much *normal* about being Amoveo."

"How much do you know about the mating process or the Purists and what happened?"

"I'm not really involved in the Amoveo side of my parentage, so I'm not familiar with the whole story. Basically, I know that since I'm a hybrid, I have Purist Amoveo who hate me, *and* because I'm part Amoveo, I have humans who hate me. *And* I'm supposed to drop everything to *mate*," she said, making air quotes with her fingers, "with some guy I don't know just because the universe says so." Tatiana let out a sound that hovered between a growl and a sigh. "So, to be really honest. I have *zero* idea what normal is anymore."

"I know what you mean," Courtney said humorlessly as they slowly walked along the dirt road. She ran a hand over her stomach and looked at Cass as he ran to her and rubbed against her leg. "All I can say is that Steven and I didn't conceive our child by traditional methods."

Tatiana gave her a quizzical look.

"The Purists had a breeding program to genetically

engineer pure-blood offspring. I was one of the women forced into the program."

"Oh my God." Tatiana stared at her, riveted and horrified by this latest bit of information. "Layla didn't mention any of this."

"I'm not surprised." Courtney gave her a small smile. "Steven told me it took major convincing to get you to come here, so I can't blame her for keeping certain information under wraps. Also, the Purist movement is all but wiped out, so she probably figured it was a moot point. Besides, I think everyone feels sorry for me, and they don't know what to say."

Tatiana nodded, but her sister had explaining to do, and she couldn't help but wonder what else she didn't know.

"So, when you say you were forced into this breeding program—" Tatiana looked at Courtney's stomach. "Does that mean..." She trailed off, unable to say what she was thinking.

"Steven was a spy. He was at the compound posing as a Purist so he could get information for Richard." Her voice shook, and she kept her eye on the horizon as they walked, unable to look at Tatiana while she spoke. "Apparently, he saw me there and tried to help me escape, but before he could get to me, they captured him. They used Steven's sperm to artificially inseminate me."

"So you two didn't..."

"No." She shook her head and glanced briefly at Tatiana. "You see, the other women they used in the program died before they reached full-term. They weren't pregnant with the children of their mates, so apparently, it wasn't working."

"Jesus Christ," Tatiana said under her breath. "This keeps getting worse."

"Yeah." Courtney let out a short laugh. "Well, they captured Steven as he was trying to break into my room and rescue me. He told them I was his mate, and well, you can imagine how thrilled that made them, especially since we're both pure-bloods. They held us captive and heavily sedated." Bitterness edged her voice, and a single tear rolled down her cheek, but she continued looking straight ahead. "At least that's what everyone told me."

"Wait a minute." Tatiana touched Courtney's arm, and they stopped walking as the main compound came into view. "What do you mean, that's what they told you."

"I don't remember anything." She sniffled. "I woke up here on the ranch, and I was pregnant and alone. Eric found me wandering in the mountains two months ago, and I've been here ever since."

Courtney swiped at the tears with the back of her hand, and a smile cracked her face as the puppy nuzzled her feet again.

"Steven was thrilled, of course. He thought I was dead. They all did. Everyone wanted to know where I'd been and what happened, but I couldn't remember anything. I mean, the last thing I remember is getting ready to go out for drinks with my girlfriends, and then I wake up like this." She rubbed her stomach and let out a shaky sigh. "The truth is… maybe everyone would be better off if I had died." Her voice quivered. "Especially Steven."

"Courtney," Tatiana said gently. "Don't say that. You're carrying his baby. You're his mate, and he's obviously crazy about you."

"I know," she whispered. "He's an incredible man."

"Look—I obviously have no idea what you're going through. I mean, I've only gotten a taste of this whole mate thing, and it's got my head messed up."

Courtney studied her closely. "It's Dominic, isn't it?"

Tatiana nodded but said nothing.

"I could tell as soon as I saw you together," she said through a teary smile. Her green eyes, edged with sadness, searched Tatiana's. "That's how it should be."

Tatiana's brow furrowed. "What do you mean?"

"Nothing." She flicked a nervous glance toward the house and started walking again. "It's nice to have a friend to talk to. I've felt like an outsider, and I guess since…"

"And since I'm an outsider too, you feel more comfortable talking to me?"

"Yeah." Courtney nodded and let out short laugh. "Does that sound horrible?"

"Nope." Tatiana smiled and linked her arm through Courtney's. "Sounds human."

They walked the rest of the way with Tatiana telling Courtney about Oregon and her practice. She found herself enjoying Courtney's company and had to agree that it was nice to have a girlfriend, especially one who understood how it felt to be a bit of an outsider.

As they chatted, Tatiana wondered why Layla would keep this information to herself. However, she wasn't the only one keeping it under wraps. Dominic could have told her about it, but he chose to keep her in the dark too.

Lies. That's what the woman in the dream said. Tatiana gave Courtney a sidelong glance as she spoke about the baby and the names they were tossing around. She wondered if perhaps Courtney was the woman they had heard in the dream realm last night. If so, was she trying to communicate with Tatiana, or had they gotten their dream wires crossed?

As they walked to the barn with the summer sun beating down on them, Tatiana resolved to find out what else was being hidden. She was tired of living in an uncertain world, feeling like the rug could be pulled out from under her at any moment.

The conversation was interrupted by the unmistakable sound of people shouting and the high-pitched shriek of horses whinnying.

"Something's wrong in the barn." She grabbed Courtney's arm. "Stay here."

Tatiana ran at a breakout pace, and as she got closer, she was battered by the rippling shock waves of the animals' agitated energy signatures. She stumbled as the power of their energy knocked the wind out of her and struggled to catch her breath before continuing. When she finally rounded the corner and stepped into the barn, nothing could've prepared her for what she found.

Skidding to a halt, her hands flew to her mouth in horror. Spirit, the gorgeous white mare she worked with yesterday, lay on the ground in a massive stain of blood-soaked hay and dirt. Her dark, lifeless eyes stared blankly at the world, and her coat that had been pure as snow was now marred with blood splatter from two gunshot wounds.

Dominic had Matt pinned against the wall by the throat, and Eric, the other Guardian, stood next to them. Both men glowered at Matt through the glowing eyes of their clan. Seconds later, the air in the barn burgeoned with static electricity and a blast of heat as Richard, Steven, and Courtney materialized next to her.

"You should have done a better background check on your employee, Tatiana," Dominic seethed. He leaned closer, tightening his grip and making Matt's eyes widen. "Otherwise, you wouldn't have brought a Caedo assassin to this ranch."

Dominic jutted his chin toward the back of the stall, and Tatiana's stomach rolled when she saw the message scrawled in blood. *Your half-breed women are next*.

Chapter 6

If he squeezed Matt's neck a little more he could kill him. The words on the wall haunted him and made his blood boil. *Your half-breed women are next.* Dominic growled and fought the instinctive urge to shift into his tiger. Their women—his woman—Tatiana? It would be a cold day in hell before he let anyone lay a hand on her. Just a little more pressure, and Matt would be a nonissue.

However, after seeing the horrified look on Tatiana's face when she walked in the barn, he couldn't bring himself to do it. He could handle anything except seeing her upset, especially upset with him. He loosened his hold but didn't let go.

"What the hell is going on?" Tatiana looked frantically between them and the dead mare. "Dominic. Let Matt go. He's not Caedo. For God's sake, he doesn't even know about us." She looked at the group who had just materialized out of thin air. "Well, he didn't up until a few minutes ago."

"What's going on?" Matt squeaked out. "Tatiana?"

"Quiet," Dominic growled.

"He killed Spirit," Eric said tightly. "Dom and I heard the horses going crazy and found him here standing over the horse's body. Besides, I ran a background check on him, and he's like a fucking phantom. Hardly any information online. He could easily be a Caedo spy."

"Not everyone posts their every thought on Facebook, dude," Matt said.

"You're not good at this whole assassin thing, are you kid?" Dominic bit out. His eyes glowed brighter. "You're supposed to *not* get caught."

"This is crazy." Matt looked at Tatiana through wide, frightened eyes. "What the hell is going on? What the fuck are they?"

"Dominic," Richard said firmly as he stared at the message on the wall. "Let Matt go. Since he is unarmed and surrounded by Amoveo, he's not going anywhere. Everyone needs to calm down a moment while we look at all of the evidence."

"Fine," Dominic rasped. He dropped his hand from Matt's neck as Tatiana stepped between them and pushed him away. "You're lucky Tatiana is here. If it weren't for her, you'd be dead already."

"Stop it, Dominic." She shot him a deadly look before turning to face Matt who was shaking like a leaf and looking at them like they were from Mars. Hell, as far as he was concerned, they probably were. "It's okay, Matt," she said soothingly. "No one is going to hurt you."

"Tatiana," Matt said in a shaking voice as he hugged her and buried his face in her neck. "I didn't hurt Spirit. I swear to God. I found her like this, and then these guys fucking attacked me."

A knot formed in Dominic's gut as he watched Tatiana hold Matt in her arms and comfort him. She released him, turned around, and stood protectively in front of him, her eyes glowing brightly in their clan form.

"Someone tell me what happened." She looked at Eric, ignoring Dominic. "Matt would never hurt anyone, especially an animal. He's one of the kindest, gentlest men I've ever known and doesn't have a mean or aggressive bone in his body." She shot Dominic an accusatory look. "Unlike some people, *he's* never killed anyone."

"I went into town to get coffee because we didn't have any in the cabin, and I know how much you like hazelnut. I found Spirit like this when I came back," Matt sputtered, peering over Tatiana's shoulders. "I freaked out when I saw her like this and dropped the tray of coffee. I went to see if she was still alive, and two seconds later these two tackled me." He lowered his voice. "What's wrong with their eyes?"

"Bullshit," Dominic spat. "There aren't any other energy signatures on the property except for ours. If another assassin invaded the ranch, we would've sensed it, or at the very least, there would be a trail left behind." He folded his arms over his chest and looked at Richard. "Your Highness, we don't know this human, and as soon as he shows up, one of the horses is murdered."

"Yes. That is all true." Richard looked grim and turned his glowing lion eyes on Matt. "However, I am inclined to believe his proclamation of innocence. Aside from the fact that it's far too convenient to catch him in the act." He looked at Eric and Dominic. "Where is the weapon?"

They all looked at each other and then to Matt, who was still cowering behind Tatiana. The horses whinnied and shuffled nervously in their stalls, but Cass trotted up and down the aisle, calming them as he went.

Dominic swore, and his jaw clenched. "He doesn't have one, and I checked the car too, but nothing. However, that doesn't mean he couldn't have ditched it somewhere else."

Stalking toward the stall, Dominic brushed past Tatiana who moved her body in a protective stance in front of Matt. He scanned the area around the horse and the rest of the stall but didn't see anything.

"I want to go home," Matt whispered. "I won't tell anyone about you guys or this place. Please. Just let me leave."

Tatiana pushed past Dominic and went directly to Spirit's body. She said nothing but took several minutes running her hands over the blood-splattered coat of the fallen beast with reverent strokes. She squatted by the animal's head for a moment with her eyes closed, and Dominic's gut clenched as he saw her swipe at her eyes. Sadness and anger rippled in her energy waves as she stood and faced the others.

"Matt couldn't have done this." She walked over to Richard, and her voice remained strong. "Spirit has been dead for hours, and if I had to guess, I'd say she was killed in the middle of the night. Not this morning. Did anyone hear anything last night?"

Dominic locked eyes with Tatiana briefly as his mind went to the voice they heard in the dream realm. Could that have been the mare trying to connect with Tatiana?

"I didn't," Eric said. "It probably happened when I was patrolling the outskirts of the property."

Before anyone could say anything, Tatiana turned and faced Matt with the glowing eyes of her clan. His jaw dropped, and he stumbled backward, bumping into Dominic.

"You're one of them," he yelped and attempted to run away, but Dominic grabbed his arm and held him there. "It's the fucking pod people."

"You're not going anywhere," Dominic ground out. "Quit squirming, or you're going to hurt yourself."

Tatiana stepped closer and put a hand on Dominic's arm. Her eyes, now shifted back to their human brown, were locked on Matt and rimmed with sympathy. Her energy waves were colored with sadness, and Dominic knew she was torn up over the way Matt was looking at her.

"Please don't be afraid, Matt." She placed her hand over Dominic's and gave him a slanted glance as she urged him to let go. Reluctantly, he dropped his hold on Matt as Tatiana kept her voice calm and sent out soothing waves of reassuring energy, which helped ease the tension. "I promise I'll explain everything. No one here is going to hurt you. Isn't that right, Richard?"

"Absolutely." Richard's quiet but commanding tone filled the space. "We have many things to discuss, not the least of which is who managed to get onto the property undetected to slaughter my wife's favorite mare and threaten our mates? I think we should take this discussion to the Council chamber. I'm sure Matt will cooperate. Won't you, Matt? Besides, we have a friend who can find out if you're being truthful."

Matt said nothing but nodded, clearly aware there was little choice in the matter.

"Tatiana, are the other horses well enough to be let out to graze? I'd rather not keep them in here until we've had a chance to clean everything up." Richard cast a somber gaze at Spirit's broken form. "I had been keeping them inside until you had a chance to tend to them, but I can't imagine being kept here with Spirit's body is good for them."

"Absolutely," Tatiana answered but kept her attention on Matt. "Spirit was the sickest out of all of them. Based on the tests we ran yesterday, their feed was contaminated, so letting them out to graze would be a good idea. They're also quite disturbed by what happened to Spirit, and I don't want to leave them in here." She flicked a brief glance to Richard. "Once things are settled, I'll need to purchase new feed for the others."

"You're not going anywhere without me. Especially not after this shit storm," Dominic bit out. He turned his glowing gaze to the others. "Tatiana is my mate."

"Son of a bitch," she breathed.

Dominic spun to face Tatiana and found himself staring into a pair of furious, glowing golden eyes. A growl rumbled in her chest as she inched slowly toward him, and for a moment he thought she was going to kiss him, but instead she hauled off and smacked him across the face. Hard.

No one moved—not even Matt—but all eyes were on Tatiana and Dominic.

"I am *not* your property to claim," she seethed. Tatiana poked him in the chest and got in his face, but he held his ground. "I'm surprised you didn't try to piss on me like a dog, and quite frankly, I doubt it could feel any more humiliating. Not to mention the fact that we have slightly larger issues to deal with than your male posturing."

Tatiana spun around and looked at the others.

"I would like to take a closer look at Spirit's body to

make sure we're not missing something. There could be evidence left behind that will help us, but in the meantime, I think we should explain this to Matt before he dies of shock."

"Agreed," Richard said evenly. His somber gaze wandered over the group. "I must speak with Salinda. We will convene in the Council meeting hall in fifteen minutes. I will be reaching out to some of the others and ask them to join us. Dominic, I want you at the meeting as well. Eric, I would like you to stand guard outside the facility."

"Consider it done." Dominic kept his voice even as frustration clawed at him. He nodded at Matt. "What about him? We don't usually allow humans in the meeting hall, unless they are part of the Vasullus family."

"True." Richard moved closer to Matt, who looked terrified. Richard studied him carefully, his glowing lion eyes flickering to life. "Then I suppose Matt will be made an honorary member of the Vasullus. He's seen far too much to explain it all away. So I suppose we shall tell him everything. If Tatiana says we can trust him, then that will have to do… for now."

"That would be a refreshing change," Tatiana interjected. She flicked an irritated glance to Dominic. "I'd love to hear everything about the Caedo, the Purists, and their breeding program. *All of it*. I'm sick of getting information bit by bit."

"The Purists initiative has been disbanded right along with their breeding program," Steven said firmly. He pulled Courtney into his arms and ran one hand protectively over her stomach. "Their leader is dead, and they've lost their resolve. I doubt they had anything to do with this."

"We shall see," Richard said quietly. "I will meet you all in the Council chamber in fifteen minutes." His eyes glowed brightly as he bowed his head, uttered the ancient language, and vanished.

"What the fuck?" Matt whimpered.

Dominic looked over just in time to see him faint and fall into a bail of hay.

"Oh yeah," Dominic said with a sigh. "He's going to be lots of help."

"Shut up," Tatiana hissed. "The world he *thought* existed just got ripped away. So why don't you give him a small break? Huh?"

Tatiana squatted down next to Matt and brushed his hair off his forehead. She whispered his name a few times, but all he did was moan. Cass trotted over and sniffed at his limp hand.

"Let me get him," Dominic groaned. He thought she was going to stop him, but she stepped aside, allowing him to pick Matt up. The kid mumbled something but didn't wake up. "I hope he can handle this because the last thing we need is to babysit a human."

"He's my friend, Dominic." Her voice wavered, and her large dark eyes flicked to Matt. "Although I can't imagine he'll want much to do with me after this mess."

Dominic's throat tightened as Tatiana's energy waves, thick with sadness, washed over him. It was unsettling to have someone else's feelings directly impact his own. How the hell would he figure out how to navigate this aspect of their relationship? Shit. Who was he kidding? He didn't know how to navigate any of it.

After they let the horses out to graze and put the puppy in the main house out of harm's way, Tatiana followed Dominic and the others. The animals were clearly upset by what happened, and once they were done with this meeting, she planned on connecting with the horses again. Maybe if she could form a psychic bond with them the way she had with Spirit, she could find out who killed the mare. As that thought filled her mind, she stopped dead in her tracks as she recalled the voice from the dream realm last night.

Lies. All lies... Betrayer.

The words haunted her as she realized the feminine voice in the dream wasn't Courtney or any other person. It was Spirit, and Tatiana did nothing to help her because she was too busy getting it on with Dominic.

"Tatiana?" Dominic called her name, pulling her from her thoughts. "What's wrong?"

Tatiana shook her head and started walking again. She wasn't entirely sure about what she heard and decided to wait before blurting out her suspicions. Especially since it happened while she and Dominic were playing the dream realm dating game.

You heard it too, didn't you? Dominic's voice touched her mind gently. *Last night in the dream realm. You heard that voice in the storm.*

Tatiana didn't answer him but nodded. It was unsettling how in tune Dominic seemed to be with her. How in tune they were with each other.

As they walked across the property, she stole a glance at the men and noticed the startling similarity between them. All three of them, Eric, Dominic, and Steven, possessed a distinctly predatory air. Their energy waves rippled with tension, ready to pounce at a moment's notice, and that had her more on edge than before. Were they in that much danger?

Images of Dominic appearing in her bedroom came immediately to mind, and her fear ratcheted up a notch as she answered her own question. Of course they were in danger. If the Purists were involved, couldn't they simply blink in and out of the area with little effort? She made a mental note to bring up that little tidbit at the meeting.

They continued toward the heated barn on the other side of the property, and as she wiped the sweat from her brow, her stomach turned at the idea of being inside what was essentially a giant metal tube. The long cylindrical structure glinted in the sunlight, and she could see heat waves wafting from the steel.

"Where are we going?" Tatiana asked as she swatted at a mosquito on her neck. "I hope this meeting space isn't in that metal barn. I can't imagine it's less than a hundred and ten degrees in there right now."

Dominic glanced at her as they approached the entrance of the barn. His brown eyes stared at her intently. "As Matt learned today, not everything is as it appears."

Matt moaned again but remained unconscious in Dominic's grasp, and Tatiana noticed Dominic wasn't even winded by carrying him. The muscles in his arms bulged, stretching the army green T-shirt to its limits which, in spite of the situation, had her remembering their little tryst this morning. Her face heated with embarrassment when Dominic caught her eye and winked.

"Oh please," she said with roll of her eyes.

Eric stepped up to the massive metal doors, and the

entrance swung open silently, as if by magic. Tatiana's stomach fluttered nervously as she followed the others inside, and the doors began to close as soon as she cleared the threshold.

Tatiana glanced over her shoulder, and as the entrance closed, she saw Eric shimmer and burst into clan form. The glowing yellow eyes of a black panther were the last thing she saw before it shut, and they were sealed inside.

The temperature in the cavernous space was surprisingly cool, but that wasn't the only surprise. The high, curved ceiling of the building stretched overhead like a steel rainbow, and the floor was a checked pattern of black-and-white marble tile—a far cry from a heated barn.

"What the hell is this place," Tatiana asked as she instinctively inched closer to Courtney. Her voice echoed in the open space. She looked around as she rubbed her bare arms, which suddenly felt chilled by the dramatic change in temperature. "It's obviously not a barn."

"No." Dominic's deep voice rumbled through the air. "It protects one of our most sacred places and keeps it hidden from the world."

"Where is everyone?" Tatiana gave Courtney a smile and waved one hand around. "I mean, there's nothing in here. Not even some place to—"

"*Revelamini*." Dominic's voice, clear and commanding, cut off further conversation.

Seconds later the long white wall in front of them disappeared into the floor, and a subtle humming filled the space. As the wall vanished, a cavernous space was revealed. Tatiana inched closer to Dominic, and before she could stop herself, grabbed his arm for reassurance.

He gave her a slanted glance, and his lips curved as he looked at her fingers draped over his bicep, but he had the good sense not to say anything.

They crossed the threshold, and Tatiana let out a whistle as she took in the sight before her. They were standing at the top of a gigantic set of steps, and at the bottom there was an arena. All four sides had steps that led down to the main floor, and it conjured images of the arenas in Ancient Rome. The floor vibrated, and the wall behind them rose, immediately sealing them inside the mysterious space.

"Why do I feel like I'm being buried alive?" she whispered. Tatiana gripped Dominic's arm tighter. "Please tell me you can open that again, and get us out of here."

"You are perfectly safe, Tatiana." Dominic captured her gaze, and his eyes flickered to their clan form. "I would never let anything happen to you, and you are among friends."

Looking into those intense amber eyes, she knew he meant every word, but she couldn't shake the nagging feeling that he might be wrong. What if they weren't all friends, and there was indeed a traitor among them?

The four of them descended the steep marble stairs together with Matt still passed out through the whole thing. When they reached the floor of the arena, she was able to make out the rest of the space. However, every thought rushed from her head when she looked up and saw a starry night sky. The walls and door they entered through were gone, and if she didn't know better, she'd say they were nowhere near Montana anymore.

There were five sets of enormous marble platforms

lining either side of the arena, and it looked as though the floor, platforms, and steps were carved from one mammoth hunk of snow-white marble. At the other end of the pristine space, opposite from where they stood, there were two more platforms. The air was cool and comfortable, and the scent of pine lingered.

"Time for our boy here to wake up." Dominic set Matt on one of the platforms to the right and threw a quick look over his shoulder to Tatiana. "He'll be fine, but if you're worried, I'm sure Steven can have a look at him."

Tatiana pushed past Dominic and knelt down next to Matt. She closed her eyes and tried to tune into his energy the way she did with the animals she treated. Matt moaned, and when she opened her eyes, he was awake and looking confused. He rubbed his face, and she helped him sit up, but the instant he saw the others, his face drained of color.

"Holy shit," Matt breathed. He flicked his gaze between them, and his voice quivered. "I didn't dream all that stuff, did I?"

"No." Tatiana shook her head and sat next to him on the large marble platform. To her relief, he didn't shy away or flinch but looked at her wide-eyed. "I promise that I'll explain everything, Matt."

Seconds later, Richard and Salinda, with baby Jessica in her arms, materialized at the center of the arena in a rush of static electricity. Matt stiffened and leaned against Tatiana but didn't make a sound as they approached.

"Thank you all for coming." Richard waved his hand wide. "*Verto*."

Tatiana watched in awe as a round table and chairs, also carved from white marble, materialized in the center of the room. She had heard about the visualization skills that the pure-bloods had, but she had never seen it in action until today. Some hybrids could do it too, but from what Layla said, it wasn't an ability that came easily.

"I'm sure we'd all be more comfortable sitting here than in the traditional Council seating," Richard said, jutting a thumb toward the large platforms. "Especially since this isn't an official Council meeting. The others will arrive momentarily."

As the last word slipped from his lips, the space flickered with static again, and three more couples materialized.

In addition to Layla and William, there were two other couples, neither of whom Tatiana had never met. To the left of Layla stood a strikingly handsome pair, and while the man was unfamiliar, the woman was immediately recognizable—Kerry Smithson's face was seen in pictures all over the world, and she was even more stunning in person. Tatiana remembered Layla saying that Kerry was a hybrid from the Panther Clan, and she had the gift of sight—one touch and all your secrets were hers to tell.

The other couple was eye-catching and gorgeous in the way that all Amoveo seemed to be. The man was handsome with an unusual air of intensity. However, he definitely was not an Amoveo—not a pure-blood or a hybrid. His energy signature was distinctly different, and she could tell that he wasn't human either. He stood with one arm protectively around his mate, who was very pregnant—the poor woman looked ready to pop.

All of them took their seats around the large table with Matt staying close to Tatiana and sitting to her right. Dominic sat on her left, watching every move, and occasionally glowering at Matt. Steven and Courtney sat together but remained quiet, and Tatiana noticed that Steven barely took his eyes off his wife.

Tatiana kept her focus on Richard and couldn't stop wondering why on earth they had to meet here… wherever *here* was.

"Before we begin," Richard said solemnly. "I'd like to thank you for joining us. I realize you all have lives outside of Amoveo business, but your prompt attention to the latest development is greatly appreciated."

"Aren't you supposed to be on a photo shoot somewhere?" Tatiana asked her sister.

"I'll get there." Layla winked as William took her hand in his. "William and I want to make sure everyone is safe before we head out. I was able to postpone it for a few days. Family first, right?"

"Tatiana and Matt." Richard's voice filled the cavernous space effortlessly. "You already know Layla and William, but I have yet to introduce the others."

"I'm Kerry," said the stunning brunette. "And this big hunk of hottie is my husband, Dante. I'm a hybrid—Panther Clan—but my baby here is all Fox." She winked at Tatiana and smiled at her husband as he draped one arm over her shoulder. "Good to meet you, by the way. I just wish it was at a spa for a girl's day out and not more of this everyone-wants-to-kill-us bullshit."

"Tell us how you really feel, princess." Dante chuckled and kissed her hand, which was linked with his.

Kerry exchanged a look with the prince and nodded.

She rose from her seat and walked around the table until she stood next to Matt. She extended her hand.

"Nice to meet you, Matt," she murmured as her eyes shifted to her clan form.

Matt looked to Tatiana for reassurance.

"It's okay, Matt." Tatiana rubbed his back. "She's not going to hurt you."

"I'm only going to put everyone's minds at ease." Kerry smiled sweetly. "If you have nothing to hide, then you have nothing to fear."

"O-okay," Matt sputtered.

Placing his hand in hers, Kerry's body jolted as the link was made. After a few minutes, her eyes fluttered open, and she dropped Matt's hand. She flicked her glowing gaze to Tatiana, and a wide smile cracked her face.

"Other than harboring a serious crush on you, the kid is clean." Kerry breezed back to her seat as Matt rubbed absently at his hand and blushed. "He didn't shoot the horse, and as far as I can tell, he's got no connection to the Caedo."

"Thank you." Tatiana nodded and let out a sigh of relief. "It's *very* nice to meet you, Kerry."

"This is Pete Castro and Marianna Coltari." Richard gestured to the expectant woman and her unusual mate. "You may have noticed that Pete is not Amoveo."

"Yes." Tatiana swallowed hard and flicked her gaze to the intense man with the pale blue eyes. "I picked up on… something."

"Vampire and part demon," Pete said with a shrug. "I promise I won't suck your blood. Up until a few months ago, I was human like you… well, except for the whole demon lineage, but to be fair, I didn't know about it so it doesn't really count."

"Vampire?" Matt whimpered and put his head in his hands as he rocked in his seat. "This is fucking crazy."

"You'll be okay, kid." Pete winked and chuckled. "I know you think you're going nuts, but it's gonna be fine." He tilted his head and smiled at Tatiana. "Nice to meet you too, Tatiana. Wolf Clan. Right?"

Tatiana nodded but didn't say anything as she looked at the man who admitted to being a vampire. She'd never met a vampire, but unlike Matt, she knew they existed, along with a multitude of other supernatural creatures. Tension, and an overall sense of unease, settled over her.

Pete won't hurt you. Dominic's voice, calm and commanding, floated into her mind. His energy waves wafted around her like a blanket, comforting her. She ducked her chin and slanted a glance in his direction. *I know… but I won't deny that I'd feel safer if a vampire wasn't sitting across the table from me.*

"I'm Marianna. Pete's *extremely* pregnant wife and member of the Bear Clan." She ran both hands over her enormous belly and let out a long, slow breath as she squeezed her eyes shut. "Oh baby. There's another one."

"Holy shit! You're having a contraction?" Pete's eyes flickered and glowed bright red. "I'm getting you out of here."

He stood, but she grabbed his arm and pulled him back down into his seat without even opening her eyes. Tatiana suppressed a grin as she watched Pete, a strapping vampire, reduced to a pile of mush by his wife. His eyes continued to glow, and his body was wound tight, ready to spring into action, but he did as she asked and sat next to her.

"I'm fine," she said calmly as she opened her eyes. Marianna turned her surprisingly serene gaze to Richard. "It's those Braxton Hicks thingies."

"Are you sure?" Steven asked.

"Yes," Marianna said evenly. "They only happen every so often, but they're getting stronger. So while I'm all for helping out, I'd really like to go back to New York City to get ready for the big event. Now, what's going on, and what can we do to help?"

All eyes turned to Richard.

"Of course. I'm sure Tatiana is wondering why we are meeting here instead of the house," Richard said with the hint of a smile as he took his wife's hand and looked lovingly at baby Jessica. "This is a sacred space. It is shielded from psychic invasion, or any type of unwanted intrusion, and given our situation, I felt that kind of assured privacy was important."

"Where is *here*, exactly?" Tatiana looked up at the starry sky and then to the prince. "Where are we?"

"This space has housed our Council, the governing body of the Amoveo, for a millennium. The people seated around this table right now, aside from yourself and Matt, are all members of our new Council."

The air flickered with static again, and seconds later, another Amoveo couple materialized in the room and, like Salinda and Richard, they had an infant with them. The man was tall and well-built like most Amoveo men, and his wife was a petite blonde with large blue eyes. Their child couldn't have been more than a couple of months old, and she gurgled happily in her mother's arms.

"Apologies for being late, Richard," said the man with the tousled chestnut hair. "Jane needed a diaper change, and given what's been going on, I didn't want to leave my girls alone."

"Understood," Richard said. He waved his hand and uttered the ancient language, making two more chairs appear at the table next to himself and Salinda. "Malcolm and Samantha, this is Tatiana and her friend Matt, who is now part of the Vasullus family."

Tatiana braced herself, waiting for the prince to introduce her as Dominic's mate, but to her surprise, he did not.

"Hi," Matt said through a shuddering breath and a strangled giggle.

"Hello," Tatiana said before turning her gaze back to Richard.

Amoveo were multiplying by the second, which only made her want to run the hell out of this place. However, since the door seemed to have disappeared, she figured her best chance of getting out was to move this little meeting along.

"So, we're in a super-secret, whammy-proof bunker." Tatiana fought to keep her voice calm and controlled. "Now, with all due respect… what the hell is going on? Why would the Caedo, or anyone else for that matter, want to kill your horses? I don't get it."

"I'm not convinced the Caedo are behind this particular incident," Richard said.

"Purists?" Dominic's voice cut in, suddenly making Tatiana jump. "Could they be working with the Caedo again?"

"That's entirely possible, but whoever did it got onto the ranch undetected, which would lead me to believe it's another Amoveo. A Caedo—a human—would not be able to do that, at least not without help."

"Fine." Tatiana sighed with frustration. "Then why would a Purist want to kill your horses?"

"It was a warning, and it wasn't just any horse." Richard squeezed his wife's hand as she wept quietly. "It was Salinda's mare, and until Spirit got sick, she rode her every day."

"Agreed," Dominic said tightly. His energy waves rippled with tension as he leaned back in the chair and folded his muscular arms over his chest. "Whoever was poisoning the animals must've realized that Tatiana was here to treat them, and obviously, they ended up resorting to more drastic measures."

"Shock value," Dante interjected. "Slaughtering the horse like that and leaving a bloody message? That has definitely got the marks of a Purist. They use the love we have for our mates against us. Whoever is doing this wants us to be terrified for the safety our women." He looked at Kerry through worried eyes. "I have to be honest… it's working."

"They want us off our game." Dominic flicked a brief glance to Tatiana before turning his attention to Richard. "They know how intense the bond between mates is, and they are using it. Our enemies want us on edge and so fucking freaked out that we'll make mistakes." He straightened his back and avoided Tatiana's gaze. "Fatal mistakes."

"True," William said slowly. "However, the Caedo are well-schooled in our ways and know how important our mates are to us. They could be involved as well."

"You saw the message yourself," Dominic insisted.

"It's about the *women*, and a Purist, not a Caedo, is going to target our women. The Caedo hate all of us equally, but the Purists are driven by their hatred for hybrids and lack of pure-blood mates."

"Yes." Richard nodded solemnly. "I tend to agree, and given the fact that this individual got onto the ranch undetected… it leads me to believe it is one of our elders." He turned his serious eyes to Tatiana. "Amoveo over two centuries old, like myself and Salinda, have the ability to mask their presence from others. My money is on one of the Purists."

"I don't understand." Courtney looked at Steven through frightened eyes. She'd been quiet for so long, Tatiana almost forgot she was there. "You told me that the Purist group was dismantled. You said they couldn't hurt anyone anymore."

"The Purist compound was destroyed, and most traitors went back to their clans and begged forgiveness." Steven's features darkened. "They're lucky that their clans were willing to give them another chance."

"Not everyone came back or has resurfaced. There are still two high-profile Purists unaccounted for, among others." Richard's mouth set in a tight line. "Dr. Moravian and his daughter, Savannah, have not been heard from since the compound was overthrown."

"You mean Dr. Frankenstein?" Steven's eyes glowed brightly, and his energy waves fluttered violently around the room.

"Yes." Richard gave Steven a sympathetic look. "We cannot discount the fact that Moravian and his daughter could be gathering supporters, trying to reignite their cause. Possibly working under the radar again."

Richard's face was carved with intensity as he turned to Marianna.

"That is why I especially needed to speak with you, Marianna. You spent time with Savannah and Moravian. I realize that it was a horrendous experience, but given your exposure, I thought you might be able to help us. You said that Savannah actually helped you while you were there. Do you have any idea where she and her father might be?"

"No." Marianna shook her head, and a pained expression crossed her face as she looked at Courtney. "I would recognize her energy signature if I came across it, but I have no idea where she is now."

"Wait a minute," Tatiana interrupted. Everyone stared at her as though she had ten heads, including poor Matt, who looked like he might pass out again. "Courtney, you said you turned up here a few months ago. Right? So where were you during the time you were missing? Who was taking care of you?" She looked around the table at the rest of them. "Think about it, people. You said no one knows where the doctor and his daughter are. Did it occur to any of you that was who Courtney was with when she was missing for all those months?"

"Yes." Courtney sniffled and swiped at the tears that fell freely down her cheeks. "I can't remember anything."

"Steven?" Kerry asked in a gentle tone. "I know you were opposed to letting me play peekaboo in Courtney's head when she first came home." She held her palms up and stopped him from protesting. "I get it. She was super-fragile and freaked out when she got here. Shit. You were in a damn coma until she showed up at the ranch, so I totally get how protective you feel, but—"

"No," Steven insisted as his eyes shifted and glowed brightly. "She can't risk it."

Courtney quietly said, "I'll do it."

Steven and Courtney spoke in unison, and although Courtney's voice was far softer than Steven's, it carried a bigger wallop. Tatiana's heart was in her throat as the drama played out before her. She fought the instinct to seek comfort and touch Dominic's mind with hers.

The room fell silent. All eyes were on Courtney. Steven placed one large hand on her shoulder and turned her face toward him with the other. "Are you sure? It could be dangerous for you and the baby."

"We have to." Courtney squared her shoulders and looked around the room. "I want to know what happened when I was missing as much as the rest of you do. I can't help but feel like I've been nothing but a burden on everyone, and I want to do this. It's the least I can do." She faced Steven again. "Besides, the baby is due in a month or so. If labor did start, he would be okay. Especially with his brilliant daddy to take care of him."

"Then it's settled." Kerry clapped her hands and pushed her chair back. "You have second sight too, right?"

It took Tatiana a minute to realize that Kerry was speaking to her. She looked around for a moment, and everyone was staring at her.

"Who, me?" Tatiana's hand went to her chest, and she shook her head as she laughed nervously. "No way. I mean, I can read animal energy…"

"That's why you're such a good vet," Matt said as he looked at her through wide eyes. He looked slightly less frightened, but she thought he was probably in shock. "That's really wild."

"Fine. Call it whatever you want," Kerry said with a shrug as she stood from her chair. "That's still second sight, and I'm going to need help breaking through to read Courtney's memories. I can read humans and hybrids easily, but pure-blood Amoveo are tougher nuts to crack. Pete used to be able to help me with that stuff, but now that he's on Team Vampire, it doesn't work that way anymore. So, whaddya say?" Kerry asked.

"I—I don't know…"

An overwhelming sense of panic and suffocation came barreling back as Tatiana confronted the idea of diving headfirst into her Amoveo powers, of embracing what she was with no limits.

It was terrifying. She used her Amoveo abilities only on her terms, and breaking that streak unnerved her. If she accepted it and allowed herself to fully embrace her Amoveo heritage… how far behind was the life-mate bond?

How long until her life was no longer her own?

Fear and self-doubt swamped her, and just when she thought the darkness would pull her under, a strong, warm hand encircled her own, invoking an immediate sense of calm.

Tatiana looked down to see Dominic's long fingers wrapped around hers. His thumb brushed her lightly as his voice drifted gently into her mind. *You can do this, Tatiana. You are more than capable, and Kerry will help you navigate.* He gave her hand a reassuring squeeze as her eyes met his. *If you don't want to, you don't have to. I've got your back either way.*

Staring into the seemingly limitless depths of his warm brown eyes, a million thoughts raced through

Tatiana's mind, many laced with fear and uncertainty. However, in spite of that, one phrase rose to the top and drowned out all the rest... *I've got your back either way*.

Dominic meant what he said. She'd seen evidence of his devotion to his people, and in that moment she knew, without hesitation, that the same fierce loyalty applied to her. He had her back. Mated or not.

"Okay." Tatiana squeezed Dominic's hand in return and sucked in a cleansing breath. She looked at Kerry. "What do I do?"

Chapter 7

Tension settled in Dominic's neck as he watched Tatiana get the lowdown from Kerry about what to expect on their psychic trip into Courtney's memories. The table and chairs were gone, replaced by a pillow-strewn chaise lounge, which Courtney now sat comfortably on. Steven sat on the edge next to her, holding her hand and speaking soft words of encouragement.

Dominic inched closer to Tatiana but fought the urge to touch her, to reach out and place a reassuring hand on her lower back. She listened intently to Kerry, her face a mask of concentration as she absorbed the direction. He wanted to wrap his arm around her, hold her and tell her that everything would be all right, but somehow, he knew that's not what she needed. She required enough space so that she didn't feel suffocated, but not so much that she felt abandoned.

At least that's what his gut told him.

Dominic ran one hand over his stubble-covered jaw as he wrestled with his conflicting emotions. Looking around the meeting hall, he observed the other men with their mates and bit back a surprising surge of jealousy as he watched how easy they were with one another. There was a seamless fluidity to the way they moved, spoke, and even looked at each other. He couldn't help but worry he and Tatiana may never have that.

The two of them had been making decent progress,

but he knew he'd blown up in the barn when he blurted out that she was his mate, announcing it for the world to hear. What a dope.

Dominic couldn't blame her for being upset, but in that moment, all he could feel was fear. Fear that she could be stolen before he had a chance to really know her—for them to know each other.

Assuring Tatiana's safety and happiness had quickly become his number one mission—it even ranked above being Guardian. His serious gaze swept across the room and landed on Richard, Salinda, and little Jessica. What would he do if he had to choose? If he was faced with protecting Tatiana, or the prince and his family…

"Is she gonna be okay?" Matt's shaky voice interrupted his thoughts.

"What?" Dominic snapped. He looked to his left and realized Matt was standing next to him with a concerned expression.

"Tatiana?" Matt stuffed his hands in the front pockets of his jeans and jutted his chin toward Tatiana as she took her place by Courtney's side. "Is this—this séance thing or whatever it is—is it going to hurt her?"

"No," Dominic bit out. "Trust me. If I thought Tatiana were in danger, there's no way I'd let her do this."

"*Let* her?" Matt let out a huffing sound, and for the first time since this fiasco began, humor laced his voice. "Man, you may be some kind of badass, ninja pod-person, but you're gonna get your butt kicked if she hears you say that."

Dominic glared at Matt, but before he could say anything, Richard called for silence.

A hush fell over the meeting hall, and everyone

gathered around the bed holding hands, creating a protective circle, except for Matt. He could have joined them. Richard invited him, but he shook his head and stepped back.

Courtney sat propped up by pillows on the chaise with her eyes closed, and Steven sat next to her with one hand resting protectively on her belly. Dominic knew he was also tuning into her and the baby so he could monitor their physical reactions.

Kerry and Tatiana stood on either side of Courtney's bed. All three women held hands, creating their own small circle, which directly linked their energies. Tatiana briefly flicked her eyes to Dominic and gave him a tight smile. *Here goes nothing*. Her voice floated into his mind hesitantly. *Don't go anywhere, okay?*

Not a chance. He winked at her. *I've got you*. Dominic's body tensed as their mental connection was severed, and she focused on Courtney. It had only been twenty-four hours since she first touched her mind to his, and now the absence made him uneasy. There was a strange void, an emptiness that could only be filled by her.

Tatiana let out a long, slow breath as her eyes fluttered closed, and her jaw set in concentration. Within seconds, both Kerry and Tatiana's bodies jolted as the connection with Courtney solidified. A low humming sound filled the space as their joined energies flickered. Dominic sent soothing waves to Tatiana, hoping to ease her through it, although he wasn't sure if his comfort would get through.

The humming grew louder, and the tendrils of power pulsing from the three women throbbed in thick ribbons of invisible energy around the group. Courtney's brow furrowed, and she whimpered, softly at first, but it quickly grew louder until she was crying and tears streamed down her cheeks. The humming sound pulsed like a deep bass beat and reverberated through Dominic's chest, but he didn't take his eyes off Tatiana.

An impending sense of doom crawled up Dominic's back, and just when he thought he would scream with frustration, break the circle, grab Tatiana, and run—the room fell silent and everything stopped.

No one moved, and for a second, Dominic thought the women were still in the trance. However, a moment later, they released Courtney's hands, and Tatiana opened her eyes, instantly locking her gaze with Dominic.

"It worked. We followed Courtney's memories back to Moravian and Savannah." Kerry's voice trembled as she spoke and leaned against Dante for support. "I was able to merge with Moravian's energy signature briefly." Concern and anger edged her voice. "He's coming, Richard, and he's not coming alone. I saw five or six other Purists with him."

"They're coming for Courtney," Tatiana whispered as unshed tears filled her eyes.

"And the baby."

Dominic held her stare as he pulled his hands from the others and crossed to Tatiana. Tears fell freely from her large brown eyes as he wrapped her in his embrace. She buried her face against his chest, sobbing quietly as he stroked her hair and rocked her gently.

"Courtney," Steven whispered. He held her hands and kissed her fingers as they all waited patiently for her to wake up. "Baby? I'm here. It's okay."

Tatiana's body tensed in Dominic's arms, and he could feel her holding her breath as they waited for Courtney to respond. As the young woman's eyes opened, everyone let out a collective sigh of relief, and Tatiana allowed her body to sag against him. He held her closer and noted the way her body fit so perfectly against his, every curve and plane in just the right place.

Courtney looked at them through wide eyes as Steven helped her adjust her position on the chaise. She swiped at her wet cheeks and let out a shaky breath. However, her expression swiftly changed to terror, and she grabbed Steven's arms.

"Oh my God." Her voice sounded small and scared as she tipped her chin and squeezed her eyes shut. "I saw him, and I saw where they kept me... I saw what they did." A sob choked her, keeping more words from coming.

"We broke through to some memories, but don't be surprised if you remember more as time passes," Kerry said gently. "Chances are, you'll remember everything eventually. Repressed memories are pretty common when someone has a traumatic experience, and I'd say yours sure as hell qualifies."

"Savannah was the one who brought you back here," Tatiana said.

"I know. I saw it too." Courtney's confused expression bounced from Steven to Tatiana. "I don't understand. Why would she leave me here alone?"

"You're not alone," Steven whispered.

"I knew it." Marianna sighed. "I knew she wouldn't help her father if she didn't absolutely have to."

"I'm not sure why she did what she did." Tatiana's

voice, now calm and controlled, filled the room as she gave Courtney a reassuring smile. "All I know for sure is that she's the reason you're here with Steven and not still held captive by her father."

"It's true," Kerry added. "Savannah's definitely the one who got you out, and from what I saw, she's not in cahoots with dear old daddy. I'd bet that she's in a world of trouble at the moment, but I couldn't get a bead on her signature."

"Be that as it may," Richard said tightly, "we still have Dr. Moravian to deal with."

"They won't touch you again." Steven pulled her into his arms, his eyes glowing brightly and determination edging his voice. "And they sure as hell aren't getting their hands on our son."

"I couldn't agree more. I promise that we will do everything within our power to keep you and your child safe." Richard paced to the front of the group as he spoke. "I have always considered our ranch a safe haven for our people, and until recently, that was the case. We will not run. We will wait for them to make their next move, and when they do, we will be ready."

"Absolutely." Dominic kept one arm linked around Tatiana's waist and held her tight as he addressed the others. It felt natural and perfect to have her next to him. "However, the ranch is over three hundred acres, and I'd feel better if we had more eyes on site to keep watch. Moravian and the Purists are getting more aggressive, and I doubt they'll wait much longer to try something else."

"There's one other issue," Tatiana interjected. "I don't think Moravian or Savannah are responsible for what's been happening with the horses. I didn't sense any connection to that at all. If it's okay, I'd like to bond with the animals again and see if there's something else they can tell us."

"You mean we could be dealing with two different attacks at the same time?" Pete asked. "Two enemies at once?"

"We had a Caedo assassination attempt on the ranch, but unfortunately, one of them escaped." Dominic's back straightened as he mentioned his failure. "The other died before I could interrogate him."

"Goddamn it." Pete's mouth set in a tight line as he looked into the eyes of his mate, Marianna. "I don't mean to be a dick, and I love a good, ass-kicking fest as much as the next guy, but my wife is about to give birth to our twins. I'd rather that *not* happen in the middle of a battle zone."

"Absolutely." Richard nodded. Hands behind his back, he scanned the rest with his glowing lion eyes, finally stopping with his wife. "None of the children should be in the middle of this."

Richard's bright blue eyes turned back to Pete.

"Pete, since you are a sentry in New York City and work with the vampire government, would you be able provide protective asylum for the women with children?" A wry smile hovered at his lips. "I realize this is an unusual request, but since you act as a liaison between our two races, I thought—"

"Consider it done," Pete responded before Richard could finish the question.

"Thank you." Richard's lips tilted. "I doubt even the most brazen Amoveo would attempt an attack on a vampire stronghold. It's settled then."

Several voices, mostly female, spoke all at once, but Richard held up both hands, and the space fell silent once again. Tatiana's fingers curled against Dominic's stomach, and he could tell she was doing her best to keep a brave face. In spite of that, she leaned further into him, seeking reassurance.

"This is nonnegotiable." Richard, gaze fierce and hands held tightly behind his back, turned to the rest of them. "Salinda and Samantha, along with the babies, will stay with Pete and Marianna at the vampire's New York facility. Courtney, you will go as well."

"No." Steven stood up and faced the prince. His eyes glowed the bright green of the Coyote Clan. "Richard, with all due respect, I am a healer, and if there's going to be a fight, then I need to be here to help anyone who might need medical attention, but Courtney is staying with me. Too much has happened, and I don't want her out of my sight."

Steven knelt down and pulled Courtney into his arms. His eyes glowed, and determination edged his voice as he looked past her to Richard.

"Courtney stays with me."

Dominic could tell the prince was weighing his options as looked at the beleaguered couple. Steven wanted to do his duty as an Amoveo healer, but he also wanted to protect his wife. The man was torn by duty, love, and loyalty, and Dominic could only imagine how he felt.

Dominic's fingers brushed Tatiana's lower back, and as her heart beat in time with his, he knew he would have made the same choice Steven did. Leaving his mate would never be an option. Even if she ends up rejecting him, he would stand by her and lay his life down for hers.

"As you wish." Richard tilted his head in deference to Steven's request. "The rest of us will remain on the ranch and stand our ground."

"You're not insisting us gals take cover with the vamps?" Kerry asked with genuine surprise. "How very un-Amoveo male of you."

"True." Richard's lips curved into a smile as he looked from one man to the next. "Keeping Amoveo mates apart is never a good idea, *but* if things get worse, I will insist the women leave for safer surroundings. Call it a royal prerogative."

"Now that's what I call progress," Layla said with a wink to her sister. She elbowed William. "You should take a page or two out of Richard's book, babe."

William shook his head and gave his wife a doubtful look.

"We will take turns patrolling the property in groups of two or three. No one goes anywhere alone." Richard turned to Tatiana, and his voice softened. "I would understand if you wanted to leave, to go home to Oregon and forget you were ever here, but I think it would be unwise. As much as you loathe to acknowledge it, you are half Amoveo, and that makes you as much of a target as the rest of us."

"I'm not leaving." Tatiana tightened her hold on Dominic though he sensed she was fighting the urge to bolt. "I want to find out what the hell is going on as much as all of you do. My life will never feel like my own unless I face this head on. I can't live with the unknown hanging over my head. Not anymore."

"Yeah, girl." Kerry winked as she rested her head on Dante's shoulder. "Let's kick some ass."

"That shoot was gonna be a big old bore anyway," Layla said on a heavy sigh. William looped one arm around her waist and straightened his tie with the other. "I'm sure William and I are going to enjoy stamping out these Purists once and for all, right?"

"Correct." William planted a kiss on the top of her curly red hair. "I would suggest we take stock of our weapons and lay out the patrol shifts as swiftly as possible."

"I'll fill Eric in as soon as we get back to the ranch." Dominic gave Richard a solemn look. "Your majesty, I think it's best if the others leave directly from here. I don't think they should risk time exposed on the ranch if they don't have to. Besides, if they leave from here, their energy signatures will be untraceable."

Dominic held Tatiana closer as they watched the others say good-bye to their mates. Malcolm and Richard kissed their wives and snuggled their daughters before the air filled with static, and they vanished. A lump formed in Dominic's throat as he saw the somber but resolute expressions on the two men.

"We'll finish this, Richard." Dominic's voice cut through the heavy silence. "I promise you, we'll finish this and bring your family home."

"Would someone please tell me what's going on?" Matt whispered from the back of the arena. Urgency laced his voice as he tapped his fingers on the smooth surface of one of the platforms, and guilt tugged at Dominic because he'd forgotten Matt was even there. "I'm getting the fact that you are about to have some kind of holy war, but I gotta tell you, I feel like I'm going crazy. Who, or what, are you people?"

"You are not crazy, Matt," Richard murmured. "We are not pod-people or aliens, but we *are* shapeshifters. Welcome to the world of the Amoveo."

A low, rumbling growl filled the room, and everyone looked at Richard. His blue eyes glowed brightly and were locked on Matt. He uttered the ancient language, and the air around him shimmered as he exploded with an earsplitting roar into a massive lion.

Matt gaped, but no sound came out as Richard approached. Dominic was certain Tatiana wanted to say something reassuring, but she didn't. She, like everyone else, was in awe of the magnificent beast.

Richard stalked slowly toward Matt, muscles rippling beneath his tawny coat, his proud face surrounded by a thick, dark mane. A growl rumbled in his throat as his eyes glittered. As Richard moved closer, Matt mumbled something incoherent and passed out cold.

Oh, yes. Richard's voice touched their collective minds. *He'll be a big help*.

Once they left the council chamber, Tatiana wasted no time getting back to the barn to take a closer look at Spirit's body, but the examination didn't yield new information. Richard and Malcolm used their Amoveo visualization abilities to remove the animal's body, and though she was curious as to where it went, she couldn't bring herself to ask.

Tatiana wanted to connect with one of the horses but wasn't sure which, so she decided to observe them for a while to get a bead on which one would be most receptive to that type of connection. She suspected the mares would be more receptive than the stallions and had her eye on Obsidian, a gorgeous, jet-black mare who seemed the most disturbed by Spirit's absence. However, as much as she wanted answers, Tatiana knew that pushing the issue wouldn't get her anywhere.

Matt didn't leave Tatiana's side for the next few hours as they worked in the barn and tended to the horses. The stalls, usually cared for by Salinda, were getting dirty, so they worked together to muck the stalls and reevaluate each horse. Matt said little—most was in response to direct questions—but she had to give the guy credit for sticking around. It's not every day that a person discovers the world is full of supernatural creatures or that his friend is one of them.

Tatiana's only regret was the distance that now lingered between them. She could only hope that with time, he would come around, and things could be like they were before, but she had a gut feeling that wouldn't be the case.

Matt wasn't the only one hanging around.

Dominic became her shadow the moment they emerged from the council chamber. On one hand, she was comforted by his presence, but on the other, it was a bit unsettling to have anyone watch her so closely. To his credit, he didn't simply stand guard and watch them work. He actually pitched in and got dirty right along with them.

The man was nothing if not tenacious.

Tatiana wiped the sweat from her brow with the back of her gloved hand as she stole a glance at Dominic, and when she set eyes on him, all the breath rushed from her lungs. At some point when she wasn't looking, he'd disposed of his T-shirt, which left his broad, well-muscled back exposed in all its rippling glory.

Sweat glistened across his hulking shoulders and trickled a tempting trail down his spine as he hoisted a bale of hay to one of the stalls. She couldn't help but stare as the thick layer of muscle moved beneath suntanned skin, and the veins in his arms bulged with effort.

Tatiana rested her chin on her hands, gripped the top of the rake, and simply allowed herself to enjoy the sight of him. Memories of his skin rushing beneath her fingers came flooding back, and as she sucked in a slow breath, her eyes tingled and snapped to their clan form.

"I'm sorry, Tatiana, but that's totally fuckin' weird," Matt whispered.

Tatiana jumped at the sound of his voice. Her chin slipped off her hands, making her stumble awkwardly over the rake. Dominic smirked at her over his shoulder as he tossed the last bale of hay into the stall.

What were you thinking about? His teasing voice drifted into her mind. She steadied herself and let out a nervous laugh as her eyes shifted back to their human form. *Nothing I care to admit to right now*, she responded playfully.

However, her smile faded when she saw the way Matt was looking at her.

He stared at her as though she was a complete stranger, and in a way, she was.

Tatiana barely recognized herself. Somehow, over the past several hours, she had begun to embrace her Amoveo nature. She looked briefly at Dominic. Yup. Embraced her powers along with everything and everyone who came with it. Yet what surprised and unsettled Tatiana the most was how natural and absolutely *right* it felt.

"Matt," she said, reaching for his arm, wanting to reassure him she was still the same person. He stepped back, avoiding her reach. Tatiana dropped her hand. "I'm still me."

"Right," he said in a shaky voice. "You're you, but you can make your eyes glow, and apparently, you turn into a wolf." Hurt carved into his features, and his mouth set in a frown. "You lied to me."

"I didn't lie exactly." Tatiana leaned the rake against the wall and pulled the work gloves off, wishing like hell a cool breeze would come along and calm her body and mind. "It was more like an omission."

"Same thing." He glanced past to her to Dominic, who she sensed behind her. His presence was thick and radiated heat. Like the sultry summer air she felt him there, strong and ever-present. "What about you?" Matt jutted his chin and gave Dominic a defiant look.

"Tiger Clan." Dominic's voice, deep and gravelly, skittered around Tatiana temptingly, and she fought the urge to growl. Amazing how one note from that voice made her want to strip naked and maul him. "Bengal Tiger to be specific."

"Besides," Tatiana said through a shaky laugh, "I'm only half Amoveo."

"Right," Matt scoffed. "That's like saying you're a little bit pregnant."

"Tatiana and I might be from two different clans," Dominic interjected, "but we are both Amoveo."

And mates…

The unspoken words hung in the air, but he may as well have said them out loud again. He may not be claiming her with his words, but his meaning was clear.

Dominic moved silently as he took his place beside her but kept his gaze on Matt, who looked as though he might throw up. Tatiana could tell Dominic still didn't trust Matt, and she supposed there wasn't much she could do about that. Truthfully, she felt like there wasn't much she could do about anything, and feeling helpless sucked.

"The horses need new feed," Matt grumbled. He took his rake to the tool rack and hung it in its place. "I can go pick some up if you'll tell me where it is."

"No," Dominic said in a surprisingly sharp tone. "Richard already placed an order, and it will be delivered this afternoon. Besides, I think it's best if you stay here on the ranch. Given everything that's going on, we can't guarantee your safety if you leave the property."

"Bullshit." Matt's eyes narrowed, and he threw his work gloves onto the tack table by the open barn doors. He shot a look of pure hatred at Dominic. "You aren't worried about me at all. You still think I had something to do with what happened to Spirit, don't you?"

"No," Dominic said evenly. "However, it's not just your safety I'm concerned about. If Moravian or any other Purist Amoveo makes a move, then abducting a human that Tatiana cares about would be a good way to get to her." His body tensed, and his eyes flickered to their clan form. "No one leaves the ranch."

"So, what? Now I'm prisoner here?"

"No, Matt." Tatiana closed the distance between

them and placed her hands on his shoulders. "That's not what he's saying." She glanced at Dominic. "Right?"

"Of course not." Dominic's jaw clenched, and his eyes flickered back to their human brown. "As soon as we eliminate the threat, he is free to leave."

Tatiana looked at Matt and saw hurt in his eyes.

"But you're not leaving, are you?" His face twisted in anger as he nodded toward Dominic. "You're staying here with him, right? So I guess I'll have to find another job."

"I—I didn't say that," she said hesitantly.

Tatiana dropped her hands and turned her body as she looked between the two men who were staring at her intently. She hadn't thought that far ahead. The truth was, she hadn't been thinking about anything. Her hormones and emotions had been running her from the second she arrived at the ranch and found Dominic.

"Right," Matt said under his breath. He walked to the back door of the stable and stopped. "I'm going back to the cabin to take a shower." He glared at Dominic. "If that's alright with you."

Tatiana watched him disappear around the corner, and her heart sank. How could she go back to her life in Oregon? Her practice? Any of it?

Everything was different, and the very thing she had been fearful of had actually happened. The rug had been pulled out from under her, and her existence was turned upside down because of the Amoveo and their insane world.

"He shouldn't walk back to the cabin alone. Eric's patrolling with Malcolm and Richard—I'll ask him to split off and keep an eye on Matt." Dominic stared at her intently and scoffed, "I can't blame him for being upset. I mean, obviously you're going to stay here."

"I'm sorry." She blinked, not quite sure if she heard him correctly. "What did you say?"

"I'm Guardian of this ranch." He inched closer, his large frame invading her space easily. "And given the climate for our people right now, I certainly can't leave."

Tatiana took a breath to steady herself, but his spicy, masculine scent filled her head, making concentration difficult. Hay and sweat with a touch of something else she couldn't quite put her finger on filled her head. Based on the shameless way her body reacted, it was likely some kind of pheromone.

"Tatiana," he breathed. Dominic brushed a sweaty lock of hair off her forehead and ran his thumb along her cheek. Heat rippled off his chest as muscles flexed beneath damp skin. His fiercely intense eyes glowed down at her from under thick dark lashes. "You are my mate, and your place is with me."

"What did you say?" Tatiana blinked as the words came in a rush.

Lust was swiftly replaced with anger, and her body stilled as she grappled for the ability to speak. Her brain and body were at odds as she tried to form a coherent response, opposed to simply punching him in the nose.

"My *place*?" Tatiana seethed as she batted his hand away. Hands on her hips, she glared up at him furiously as familiar fears and pent up emotions rose to the surface. "My *place* is wherever the hell I say it is. You and I may be mates, but I will be goddamned if you or anyone one else tells me where my *place* is. I refuse to have my future dictated by you, the Amoveo, Purists, Caedo, or some stupid fucking legend that I had no say in being a part of."

Dominic didn't flinch. He held his ground as he stared at her, meeting her challenge and not backing down. He stood there like the immovable force he was, and it made her crazy. Strong and silent? Hah! More like stubborn and irrational.

"Say something, for Christ's sake."

Frustrated, she shoved at his shoulders, but her hands slipped off his sweaty skin. As she fell forward, he grabbed her wrists and yanked her body against him.

Heat from his torso seeped through her thin tank top and rippled straight to her very core, causing her body to respond on a primal level.

A pulsing need throbbed between her legs, and her eyes shifted to their clan form as ferocious, carnal desire burned through her. Tatiana's heart raced as she stared at him, but she'd be damned if she'd show any sign of giving in.

Movement over Dominic's shoulder caught her eye as the horses galloped past. That's what she needed—to run free and embrace the wolf. Her wolf was fearless and invisible, capable of disappearing into the woods and hiding from the world.

"Tatiana," Dominic breathed her name. He leaned down and brushed her lips with his before resting his damp forehead against hers. "Do you have any idea what you do to me? Any clue what you've done to my life, my perception of myself, or my place in this world?"

Dominic loosened his hold on her wrists and held her hands against his chest, their bodies still pressed tightly together. He pulled back and looked her in the face.

"You aren't the only one who's feeling confused," he rasped. "Before you came along I had a really clear bead on things."

Dominic's fingers trailed along her bare arms, sending shivers through her as he stared at her through glowing eyes. He cupped her face with one hand as the other wandered down her side and finally rested at the dip of her waist.

"I think it's safe to say I'm in touch with that emotion," she murmured.

Tatiana's hands rested on his chest, and she tried not to notice how his muscles moved beneath her fingers, or the erotic way his body hardened as it pressed against hers. He hummed with power, desire, and restraint. His jaw clenched, and a tiny muscle flickered beneath the ever-present five o'clock shadow as his fingers gripped her hip.

"I want you, Tatiana," he ground out. "I can't escape you. No matter how hard I've tried to get you out of my head, it's no use. You've bewitched me, put me under a spell so that I can't see, hear, or feel anything but you."

As Dominic spoke, he walked her backward, toward one of the freshly cleaned stalls, and she moved with him, knowing what his intentions were. His hands drifted up her rib cage, brushed along her arms, and found their way once again around her wrists.

Tatiana's breath came quickly, and her skin tingled as he branded her with his stare. She let out a gasp as her back bumped into the wall, and Dominic pinned her there. His erection pressed enticingly against her belly as he lifted her arms over her head and leaned his taut body against hers.

"Before you," he whispered, his face hovering an inch away, "the only thing that mattered was doing my job as Guardian, but now… it's you, Tatiana."

Dominic ground himself against her as he nudged her legs apart with his knee, trailing kisses along her neck. With every breath, her breasts crushed against his chest, sending jolts of pleasure through her. Dominic had her wet and panting, and if he didn't kiss her soon, she might scream.

Yes. Her mind touched his on a whisper.

A growl rumbled in his chest as Tatiana tilted her head to the side, allowing him better access to the hypersensitive skin on her neck. She wrapped one leg around him, pulling him against her most sensitive spot. Dominic lifted his head and locked eyes with her, their lips a breath apart, and she whispered the words into his mind… *I want you, Dominic*.

On groan of pleasure, he covered her mouth with his, running his tongue along the seam of her mouth as she opened to him. Warmth raced through her as he linked their fingers, pressed her wrists against the wall, and drank from her greedily. His kiss was hard and demanding, taking everything she had to give and more. Her body screamed with need as the fire he started raged out of control.

Tatiana yanked her hands from his, needing to touch him and hold him. She ran her fingers over the slick planes of his chest and then trailed them over his rippling, six-pack abs as she licked and nibbled at his lips. Fumbling with his belt, they laughed through their kiss, and he groaned as she finally released him.

The sight of him fully aroused was almost as much

of a turn-on as hearing him moan when she ran one finger up the hot length of skin—scorching satin over steel. Dominic breathed a sigh of pleasure against her lips as she took the heavy weight of him in her hand and stroked.

"Oh God, yes," he whispered as she massaged him.

Dominic deepened the kiss as she worked him, and his talented fingers slipped beneath her sweat-soaked top. He lifted it over her breasts and pushed her bra aside before capturing her swollen breast in his eager hands. The rough skin of his palm braised the sensitive nipple, sending shocks of pleasure to her feminine center. Erotic waves swamped her as she worked the hot length of him and ran her thumb over the swollen head. He pinched her nipple as she arched into his hand and kept massaging his engorged cock.

Dominic broke the kiss, and in one swift movement, pulled her shorts and underwear down past her hips, which she quickly stepped out of and kicked aside. Tatiana let out a soft cry of pleasure as his fingers slid between her slick folds, and he slipped two inside of her. Holding her gaze, his thumb worked the tiny bundle of nerves, making her wet and ready.

Sensing they were both nearing the edge, Dominic gently removed her hand from him and once again linked his fingers with hers. A sly grin cracked his face as he held her hands over her head with one hand and pinned her body against the wall with his much larger frame. The look in his eye was feral and predatory and made her moan as she waited for the only thing that could satisfy her.

This was what she needed—what they both needed.

Tense with unfulfilled desire, she quivered with anticipation as one strong hand slid along her bare thigh and lifted her leg over his hip, opening her. Dominic reached down between their sweat-covered bodies and prodded her swollen entrance with the tip of his erection. Then in one swift stroke, he buried himself deep inside.

Tatiana's cry of pleasure was muffled against his shoulder as he filled her in one thick, satisfying thrust. He sought her mouth, licking and suckling her lips as he pumped into her. Slowly at first, the kind of long, deep, languid strokes that can make a woman scream and beg for more. Dominic rolled his hips and ground against her, putting pressure on the right spot, which sent white-hot streaks of lightning through her.

Tatiana whimpered and rolled her hips, needing more. "Fuck me harder," she whispered as she flicked his earlobe with her tongue. "Faster, Dominic."

Dominic dragged her leg higher over his hip so he could dive even deeper and give her exactly what she asked for. Carnal need swamped them. Like a man possessed, Dominic pounded into her faster, and with every stroke, the passion peaked higher.

Their energy waves mingled wildly in the air like a tornado as the orgasm exploded and carried them both over the edge. As the final burst of pleasure shot through them, their bodies shuddered in unison, and Dominic's mind touched hers on a growl. *Nos es unus. Materia pro totus vicis. Ago intertwined. Forever.*

Tatiana's eyes flew open, and she gripped Dominic's shoulders as the delicious weight of him pressed against her. Both of them were completely spent and shaking from the aftershocks of the shared orgasm. However, through the blinding fog of lust, the reality of those whispered words—and what they meant—came crashing down.

"Did I just hear what I thought I did?" Tatiana asked through huffing breaths as her hands gripped his shoulders and pushed him back, forcing him to look her in the eyes. Her voice shook with disbelief and a touch of fear. "D-did you say the mating rite?"

Dominic's face fell, and he swallowed hard, but he didn't release her. His body remained locked inside of her. He looked as though he didn't realize he did it, but even if that were the case, it didn't change the outcome.

If he said it, they were mated.

"Answer me," she seethed. "Dominic?"

"Yes." His features hardened as his mouth set in tight line. "I did."

Tears pricked the back of her eyes, and all the air rushed from her lungs as she stared at him in shock. Her body cooled swiftly, and a knot formed in her chest as the weight of this betrayal washed over her.

"How could you do that?" she asked in a quivering voice as the tears fell, and she choked on the words. "How could you betray my trust like that?"

Tatiana shoved him away and scrambled to get her shorts on. She turned her back on him and said nothing as she got dressed, but she could feel him there, watching her. She spun around and faced him but did not find the contrite or regretful look she expected. Dominic, now fully dressed, stood with his arms folded over his chest in that cold, arrogant, alpha-male stance. Emotionless.

"We are mates, Tatiana." His voice was cold and

matter-of-fact, but for a moment, the mask slipped away, and she could swear she saw regret. "It is what it is."

Tears filled Tatiana's eyes, the weight of his words shrouding her, and she shook her head.

"So that's it?" she said in a teary voice as anger crawled up her back, and she stalked toward him, her eyes glowing brightly. The urge to shift pulsed beneath her skin. "You go ahead and bind our lives together without discussing it with me?"

"Tatiana," he said gently. His features softened, and he reached out to touch her, but she shoved his hand away. "Let me explain."

"You've done enough."

Tatiana raced out of the barn. Panic swamped her as she tore across the field and past the grazing horses. Their energy washed over her, and two of the mares, Obsidian and Poppy, ran alongside her. Tatiana smiled through her tears as the horses trotted with her because she knew they sensed her pain and sought to soothe it.

As she approached the fence, the animals slowed and watched as she slipped between the rails. Tatiana sent them gentle waves of energy, reassuring them before she continued toward the mountains. She needed space. She needed her wolf.

Tatiana didn't know if Dominic was following—truthfully she didn't care. Right now, the only thing she could focus on was shifting. Stopping along the tree line, she closed her eyes and pictured her clan animal—the timber wolf. The summery Montana air surrounded her, and moments later, static rippled over skin as the familiar flutter of the shift consumed her.

She threw her arms out and tilted her face to the sky

as her body arched and stretched into the beast. Within seconds she burst into the form of her wolf. Skin was replaced by soft brown and white fur with four legs replacing two.

Energy surged through her as she reveled in the power of her canine body. She lifted her snout, breathing deeply, allowing the crisp scents of nature to fill her head, and then she ran.

Power surged through her as she raced through the tall grass and headed into the wooded area. She moved faster, keeping her head low and her gaze sharp. As much as she hated to admit it, shifting into her wolf always put her at ease. Perhaps it was because no one in her life, other than her family, knew what she could do. But when Tatiana became the wolf… nothing and no one could touch her.

Not even Dominic.

Tatiana had, after all, hidden from him in the dream realm for years, and she would have remained that way if she hadn't set foot on this damned ranch. Now, here she was mated to an overbearing, alpha-male Amoveo who decided to choose what her future would hold. Tatiana whined as the reality of what had happened settled over her, but in spite of it, she couldn't deny the way he made her feel.

Trotting up the hill, she barely felt the rocks and dirt beneath the pads of her paws. Lost in her thoughts and the exhilaration of the shift, it took her a moment to realize she wasn't alone.

Tatiana stopped by a large pine tree and stood motionless as she reached out, attempting to identify the subtle ripple in the air. It was a tickle, almost a phantom, as though someone she couldn't see was trying to disguise his or her presence. She crouched low and pressed her furred body into the brush, praying it provided the cover she needed. Her heart raced as she fought to identify the source of the energy pattern.

Eyes closed, Tatiana used all of her effort to pinpoint it, and as she breathed deeply, the flutter of energy became distinct and vaguely familiar. The sound of leaves and branches cracking beneath feet broke through the usual noises of nature and sent her heart into overdrive.

Tatiana definitely was not alone.

If she weren't such a chickenshit, she could try to use the visualization skills of the other Amoveo and get the hell out of there, but she hadn't a clue how to do it. She could call Dominic, but after running out like that... why on earth would he want to help?

Chapter 8

Dominic watched her race across the field with the horses matching her speed, and any anger he felt flew away on the summer breeze. Tatiana was beautiful, stubborn, and spirited, but she was still scared. She was frightened, and instead of reassuring her and letting her figure things out on her own time, he said the mating rite.

"Fuck," he shouted. The horses lifted their heads from grazing and looked at him as though he were crazy. "I'm in deep shit, you guys."

The truth was that he didn't mean to say the mating rite. Hell, he didn't think he'd really said it until she confirmed it. Dominic didn't know what came over him, but in that moment, he had to bind her to him. It wasn't a matter of want, to—he *had* to—and it scared him as much as it did her.

Dominic ran both hands over his face as he strode out to the field, keeping her in his sights. The afternoon sun beat down relentlessly as he stalked through the grass, but unlike with Tatiana, the horses kept their distance. Perhaps it was the predator in him, but they never cared to get too close.

Could that be why Tatiana didn't want to mate with him?

Dominic stopped dead in his tracks and stared after her as the reality of what he'd done hit him like a ton of bricks. God, he felt like such a dumb-ass. She was afraid of him and of binding her life to his, and now, what did he do? He went ahead and confirmed all of her fears by saying the mating rite without her consent. She'd given him permission to take her body, but not her heart, and it made him feel like a thief.

Dominic stilled as he watched her slip through the bars of the fence. Tension settled in his shoulders.

"Son of a bitch," he breathed. "Where the hell is that woman going now?"

Tatiana clearly wanted to be alone, and giving her space to run in the fields was one thing, but going into the wooded area—well, that was another. She may want to get away, but that was too damn bad. There was no way he would allow her to wander around the outskirts of the property without him.

However, every coherent thought was ripped from his head as he watched her stretch her arms out wide and erupt into her clan form. He knew she'd be breathtaking in the shape of her wolf, but nothing could have prepared him for the elegant beauty of his spirited mate. Her brown and white coat fluttered with the summer breeze as she trotted through the tall grasses toward the woods.

Fear gripped his heart as she vanished into the trees.

Dominic burst into a run, and as he tore across the field, his eyes flickered to their clan form. He growled the ancient language, "*Verto*."

In a burst of static, Dominic erupted into his tiger and leapt over the fence in one fluid motion. Landing easily on all fours, he followed Tatiana's familiar energy signature into the woods, and as he hurried up the hill, a dark stream of energy captured his attention.

Dominic froze. Scanning the area, he spotted Tatiana at the crest of the hill, still in her wolf form, lying low and stone-still. *Tatiana.* He touched her mind with his, shielding his thoughts from anyone else who could be in the area. *Don't move and stay calm.*

There's someone else up here, Dominic. Her frightened voice quivered, and the sound of it nearly did him in. *The energy signature seems familiar, but I can't quite get it.*

Dominic moved painstakingly slow, making no sound as he crept through the sun-dappled trees. Movement, about fifty feet to the left, captured his attention. He sharpened his focus and watched as the air in that vicinity pulsed and shimmered, like heat coming off pavement.

Purist! Dominic roared to the collective minds of his friends.

As he exploded into action, an unfamiliar male from the Bear Clan materialized before him and immediately charged Tatiana.

We're under attack. Eric's gravelly, focused voice sliced into his consciousness.

We have two more at the main house. William's voice shot into his mind.

In an instant, Dominic's worst fears were realized. His mate and the prince were in danger—but the choice was far simpler than he thought it would be because there was no choice.

It was her. It would *always* be her.

Blinding rage consumed him as he watched the massive beast descend on his mate. Tatiana scrambled backward as Dominic roared and leapt onto the back of the enormous Kodiak bear. He and the bear went tumbling down the hill. In a blur of claws and fur, they slammed into the trunk of a tree, which momentarily dislodged Dominic from the Purist's side.

Snarling, Dominic leapt to his feet as his opponent reared up on his hind legs and bellowed into the air. Tatiana's frightened voice tore into his mind. *There's another one.*

Run up the mountain, Tatiana. Just keep moving. I promise I'll get to you.

With every ounce of power he had, Dominic pounced on the Purist and latched powerful jaws around his neck, tackling him to the ground. Pinning him with a stranglehold, he sank his razor-sharp teeth into flesh. The coppery taste of blood bathed the inside of his mouth. Knowing he was delivering a mortal wound, Dominic bit down with all his strength and growled as the neck of his enemy broke.

Dominic! Tatiana's panicked voice shot into his mind. *Up here. Hurry!*

Blood dripping from his muzzle, he whipped his head around and glanced up to see Tatiana cornered by a female from the Arctic Wolf Clan. Dominic recognized her immediately as an elder and former Council member. She had backed Tatiana onto a thin ledge of rock, and the only place for her to go was about thirty feet down.

Moravian was right. The woman's voice slithered into his mind. *Your half-breed mates are pathetic.*

Just as Dominic whispered the ancient language to visualize himself to Tatiana's side, he saw the atmosphere between Tatiana and the white wolf ripple. As he vanished in a flicker of static, Courtney materialized in front of Tatiana at the very moment the wolf pounced.

What happened next, happened in a split second.

Dominic materialized on the ledge behind the white wolf in time to see Courtney and the Purist from the Wolf Clan tumble over the edge in a tangle of limbs. Tatiana changed back to her human form, screaming Courtney's name. Dominic shifted and caught her before she disappeared after them.

"Courtney!" Tatiana's hysterical cry echoed through the woods as they peered over the edge and saw two motionless bodies on the ground below.

"Hold on to me." Dominic held her close and whispered the ancient language, "*Verto*."

In a blink, he and Tatiana were standing next to the motionless bodies of Courtney and the wolf. He released Tatiana's shaking form from his embrace and squatted down next to Courtney. Her energy signature was faint but still showed signs of life.

"She's alive, but she's in bad shape." Frustration and guilt tugged at him. *Steven. Courtney's in trouble.* Dominic didn't know where Steven was, but since he didn't come immediately to his mate's side, he had to be in the midst of battle.

"This is my fault," Dominic whispered. "I didn't get up there in time."

"Here." Tatiana grabbed a bandanna from the back pocket of her shorts and held it on the bleeding wound on Courtney's head. She took Dominic's hand and placed it over the makeshift bandage. "Keep pressure on it to stop the bleeding. I'm going to see if I can read her injuries the way I do with animals."

Dominic said nothing but did as she instructed. He watched as she placed both hands on Courtney's belly, closed her eyes, and focused. Tatiana's body shuddered, and her eyes flickered behind her lids as though she were dreaming.

Covered in dirt, with blood smudged on her hands, she was still the most spectacular, beautiful creature he'd ever encountered. Her strength and focus in this moment of crisis had him in awe. She put aside their personal differences to deal with the trauma, and that was the most impressive thing of all.

"The baby's heartbeat is steady and strong," she murmured softly. Eyes still closed, her hands moved from Courtney's belly to her arms. She brushed the length of her body, tuning in with flawless intensity. Her brow furrowed. "Courtney's fading fast, Dominic."

Tatiana opened her eyes and sat back on her heels as tears streamed down her cheeks. She took Courtney's hand and kissed it. "Please don't give up, Courtney."

The air erupted in static electricity as Steven materialized next to them. His clothing was torn and bloody, evidence of a battle fought and won. His face was wracked with grief, and his bright green eyes went immediately to his mate.

Steven uttered a strangled cry and shoved Dominic out of the way as he knelt at his wife's side. He brushed blonde hair from her bruised, bloody forehead and whispered to her as Dominic stood up. He stepped back, feeling nothing but helplessness as he watched the scene before him.

Tatiana, on the other hand, knew exactly what to do. The woman was the calm in the storm.

"Steven," she said firmly. "We have to get her back to the medical facility at the main house. The baby has to come now, or you could lose both of them."

"I know." Steven nodded and wept as he kissed his mate's cheek. "I don't understand why she was here. When the Purists showed up, I told her to hide in the meeting hall. She knew she'd be safe there." He looked up at Dominic through tear-filled eyes, his voice laced with confusion. "Why did she come here?"

Dominic had no rational explanation why Courtney would risk her life, or the life of her unborn child, but she did. Courtney had sacrificed herself for Tatiana.

Why did she do this, Dominic? Tatiana's voice brushed his mind.

I don't know. Dominic kept their communication shrouded from Steven. *She had to know she was no match for that elder, especially given her condition.*

Maybe… that's why she did it.

Before Dominic could ask what she meant, Courtney moaned in pain and captured their full attention.

"We'll get you out of here." Steven kissed her forehead and rested one shaking hand on her belly. "Please don't leave me."

Dominic. Tatiana's strained voice touched his mind as she looked at him through worried eyes. *We have got to get her out of here!*

I know. Dominic had to reach out to the others. *I have no idea what's going on back at the house, and the last thing I want to do is to land in the middle of another fight*. Anger gripped him as he glared at the dead body of the Purist. The traitor had shifted back to her human form. Her eyes were open, her head tilted at an unnatural angle. *That bitch, Elvira, from the Arctic Wolf Clan—another fucking traitor.*

I don't give a shit what clan she's from. She's dead, and Courtney will be too, if we don't do something.

Static filled the air again as Malcolm and Richard appeared, bloody and disheveled, having clearly fought similar battles. Their faces twisted in fury when they saw Steven's fallen mate and the bodies of the dead Purists.

"Richard." Tatiana scrambled to her feet urgently. "We have to get her to the medical lab and deliver the baby right now. We really don't have much time. Is it safe to take her?"

"Yes," Richard bit out. His fierce, glowing gaze wandered over the dead bodies of their enemies and lingered on the former Council member. "I suspected there were other elders still involved. I should have known. Elvira was able to break through the shield I placed around the property, but this serpent's days of treachery are over." His eyes burned brighter as he waved one hand and growled, "*Ardebit in Inferno.*" The bodies of both Purists erupted in flames and vanished with a cloud of smoke.

All of them laid hands on Courtney and Steven as Richard whispered the ancient language. As they vanished, one thought ran through Dominic's mind.

Come hell or high water, he would find Moravian and kill him.

Dominic paced the hallway outside the surgical suite as William, Kerry, and Dante watched him through concerned eyes. He kept his intense gaze on the door of the operating room and growled with frustration. It seemed as though they'd been in there for hours. The other men were patrolling the property, disposing of the other three bodies—none of which were Moravian or his daughter, Savannah.

"What's taking so goddamn long," he seethed.

Dominic sensed Tatiana's strained energy signature and attempted to send her soothing waves, but she cut herself off from him, leaving him with that odd void and sense of loneliness. He rubbed his chest absently, but dropped his hand abruptly when he saw William studying him.

"It's unsettling, isn't it," William mused. He was leaning against the wall, cool and controlled as usual. "Makes you feel out of your element."

"What?" Dominic asked with mild annoyance.

"Connecting with your mate," William said in an irritating matter-of-fact way. "We've all been there."

"I don't know what you're talking about," Dominic said tightly.

"Ha," Kerry said loudly. "Your goose is seriously cooked. I can't believe you're actually going to deny it. Before you get all macho and offended, take a deep breath and relax. All of us have been where you guys are now." Kerry winked at Dante and linked her hand with her mate. "She'll get there, big guy, but you have to let her figure it out on her terms, and then you can say the bonding rite to make it official."

Dominic averted his eyes and crossed his arms as he leaned against the wall. He grumbled something inaudible under his breath but stopped short of coming right out and telling them. However, in Kerry's usually perceptive fashion, it didn't take long for her to figure it out.

"Oh shit," Kerry said through a short laugh. She covered her mouth quickly when he shot her a disapproving look. "I'm sorry. I didn't mean to laugh but… oh dear."

"What?" William asked, looking confused as he smoothed back strands of his long blonde hair. The guy had ditched the shirt and tie, but even in jeans and a T-shirt he looked uptight.

"Oh man," Dante said on a sigh. He gave Dominic a pained expression. "You're screwed."

"Will someone please tell me what on earth you're going on about?" William said in exasperation. He looked at Kerry, who arched one eyebrow and looked at him like he was the class dunce. Awareness flickered over his features, and he raised his brow. "Did you say the bonding rite without her consent?"

Dominic nodded.

"Yes," William mused. "You *are* indeed screwed."

"I know." Dominic butted the heel of his boot against the wall and let out a huffing breath as he looked at the tiled ceiling. He squeezed his eyes shut against the fluorescent lights. "I don't know how it happened. It's like I was possessed. I didn't plan on saying it, but I sure as shit did, and now she hates me." He ducked his chin and glanced at Kerry. "I can't really blame her. I feel like a fuckin' thief."

They were all silent, which only made Dominic feel like a bigger douche. His inner voice berated him, and when he thought he'd go insane, the door opened, and Tatiana emerged looking completely drained. Any concern for himself evaporated, and all he could see was her.

Tatiana's dark hair was tousled, her energy signature bathed in weariness. Yet in spite of it all, her beauty stole his breath, and it took Dominic a moment to realize he was standing there with his mouth open.

"It's a boy," she said smiling as tears filled her eyes. "A healthy baby boy."

Everyone gathered around, but Dominic didn't get too close. He knew she was upset with him for what happened in the barn, and he had zero idea how to make it right.

"The C-section went well, considering I've never done that on a person before. Thank God Steven was able to hold it together and help me through it."

"Is Courtney…?" Kerry trailed off, unable to say what they had been worried about.

"She's still unconscious," Tatiana whispered in a quivering voice. She let out a slow breath, clearly trying to steady herself. "Steven's with her now, and I doubt he'll leave her side." She smiled and ran a hand through her hair. "Steven wouldn't even hold the baby. He said he wants to wait until Courtney wakes up so he can share the experience with her."

"Speaking of which, where is the baby?" Kerry asked expectantly.

"Steven reached out to Richard and asked him to bring the boy to Salinda. He figured that since she and Samantha were still nursing, there would be no shortage of milk. Besides, based on everything that's happened, it's safer if he stays there, at least for now."

Layla came out of the room and closed the door quietly behind her.

"How's she doing?" Dante asked.

"Courtney is hanging tough," Layla said. "We moved her into the recovery room next door, and Steven is right there with her."

"I bet," Dante said. "He's not gonna move from that spot until she's in the clear."

"I gotta tell ya, sis. That was pretty incredible." Layla rested her chin on Tatiana's shoulder and gave her a hug from behind. "You did a great job in there and managed to keep Steven calm through the whole procedure. I just wish I was a more skilled assistant." She looked at Dominic. "Anyone find Matt yet?"

"Not exactly," Dominic said sharply. He looked at Tatiana, but she avoided his gaze. "He left."

"No way." Tatiana looked at him briefly and then to the others. "I know Matt was upset and freaked out, but I can't believe he'd leave without saying something."

"Your rental car is gone and so are his things." Dominic slipped the note from his pocket and handed it to her. "Richard found this on the porch after all the dust settled."

"What does it say?" Layla asked.

"*Dear Tatiana*," she read as the paper quivered in her delicate fingers. "*I'm sorry, but I can't handle this. I'm leaving, and will try to forget I ever saw or heard any of this crazy shit. Please don't try and find me—Matt*."

Dominic stuffed his hands in his pockets and kept his eyes on Tatiana as she read the note. The tears fell silently as she let out a shuddering breath and nodded. He was torn between wanting to beat the shit out of that little jerk for hurting her or sweeping her into his arms and comforting her. "Well," Tatiana said with a sigh as she lifted one shoulder, "I guess I can't really blame him." She sniffed back her tears and cleared her throat. "However, we have bigger issues to deal with. I'm worried about Courtney's condition. To be honest, I'm surprised she survived the delivery, and her Amoveo healing process doesn't seem to be kicking in. I mean, the physical healing has begun, but she's not waking up. It's like she's… giving up or something."

Tatiana's lashes fluttered, and she pushed her bangs off her forehead as her small form wavered from exhaustion. Dominic caught her before she fell over and swept her into his arms, cradling her against his chest.

Tatiana let out a sound of surprise and looked at him through wide dark eyes.

"What are you doing?" She folded her arms over her breasts and sliced an embarrassed look to the others before locking eyes with him. Her voice dropped to above a whisper. "I am perfectly capable of standing on my own. I just delivered a baby for heaven's sake, and I have an unconscious patient in the other room. Now, put me down. I'm concerned about Courtney," she said as she tried to suppress a yawn.

"And *I'm* concerned about *you*," Dominic insisted. "You need sleep. You're not going to be any good to Courtney, Steven, or anyone else, if you pass out. So quit being a stubborn, hardheaded woman, and let me take care of you."

Tatiana opened her mouth to say something but must have thought better of it and snapped it shut. Her contrite look almost made him laugh out loud, but he had a sinking suspicion that would do nothing to help his cause.

"Thank you." Dominic looked at the others, who all did their best not to smile—except for Layla, who gave him two thumbs up. "I'm sure the four of them can handle things here, and if anything major changes with Courtney's condition, Layla will alert us immediately."

"No doubt." Layla winked. "Be a good girl, Tatiana. There are worse things you could be doing right now. We'll keep an eye on things here."

"Fine," Tatiana said on an exasperated sigh.

"We will be in my cabin," Dominic said firmly.

As he uttered the ancient language, they vanished in a rush of static. Kerry's voice touched his mind. *Keep hanging on to her, Dominic. Everything will work out as long as you're there to catch her.*

Chapter 9

THE SMELL OF BACON COOKING FILLED TATIANA'S HEAD as she emerged from the deepest sleep of her life. Rolling onto her back, she peeled her eyes open while struggling to get her bearings. The last thing she remembered was that odd sense of displacement as Dominic used the visualization skills to transport them here.

Tatiana shuddered at the memory of the bizarre sensation. It reminded her of being on a roller coaster, that nauseating moment when your stomach drops to your feet. It would be just fine with her if she never used that particular ability again. The mere thought made her queasy.

Pushing herself up onto her elbows, she looked around the unfamiliar room. When she saw the pile of men's clothing discarded in the corner she realized where she was—Dominic's bedroom. The room was typically male. Sparsely furnished with only the essentials and no sign of a laundry basket anywhere.

The space next to her on the bed looked as though no one had slept there. Interesting. Mr.-I'll-say-the-mating-rite-without-asking didn't sleep with her in his own bed. Memories of their tryst in the barn came flooding back, but she shoved them aside. Toe-curling sex aside, he had no right to say those words without her consent, but in all honesty, given the dire, life-threatening situation they all went through, there wasn't any room in her heart for anger.

Moonlight streamed in through the window, and she wondered how long she'd been asleep. Glancing at the clock, she saw it was just after midnight, and since Dominic wasn't next to her in bed, it was a pretty good bet he was responsible for the fantastic aroma filling the cabin. Her stomach growled loudly, and it dawned on her that she hadn't eaten anything but that apple yesterday morning.

Tatiana sat up and pushed the sheets aside to discover that she was wearing nothing but one of Dominic's black T-shirts. Her first instinct was to be annoyed that he'd undressed her, but under the circumstances, she figured it was the least of their problems. Besides, it wasn't like he hadn't seen her body before. She sat quietly on the edge of the bed and ran her fingertips along her lower lip as she recalled his kisses and the erotic feel of his mouth.

A shiver ran up her back, but she shook it off.

"Get a grip," she whispered to herself.

Tatiana opened the bedroom door and was hit by another wave of deliciousness. She padded silently across the wooden floor and tiptoed down the steps, doing her best to be quiet, but as her toes hit the first floor landing, Dominic's deep baritone tumbled around her.

"I was wondering when you were gonna wake up," he called from the kitchen. "Better get your cute butt in here, or I'm going to eat this midnight snack all by myself."

Tatiana smiled in spite of the fact that she wanted to be annoyed. Funny. The only other person who could get her to smile when she was pissed was her twin brother, Raife. The sound of Cass's whine caught her attention, and she entered the kitchen in time to see Dominic about to feed bacon to the puppy.

Standing at the island in the middle of the kitchen wearing only a pair of red gym shorts, Dominic gave Tatiana an eyeful of his incredible torso and long, well-toned legs. He was holding a piece of bacon out as a bribe to get Cass to sit—and it was working. The little beagle sat motionless but kept his keen eyes on the crispy bit of goodness.

"Stop right there," she said sternly with her arm outstretched and her finger pointed accusingly at Dominic. "Don't you dare feed him that!"

Caught in the act, both Dominic and the dog froze before Cass whined, and Dominic dropped his hand onto the counter. He made a face of disapproval at Tatiana and shook his head before giving the puppy an apologetic look.

"What?" Dominic asked innocently as his gaze slid to the hem of her T-shirt and down her bare legs. A smile played at his lips. "It's just a little bacon."

"It's *not* just a little bacon." She sighed and self-consciously tugged the shirt down to assure it covered her bottom. She moved around to the other side of the island and looked at the puppy in an attempt to avoid Dominic's heated gaze. "It will start a lifetime of bad habits. If you do that, you'll make him a beggar, and he'll annoy anyone who tries to eat a meal. Besides, I think he'll make a great therapy dog, but he'll need to be trained. Let's not start him off on the wrong foot."

"Whatever you say, Doc." He shrugged and popped the bacon in his mouth. "I still say it's just a little bacon."

"I guess he wore out his welcome at the main house?"

"Nope." Dominic lifted one shoulder. "I figured you'd want him here with you, so Kerry brought him over."

Cass whined again and let out a dissatisfied groan as the scent of the bacon undoubtedly taunted him.

"Sorry, little buddy." He dropped his voice to a conspiratorial whisper. "She won't let me, and as much as I want to give it to you, I don't want to be in the doghouse."

Tatiana suppressed a grin and sat at the bar stool on the other side of the island from Dominic. She fiddled with the salt and pepper shakers as he stared at her with a look that told her he hungered for more than food.

"Any word on Courtney?" she asked, needing to get her mind off him and his bedroom eyes.

"Status quo. She's still unconscious, and Steven is still right by her side." He ate another piece of bacon. "Salinda said the baby is doing great and eating like a champ."

"I'm not terribly surprised that Courtney's unconscious. I swear, Dominic. It's like she wanted to die or something. I mean, jumping in between that crazy Elvira chick and me? It was a total kamikaze move."

"True." Dominic nodded his agreement. "But why? She's got her mate, and she was carrying his baby."

"I don't know." Tatiana sighed wearily. She leaned on the counter and rested her chin in her hand. "With all the commotion yesterday, I never did get the lowdown on exactly how many Purists invaded. Where do we stand with that mess?"

"There were five." Dominic snagged four slices of bread and popped them in the toaster. "Two elders—both former Council members—and three lower-ranking members from the Falcon and Bear Clans. Richard reinforced the shield around the property, but he fully expects them to try again. Moravian obviously wants Courtney's baby and is willing to make a big mess to get him."

"What a shit show." Tatiana let out a sound of frustration. "I still want to connect with the horses," she said as she ran her hands over her face. She leaned both elbows on the granite countertop, closed her eyes, and took a deep breath. "I'm going to see if I can link to Obsidian the way I did with Spirit."

Dominic made a sound of understanding as he finished making the scrambled eggs and scraped them onto two plates.

"Remember what happened in the dream realm the other night?"

"Which part?" He stilled and gave her a sly look.

"Not the part you're thinking of." Her face heated with embarrassment, and she looked at the saltshaker, which she immediately started fiddling with again. "That woman's voice. I'm not entirely sure… but I think it was Spirit. Which is another first for me because I've never had an animal communicate with me in the dream realm." She flicked her eyes to his. "My abilities seem to be taking on a life of their own."

"Mmm-hmm. I was thinking the same, about the voice, I mean." He put the dirty pan in the sink and captured her gaze. "Okay, so if Spirit was in the dream realm, what was she trying to tell you?"

"A warning of some kind, but I can't shake the feeling that whoever killed Spirit had nothing to do with the Purists. Richard confirmed that no Purists had been on the property at that point, so that means it was either a Caedo or…" She trailed off, afraid to say what she was thinking.

"What?" Dominic scoffed and tossed the dish towel onto the counter. "Someone already here on the ranch?

No way. Unless, you think that dear old Matt isn't as innocent as we believe he was. He *did* take off, after all."

"Damn." Tatiana let out a growl and put her face in her hands. "I don't know what I think."

"Yeah? Well, it's the middle of the night, and you need to eat. So the horses and everything else can wait, at least until we get some food into you."

"That does smell incredible," she said as she rested her chin in her hand again.

"I figured you'd be hungry." Dominic made quick work of fixing her a plate with eggs, bacon, and toast. "I don't think you had much to eat yesterday, and when we got back here you passed right out."

"Mm-hmmm." She arched an eyebrow and gave him a doubtful look. "I don't remember changing my clothes."

"That's because I did it," Dominic said without looking up. He moved to the end of the counter and placed the plate of food in front of her. "It was a tough job, but someone had to do it."

"I'm sure," Tatiana said.

Dominic went to the fridge and pulled out a carton of orange juice. She watched as he moved effortlessly around the kitchen and served her juice before getting back to his own food, which he was devouring.

"You do this a lot?" she asked, gesturing with her fork.

"What?" He leaned on the counter with one hand and ate his toast with the other. The muscles in his chest flexed, and it took considerable effort to look him in the face. "Cook breakfast or undress women who are in my bed?"

Tatiana choked on a sip of orange juice. She wiped her mouth with the napkin he held out for her and didn't miss the mischievous twinkle in his eyes.

"Thank you," she said through a cough. "I was referring to cooking breakfast at midnight." She buttered her toast, hoping a mundane task like that would take her mind off the taste of him that lingered in her memory. "But since you brought it up, do you make a habit of undressing women you barely know?"

"Yes and no."

"Which is which?" She took a bite of her toast and leveled a challenging gaze at him. "Yes to the midnight cooking, or the naked women?"

"You don't get it, do you?" Dominic let out a chuckle and shook his head. "Shit. I can't do anything right."

His smile faded as he cleared his dishes into the sink. He leaned both hands on the edge of the sink, keeping his back to her. The muscles in his shoulders bunched, and his energy waves pulsed around the room insistently.

"I don't suppose I do," Tatiana said quietly. She wiped her mouth and pushed her plate away, watching him closely. "How about you explain it?"

"You are the first woman I've ever brought into my home," he said over his shoulder. He looked back out the window, and silence stretched for a beat or two. Quite frankly, she had no response. "I've never done this, Tatiana. I mean, I've had women before, and I'm sure you've had lovers."

Dominic held up one hand before she could respond.

"I don't want to hear about it because it will only upset me. The mere idea of you with another man makes me want to eviscerate someone. Besides, I doubt those encounters had much meaning for you. I know mine didn't."

"Agreed," she said quietly.

"Remember how you told me that you were tired of living in an uncertain world with an unknown future?" He turned and looked her in the eye as he leaned against the sink. His features were set like stone, and his voice was just above a whisper. "You said it felt like the rug could be pulled out from under you at any moment. Right?"

"Yes," she murmured. "My whole life was unsteady, and nothing made sense. It was a terrifying way to live."

Dominic nodded and walked slowly around the counter until he stood next to her. Heat from his body wafted over her, and the scent that was so distinctly his filled her head, making her dizzy with need. Her gaze skittered over his face, lingering for a moment on the scar—a blatant reminder of what he would do to protect the people he cared for.

"Well, that's *exactly* how I feel now," he rasped. His eyes snapped to their clan form and glowed at her beneath a dark, furrowed brow. Dominic leaned closer. "I'm no good at this, Tatiana." He gestured between them. "I keep fucking it up. I want to give you space, and I can't keep my hands off you. I agree we won't say the mating rite, and then I do." His jaw clenched, and he trailed one finger along her bare arm as his voice wavered. "I tell myself that sex will be just sex… and then I fall in love with you." He dropped his hand abruptly. "After what happened in the stables, it became glaringly clear that sex with you will *never* be just sex."

Tatiana blinked and stared at him. Did she hear what she thought she did? He was in love with her?

"You see, Tatiana." He stepped back, increasing the distance between them as he squared his shoulders.

"Until I met you, my world *was* clear. Firm and solid. I knew who I was, where I was going, and what I was meant to do."

A wry smile played at his lips, and he rested his hands on his hips as he spoke. It was a good thing he kept talking because she was too stunned to say a word.

"And now, the only thing I'm certain of is that I'm in love with a woman who thinks I'm a macho, overbearing, alpha-male jerk. So, to answer your questions… *no*, I don't make a habit of cooking after midnight, but, *yes*, I do like to cook. *Yes*, I've undressed women, but *no*, I've never done it out of the simple desire to care for her and make sure she's comfortable."

Cass whimpered at their feet and wagged his tail as he looked from Dominic to Tatiana. Dominic took a step forward, and for a second, she thought he was going to kiss her. But he didn't. He stopped and tilted his head as his eyes searched hers. Her heart thundered in her chest, and she hung on the silence that filled the air.

"That dark piece of myself," he said, his voice barely audible, as if he couldn't quite believe he was saying it, "the hard, demanding man who saw nothing but duty has been shattered, and now, I find myself laid bare. I am yours, Tatiana Winters. Totally and completely… if you'll have me."

Time seemed to stand still as she stared at him, attempting to process everything he said. No one had ever been so thoroughly honest with her, so clear about feelings or intentions. Yet, this man, the one she dreaded finding, bared his soul and set everything out on the table.

There was no uncertainty in what he said, and for the

first time in her life, Tatiana felt sure-footed. She knew where she stood, and there was no more guessing, no more wondering what might happen.

The one man she worried would take her independence ended up being the one to give her freedom—freedom from fear and an ambiguous future.

"So that's it." He spread his arms out and lifted his shoulders. "Now, if you'll excuse me, I'm going upstairs to take a shower to see if I can wash away my embarrassment. Based on the look on your face, you think I'm an ass."

Dominic turned to go but stopped and spun to face her again.

"One more thing. I'm not sorry I said the bonding rite. I do love you, and I want nothing more than to spend the rest of my life figuring out how to make you happy. I'm sure I'll keep making mistakes, Tatiana—lots of them. But I'll never stop trying. I'll keep going until you can see *me*—not a predestined mate you have to be with—but *me*. A man who loves you and would do anything for you." His jaw clenched. "Even if that means letting you go back to Oregon without me."

Tatiana scrambled off the stool as he turned and started to leave.

"Dominic." She placed her hand on his arm tentatively. "Please wait."

"Don't." His hands clenched into fists as he glanced over his shoulder, looking at her out of the corner of his eye. "Tatiana," he breathed her name.

"Please don't go." Tatiana inched closer until their bodies were a breath apart.

Tension radiated off him, but he didn't move, not

even when her bare knees brushed the back of his legs. She trailed her fingers up his arms, along the broad swath of his shoulders, and down his back, following the path of muscles. He remained motionless, but she sensed his heart beating faster and in perfect time with hers.

Tatiana pressed her lips against his shoulder and ran her hand over the curve of his ass as she walked around to stand in front of him. His hooded gaze glowed down at her brightly as she held his stare and rested her hands on his narrow waist. Dominic didn't flinch, but his body was wound tight, and he looked ready to pounce, to devour, and to consume her like wildfire.

"You're right," she whispered and inched closer, pressing her body against his, which hardened beneath her touch. "Before I met you, I was terrified of my future, of who I was and what I was capable of. Nothing about me made sense."

Taking a deep breath, Tatiana steeled her strength and tightened her grip. Sensing her struggle, his brow furrowed, and he cradled her cheek with one hand, showing her with that tiny gesture his innate capability for compassion. Tears pricked her eyes, and her throat tightened with emotion as she fought to get the words out.

"The truth is, Dominic, everything about me that didn't make sense before… makes sense when I'm with you."

Stark need blazed through him as the weight of her words registered, and Dominic's last shred of restraint ruptured. His mouth crashed over hers and plundered.

Tatiana opened to him, her tongue tangling with his. He picked her up as he kissed her, and she wrapped her legs around his waist, clinging to him as he drank from her sweet lips. He couldn't help but wonder if this was real. Was she truly his, was she giving herself to him forever, or just for tonight?

If tonight was all she could give, he'd take it. He'd take it all.

Dominic grabbed the hem of the T-shirt she wore and broke the kiss long enough to whip it from her body, leaving her naked in his arms. He swore as her heated skin pressed against his.

Holding her around the waist with one arm, he shucked his shorts with the other and kicked them off as she trailed hot, wet kisses along his throat, and her fingers threaded through his hair.

Dominic backed blindly into the kitchen and eagerly captured her lips again. He held her soft bottom in his hands as his cock pressed between them, begging to be inside of her. Dominic spun around, and in one fell swoop, shoved all the clutter on the counter aside and sent it flying. He barely registered the crash of the dishes as they shattered to the floor.

He placed her bottom on the edge of the counter, and in one swift thrust he was inside her. Tatiana's fingernails raked his shoulders, and her heels dug into his lower back as he pumped into her like a man possessed.

Dominic rode the wave of carnal pleasure and groaned as her velvety sheath covered him with every long, hard stroke. As her body moved with his in perfect unison, taking all he had to give, he knew there was no other woman who could satisfy him.

Tatiana cried his name, clutching him closer as he drove into her hot channel with a quick, hard thrust. In one final surge, he took them both to the crest and tumbling over the edge into oblivion as she milked him dry.

Shaking and spent, he swept his lips over hers, wanting to savor the way it felt to have her in his arms and be locked firmly inside her. Dominic suckled her lower lip before breaking the kiss and looked into the glowing eyes of her clan. Her mouth was red and swollen from their kisses, her cheeks were flushed with satisfied desire, and he didn't think she could look more beautiful than she did right at this moment.

"Yikes." She giggled breathlessly. Tatiana kissed his nose as she sliced a glance toward the floor. "If we keep this up, I think you're going to have to invest in paper plates."

"Good idea," he said, struggling to catch his breath.

A chewing sound caught their attention, and when they looked down, the sight on the floor had them laughing. Cass sat on the other side of the kitchen, making quick work of eating the bacon and eggs that had fallen on the floor during their latest encounter.

"So much for not giving him any bacon." Dominic laughed.

Cass sat on his haunches and burped.

"Great." Tatiana linked her arms around Dominic's neck and rested her head on his chest as she grinned at the puppy. "Looks like he's going to be a beggar after all."

"He's not the only one." Dominic, still buried in the warmth of her body, felt himself stirring to life again. He gave Tatiana a wicked grin and wiggled his eyebrows. "Wanna break more dishes?"

"Oh yeah." She leaned in his embrace and tightened her legs around his waist. "Something tells me," Tatiana said with a sigh as she licked his lower lip, "the only begging I'll do is when I'm begging you not to stop."

Dominic swept her up in his arms, carried her upstairs, and reveled in the feel of her flesh as it slid along his. As he placed her on the bed and covered her body with his own, he feared the only one begging would be him—when he begged her not to leave.

Chapter 10

Dominic and Tatiana walked to the main house together hand in hand with Cass running alongside. The bright summer sun beat down on them, and he squinted against the light as he stole a glance at her. No makeup, and her hair was drying in the wind, but she was still a stunner.

The freckles sprinkled across the bridge of her nose gave her a particularly youthful look. Wearing a simple tank top and shorts, she was a natural beauty, which he loved. He'd never been a fan of makeup and high heels. Give him a woman in a T-shirt and jeans, but not just any woman—his woman.

Courtney's condition hadn't changed, but Richard asked everyone to gather at the main house this morning. There had been no other attempts from the Purists overnight, but with Moravian still out there, the threat loomed. Dominic knew Richard well enough to know he wouldn't sit and wait for another strike. Chances are he was planning a counterattack.

Normally, Dominic would use his visualization abilities to go back, but Tatiana made it clear she wasn't fond of the Amoveo's usual form of travel. He'd tried to get her to try it again, but she adamantly refused.

"I can show you how to do it, you know," he said after a few minutes of silence. "You're perfectly capable of doing it on your own, and maybe it won't make you feel as strange if you're the one controlling it."

"No way." Tatiana laughed and squeezed his hand before releasing it.

Dominic fought the urge to touch her, and instead, gave her the space she obviously wanted. They made love two more times last night after their kitchen escapade. However, when she woke up this morning, she seemed distant. He was itching to ask her if she was staying with him or going back to Oregon alone, but he refrained. He told her how he felt, and the rest was up to Tatiana.

"I'll stick with the usual human modes of transportation." She avoided his gaze and watched Cass run up the hill. "That blinky thing makes me feel like I'm going to barf."

"Whatever you say, Doc," he said through a chuckle.

The main house came into view, and they saw Richard, Eric, Malcolm, Kerry, and Dante gathered outside. Cass barked and ran ahead, clearly excited to see the rest of the group. Richard waved them over, and Dominic noticed everyone carried a gun, and they were all dressed in black fatigues.

Tatiana must have noticed it as well because the instant she saw them, her energy waves rippled with apprehension. *Everyone has a gun*. Her voice touched his mind along the protected telepathic channel between mates. *What the hell is going on now?*

Just take it easy, Tatiana. He brushed his hand along her lower back. *I'm sure they're only being cautious*.

Tatiana didn't respond, but she didn't have to because her energy signature was wracked with tension. As they approached the group, she immediately trotted over to Cass and scooped him up. She snuggled the puppy in a move that was surely meant to comfort her more than the dog.

Dominic tried not to be insulted that she sought reassurance from the dog and not him. He'd hoped that after everything they shared last night, she would be more comfortable with him around the others, but apparently she wasn't.

"Morning." Eric handed Dominic a rifle and slung another over his shoulder.

"Thanks." Dominic checked the ammo chamber and gave him a satisfied look. "You know just what I like."

"I usually wake up with coffee." Tatiana shot Dominic an uneasy look as she tried to make light of a tense situation. "But hey, to each his own."

"I'm not a fan of guns either," Kerry interjected. "If I have to fight, it's all teeth and claws for me."

"Right." Tatiana kissed the dog's head and frowned as she looked around. "Where are Layla and William?"

"They're staying with Courtney and Steven," Richard said. "I'm sure you want to check on her yourself, but I am sad to say her condition hasn't improved."

"I was afraid of that," Tatiana said quietly. "Has anyone checked on the horses?"

"Sure have," Kerry said cheerfully. "The feed got delivered last night. Luckily, it was after the visit from our friendly neighborhood Purists. Dante and I fed and watered them this morning. We also let them out to graze."

"Thank you." Tatiana turned her attention to Richard. "I'll have a look, and then I should go check on Courtney."

"The horses look better to me, but I'm not a vet,"

Kerry said with a shrug. "They're still kinda agitated though. Antsy, you know?"

"Yes." Tatiana flicked her eyes to Dominic briefly. "I know exactly what you mean."

"Tell them, Tatiana," Dominic said gently. He moved closer and ran one hand down her back. "Tell Richard about the dream realm."

Everyone stared at her intently, and for a second, he thought she was pissed at him for bringing that up in front of the group. To his relief, she nodded and let out a slow breath.

"What is it?" Malcolm asked.

"My powers have grown significantly since—" Tatiana paused for a moment and straightened her back. "Well, since I came here and met Dominic."

"That's quite common for hybrid Amoveo," Malcolm added with a smile. "Once we connect with our mates, the possibilities are limitless."

"Before I came here, I could read animal energy, but now I can connect with their thoughts, and I hear actual words. It happened with Spirit in the barn, the day before she was killed, and then that night, I'm pretty sure she connected with me in the dream realm."

"What happened?" Eric asked as his brow furrowed in concentration. "What did she say?"

"Nothing that made much sense." Tatiana shrugged and gave them an apologetic look. "It was along the lines of… *lies* and *betrayer*… I think she wanted to tell me who was hurting them."

"Betrayer?" Eric scoffed and adjusted the gun on his shoulder. "It's obviously the Purists. They're the biggest traitors of all."

"I'm not so sure about that," Tatiana said slowly. She looked at each of them. "I can't explain, but it was more desperate, like she was warning me about someone specific. As though the danger was more imminent or close or something."

"Interesting." Richard's face was carved with concentration, and he nodded his understanding. "And you say that she came to you in the dream realm the night she was killed."

"Yes." She let out sigh. "I'd like to see if I am able to connect with Obsidian, one of the other mares. Perhaps she can tell us more about what happened, and maybe, even tell us who killed Spirit."

"I still think that human of yours had something to do with it," Eric muttered as Dominic shot him a look. "I didn't like the look of him."

"The kid split." Dominic lifted one shoulder. "If he was some kind of Caedo spy, he would have stuck around, gained our trust, and then made his move. Leaving like he did wouldn't benefit him." He shook his head. "No way Matt's involved."

"I already told you guys that," Kerry said firmly. "Matt was not part of this, and honestly, it's probably better he left."

"He was not involved, Eric. You know that," Richard said evenly. He flicked a brief glance to Dominic, and a sense of unease flickered up his back. "Kerry, would you and Dante accompany Tatiana to the barn. I want to be sure we took care of things properly, and since her assistant is no longer with us, perhaps you could lend a hand?"

As Richard finished speaking, a subtle change in

the atmosphere caught Dominic's attention. A familiar prickle of awareness flickered over his skin as he detected two Amoveo energy signatures. He stepped back and raised his rifle as his eyes flickered to their clan form.

"Someone's coming." Dominic pulled Tatiana behind him as Eric and Malcolm raised their weapons. "Two. A male and female..." His voice trailed off as the energy waves grew stronger, and he recognized them.

"It's alright, Dominic." Richard raised his hand, asking for calm. "I called them here."

They all stepped back and formed a circle, but Dominic and Eric kept their guns raised. The thick summer air filled with static, and seconds later, a man and a woman materialized at the center of the circle.

"Daniella?" Dominic's entire body went cold as he saw his traitorous sister held at gunpoint by Zachary, a member of the Lion Clan and newly appointed Guardian. "What is *she* doing back here?"

Is this the sister I heard about? Tatiana moved closer and placed one hand on the back of his arm reassuringly. *The one who sided with the Purists?*

Yes. He gave a curt nod but didn't take his eyes off Daniella. After her capture all those months ago and her refusal to relinquish her Purist views, Richard had her jailed and permanently bound in her human form.

Daniella wore a simple black jumpsuit, and her hair was tied back in a ponytail. His heart squeezed in his chest because for a moment he saw the young girl he used to know, the one who wanted to be just like her big brother. Not so much anymore.

Why doesn't she blink herself out of here? Tatiana's voice drifted into his mind on a tentative whisper.

The steel bracelets around her wrists aren't ornamental. A growl rumbled in his throat, and not even the touch of Tatiana's voice could soothe him. *They're made with a special powder that keeps her bound in her human form and void of her Amoveo abilities*.

"Richard thought our little jailbird might be useful to us," Zachary said evenly with his fierce gaze pinned to Daniella. "Good to see you again, Dominic. I'm glad to finally have a chance to practice all of the skills you taught me."

"Wish it were under different circumstances." Dominic lowered his weapon and linked his arm around Tatiana's waist, holding her close. "Tatiana Winters, this is Zachary Allen. A member of the Lion Clan, and currently our Guardian at the jail, where my darling *sister* has the distinct honor of being held as the first prisoner."

Zachary, in true Guardian fashion, said nothing, but tilted his head in deference to Tatiana, all the while keeping his attention on Daniella.

"You guys have your own jail?" Tatiana asked in disbelief.

"Yes," Richard said darkly. "We didn't have need of one until the problem with the Purists, but I must say it's come in handy. It's really quite nice as far as an incarceration facility is concerned."

"Better than she deserves," Dominic spat.

"Good to see you too, *brother*." Daniella glared at him and shot Tatiana a look of disgust. "What's the matter? Not going to introduce me to this *hybrid*? One is more pathetic than the next."

"Shut up," Dominic snarled. He moved toward her,

but Tatiana linked her arm with his, pulling him back. Her soothing energy waves swirled around him, quieting his rage but not extinguishing it. "You will not talk about Tatiana that way."

"It's fine, Dominic." Tatiana put Cass down on the ground, and he immediately snarled at Daniella. "Cass, you give it a rest too."

"It sure as hell is *not* fine." Dominic fought the urge to shift. "She's lucky to be alive after the way she betrayed our people. But I can see she still hasn't learned to hold her tongue." His voice dropped low. "Watch the tone you take with my mate, Daniella."

"She's your mate?" Daniella sneered. "A Guardian for the royal family is mated to a hybrid? No wonder the Caedo and Purists slipped onto the ranch so easily." She made a *tsking* sound. "You're obviously weakened by mating with this *thing*."

Before he could say anything, static flickered around them, and Tatiana erupted into the form of her wolf. Snarling, her hackles raised, she stalked toward Daniella with her teeth bared. Daniella paled and tried to back away but stopped when she ran into the butt of Zachary's rifle.

"Going somewhere?" Zachary asked.

Tatiana growled loudly as the others stepped aside, allowing her clear access to Dominic's sister. Daniella's eyes were wide with fear as she watched the wolf approach, and just when Dominic thought Tatiana was going to attack her, she shifted into her human form and got in Daniella's face. Shaking, but doing her best not to look terrified, Daniella stared at Tatiana, who now stood eye to eye with her.

"I may not be a pure-blood," Tatiana said in a surprisingly calm, sweet voice. "But I can still turn into a wolf and tear your throat out. So, if I were you, I'd watch what you say about your brother. Got it?"

Daniella said nothing. Sweat broke out on her forehead, and she licked her lips as she nodded.

"Good," Tatiana said firmly. "Come on, Kerry. I've got some animals to tend to." She stepped back and looked Daniella up and down. "I can see that this one is a lost cause."

"Ain't that the truth?" Kerry linked her arm through Tatiana's and led her toward the barn.

She's a lost soul, Dominic. Tatiana touched her mind to his as she walked away. *You can't blame yourself for her behavior. You may be a Guardian, but you're not God*. She winked at him over her shoulder. *You may have the body of a Greek god... but you're not God. So get off the cross, baby. Someone needs the wood.*

Dominic suppressed a grin at her playful teasing as he realized she'd put him at ease. He shook his head in amazement and watched as Dante escorted the two women to the barn. The woman was full of surprises.

"So." Dominic looked back at Richard and did his best to ignore his sister. "Why is she here, and why is everyone dressed for battle?"

"I have offered Moravian a prisoner exchange."

"What are you talking about?" He glanced briefly at Daniella, who looked as surprised as he did. "Who do you plan on trading her for?"

"Matt." Richard's mouth set in a firm line. "I didn't want to say anything in front of Tatiana. He was abducted by one of the Purists during the attack. The note we found is a fake. Eric discovered trace evidence of an Amoveo signature in Matt and Tatiana's cabin—a different energy pattern from the individuals who attacked us directly. This morning, Kerry detected that same signature on the paper."

"It was Savannah," Malcolm said.

"Shit." Dominic gripped his gun tighter. "Savannah was here on the ranch?"

"Yes." Richard ran a hand through his long hair, and the look on his face was nothing short of fury. "When we were dealing with the other five attackers, she was able to slip in and out of here undetected."

"Why?" Dominic seethed. "Why would she go to the trouble of helping Courtney escape, only to continue aiding her father? It doesn't make sense."

"Who the hell knows?" Eric waved one hand in the air. "Why do these Purist douche bags do any of the fucked-up shit they do? Maybe dear old daddy doesn't know she's the one who let Courtney go?"

"I doubt it," Malcolm said. "What if they're using Courtney's presence here as a way to link them to the ranch? Richard, you said yourself that the psychic shields you've been placing around the ranch haven't been working. They keep cracking the code, so to speak." He gave them all a grave look. "Perhaps bringing her here was only a way to help them get to you and your family, Richard."

The group fell silent, and they all exchanged concerned looks.

"Damn it," Dominic fumed. He locked eyes with the prince. "Richard, if they were to assassinate you and your main supporters, imagine how easy it would be for

Moravian and the other Purists to take over all of the Amoveo? Who would stand up to them after that?"

"Perhaps," Richard said quietly. "Regardless, we need to get Matt, and I'm more than happy to let Daniella go back to them. The binding bracelets can only be removed by me, and without her powers she will be of little help to their cause. In all honesty, they may kill her, but I don't suppose that's our problem."

Dominic flicked his gaze to Daniella, and his heart sank when he saw the look of pure hatred she leveled at Richard. Tatiana was right. She was a lost soul with a heart full of anger. The girl he'd known all his life was gone.

Daniella turned her hateful eyes to him. *Some Guardian you are, you didn't even know what was going on around here*. Her comment cut him to the core, but he said nothing and shielded his mind from her, preventing further telepathic connection.

"When did you figure this out?" Apprehension crawled up Dominic's back along with a sense of failure as Daniella's observation taunted him.

"I did. Last night," Eric interjected. "After you left to take care of Tatiana, I went by the cabin to take one more look around, and that's when I picked up the energy signature. It was faint, but it was there. Then this morning, Richard asked Kerry to try and pull a psychic impression from the note. It matched the one in the cabin, and she recognized it as Savannah's energy pattern."

"I see." Dominic's jaw clenched, and he leveled an angry stare at Eric. "As Head Guardian I should have been made aware of this information immediately."

"Hey man." Eric held up his hands in defeat. "I'm

sorry, but I figured since you two were still trying to figure things out, you needed some alone time."

"That was not your decision to make." His eyes flickered to their clan form, and Eric bowed his head in submission. Dominic turned to Richard. "How do you plan on offering this prisoner exchange to Moravian? We don't even know where he is."

"It's already been arranged. Kerry connected with Moravian telepathically. We will be making the exchange tonight."

"Where?" Apprehension flickered through Dominic. The more he heard, the more anxious it made him. All of this had been planned without his input. He felt as though he'd been replaced as Head Guardian, but no one told him about it. "Where is the exchange?"

"The mountains," Richard said. "Trapper's summit on the east ridge."

"Fine." Dominic nodded. He knew the spot well and had hiked those mountains countless times since he came to Montana. "When?"

"Midnight." Richard shot Daniella a look of contempt. "We wanted to be sure there was minimal chance of any humans in the area while we make the trade."

"What makes you think he'll even want her back?" Zachary snagged her arm and held it up. "She doesn't have her powers because of the binding bracelets. Shit, Richard's right. They'll probably kill her."

"I'm a pure-blood," Daniella snapped. She yanked her arm away. "Asshole."

"You kiss your mother with that mouth?" Zachary asked.

"My mother's dead. Fuck you."

"No thanks."

"I'll do it," Dominic bit out.

"I thought you might volunteer," Richard said. "However, I don't want you meeting him alone. I'm still wary, and I'm surprised Moravian agreed to this swap. Needless to say, I don't trust him. The Purists have proven time and again to be dishonorable. Moravian and the others will never keep their word, and it could be an ambush."

Dominic glanced toward the barn and instinctively touched Tatiana's energy signature. It was there—linked with his, warm, familiar, and comforting—but as it surrounded him… he knew what he had to do. Richard was right. Moravian would never stop, so someone had to stop him.

"With all due respect, your highness." Dominic stood at attention. "I will take my sister and make the exchange alone. If Moravian has been linking up to Courtney somehow, the last thing we want to do is to leave everyone here unprotected. Eric and Zachary can stay and serve as Guardians. You, Malcolm, and Pete are fathers who have children that depend on you. Dante and William are fully mated to their women, and if they were killed, the ramifications for Layla and Kerry would be devastating. You should all stay here at the ranch while I make the exchange."

"What about Tatiana?" Malcolm asked with genuine concern. "She is your mate and would undoubtedly suffer if she were to lose you."

"No." Dominic shook his head. "She never wanted to be part of our world, and if she had things her way, she wouldn't have anything to do with the Amoveo. Tatiana has no desire to commit to the life-mate bond, and I plan to release her from the obligation. If she chooses to go back to Oregon, then I'll feel a lot better about it if Moravian is out of the picture."

No one said anything, but they exchanged somber looks. They knew full well he was taking on a suicide mission, willing to sacrifice his life for the safety of his people and for his mate. He'd rather die than risk her life or force her to live in a situation she had tried to avoid.

"Understood. I've known you long enough to know there's no arguing with you." Richard extended his arm, and Dominic gripped his forearm in the fashion of the Amoveo warrior. "Thank you, my friend."

"Listen, I'm happy to fill in for you while you take sugar lips back to her pimp daddy," Zachary said. "But I heard there's a Guardian gig in Hawaii, and since I'm not a big fan of Montana winters, you better not get your sorry ass killed."

Dominic let out a short laugh and shook his head, but his smile faded as Tatiana called to him from the barn. *I'd like to connect with Obsidian now, but I'd feel better if you were here.*

Of course. I'll be there in a minute. Dominic shielded his mind from her after responding.

"I would appreciate it if you didn't discuss this plan with Tatiana." Dominic's jaw set. "She's already worried about Courtney, and she is going to connect with one of the horses, so the last thing I want is for her to be distracted. I'll tell her about the plan, but I'd like to do it on my terms."

They all nodded, but Daniella let out a snort of derision.

"Zachary," Richard said without looking at Daniella.

"Please take the prisoner into the house but keep her confined to the kitchen. I find her to be… irritating."

"No problem, chief." Zachary nudged Daniella toward the house.

"Dominic, let me know what happens with Tatiana and her attempt to connect with the horses. To be honest, I'm hoping the Purists were responsible for what happened to Spirit. The idea of worrying about the Caedo as well doesn't thrill me," Richard said. "In the meantime, Malcolm and Eric will patrol the property. Layla and William will watch over Courtney and Steven, while Dante and Kerry are available to help Tatiana. I will leave for a while to visit with Salinda and the others in New York."

"Richard," Malcolm added. "I'd like to expand the patrols farther into the mountains if you don't mind. When we were there yesterday, I believe I picked up remnants of another signature, but I'd like to go back and double-check. It may only have been an echo of the Purists who attacked yesterday, but I'd like to be certain."

"Of course. I trust all of you to do whatever is necessary." Richard slapped him on the shoulder and handed his gun to Eric. "I won't need this, and I doubt the vampires would appreciate it if I came into their territory armed."

Richard uttered the ancient language and vanished in a rush of static electricity.

"I'll be in the barn with Tatiana," Dominic said. "I'll let you know if she discovers anything else."

"You want backup?" Eric asked. "Malcolm can handle patrol on his own for a while."

"No." Dominic shook his head but kept his gaze fixed on the barn. "You two do as the prince asked and patrol the property. Eric, why don't you cover the main area, and Malcolm, you can shift into your eagle and get a broader view from the air."

"You got it, boss." Eric gave a small salute and headed down the gravel drive toward the cabins.

"Eric," Dominic shouted. "Don't keep information from me again. We're a team, but we can't do that if everyone's not on the same page."

Eric said nothing but nodded and waved as he went on his way.

"He was quite concerned about you and Tatiana," Malcolm added quietly. "It has to be challenging for him, Dominic. He's still unmated, and I'm sure he offered you the same space he would undoubtedly want for himself when the time comes."

"He thinks it's a challenge now?" Dominic scoffed and gave Malcolm a knowing look. "Wait until he finds his mate, then he'll really know what a challenge is."

"Truer words were never spoken." Malcolm laughed loudly and slapped Dominic on the arm before handing him his rifle. "I won't be taking this with me on my flight."

Dominic took the rifle and slung it over his shoulder as Malcolm spread his arms wide, tilted his face to the sky, and whispered, "*Verto*." Dominic watched as the air shimmered, and Malcolm shifted into the form of his golden eagle. He screeched loudly, and his yellow eyes glowed brightly as he stretched his wings wide, showing off an impressive six-foot wingspan.

Dominic gave him a look of approval as Malcolm

pumped his enormous, bronze wings and shot into the sky like a bullet. He watched as his friend soared across the pale blue sky.

Don't worry, Dominic. Malcolm's voice, strong and steady, filled his head and put him at ease. *I'll keep you posted*. He knew that between Eric and Malcolm, the property would be well-watched, and both men would spring into action without needing to be told what to do.

As he walked toward the barn, he glanced back over his shoulder, but Eric was no longer in sight, and one thing nagged at him. This was the first time Eric kept information from him, and Dominic wondered if there was more to it than he let on.

Did Eric really want to give him and Tatiana space, or did he question Dominic's effectiveness? He stopped outside the stables as that sense of impending dread crawled up his back. Was it possible that Eric and the others believed he was no longer suitable to serve as Guardian?

Chapter 11

Tatiana sensed Dominic the instant he was nearby and found herself comforted. She smiled at him as he strode through the open doors of the stable, and her heart skipped a beat. Wearing his usual ensemble of a black T-shirt, camo pants, and boots, he was all muscle, bone, and sinew as he stalked toward her.

The man's face was a mask of chiseled concentration, and he had a predatory look in his eye that made her wet and wanting. Images of his perfectly sculpted male body wrapped around hers flooded Tatiana's mind. Blood rushed to her cheeks as memories from last night came roaring to life.

Dominic's lovemaking had been both tender and savage. Driving her to tears with achingly gentle kisses one minute and then devouring her with unrestrained passion the next. His tanned, well-muscled arms that had been tangled up with her in bed were now draped with not one but two guns.

Tatiana's smile faltered as the dichotomy of who Dominic was came vividly to life.

This man, who could be heartbreakingly tender, touch her and cherish her as though she was made of the finest china, was also a stone-cold killer. He was a predator capable of destroying his enemies in the blink of an eye. Any doubt about how dangerous he could be was extinguished when she watched him destroy the Purist in the mountains.

In that instant, she realized something as powerful as it was frightening. She was enamored with the sensitive, vulnerable man who snuggled babies, made her midnight breakfast, and bared his soul to her. However, she was also instinctively and irrevocably attracted to the dangerous, feral beast that would kill to keep her safe.

Man and beast. Lover and killer.

Tatiana desired both sides She didn't simply desire him—she respected him. Maybe she even…

"The horses seem better." Kerry's voice snapped her from her thoughts. "Only one of them—Dover, the young stallion—hasn't gotten his appetite back, at least not as much as the others. So, does this mean you'll leave us soon and head to Oregon?"

"What?" Tatiana asked without taking her eyes off Dominic, who had stopped to speak with Dante. "I'm sorry. What did you say?" She laughed and looked back at Kerry, embarrassed she might have known what she was thinking.

"Are you going back to Oregon?" Kerry asked gently. Her large dark eyes crinkled at the corners as she adjusted her long, black ponytail. "Or might you be persuaded to relocate here?"

Tatiana's heart thudded in her chest as the reality of that question hit her. She was going to have to choose. Either go home to Oregon or stay here with Dominic?

Nibbling her lip, she looped the horse's lead line through her hands, as the question whipped through her mind. Tatiana felt torn, but when she locked eyes with Dominic the chaos swirling inside her stilled, like leaves settling after a storm.

Dominic moved toward her with a concerned look

as his energy signature whisked through the thick summer air with hers. Tatiana sighed as it swathed her in a soothing embrace.

"I don't know," she whispered through trembling lips. "How am I supposed to make that choice? Leave everything I've ever known? My home, my practice..." She swallowed the lump in her throat and fought the tears that threatened to spill over. "Or leave him."

"Can I give you a piece of advice from one freak-show half-breed to another?"

Tatiana nodded but didn't speak because it would likely release the tears she was holding back.

"Don't let fear stop you. Put everything else aside for a while and simply ask yourself how he makes you feel. I'm all for being an independent woman, believe me, but don't let your need for independence turn into an excuse to push him away. I'm still independent, and maybe even more so, since I hooked up with Dante. The question really is: Will you be happier with him or without him?"

Tatiana looked to her left and latched gazes again with Dominic. Her heart raced faster with every step he took as Kerry's question raced through her mind. *Will you be happier with him or without him?*

Everything slowed, and her heartbeat thundered in her ears as the veracity of that question settled over her. Tatiana Winters had done the one thing in the world she swore she would never do. She fell in love with an Amoveo man—*the* Amoveo man. She loved him.

"With him," she whispered, her voice thick with emotion.

Tatiana dropped the lead line, ran down the hay-strewn aisle of the barn, and launched herself into

Dominic's embrace. She linked her arms around his neck and buried her face against his throat as she breathed in his distinct scent. He smelled like soap and a hint of sweat.

"Hey," he whispered, his voice laced with concern. He stroked the back of her head as his other arm held her snugly. "What's going on? Did you connect with the horse? Tatiana, you're scaring me. Say something."

Dominic pulled back. Setting her down on her feet, he cradled her face in his hands as his worried eyes studied her closely. Tatiana's body trembled, and she pressed his hand to her cheek, struggling to find the right words. Finally, she settled on the three little words that she'd never said to another man. It made sense. Although she didn't realize it, she'd been saving them for him.

"I—I love you."

Dominic's body stilled against hers. His eyes flickered and shifted into the glowing amber eyes of his clan, but he said nothing.

"Did you hear me?" She dropped her hands to his chest and worried his dog tags between her fingers, the cool metal soothing her and keeping her grounded in reality. She held his stare and said it again. "I love you, Dominic."

Growling, he ducked his chin and rested his forehead against hers while holding her close. *I love you too, Tatiana.* The words whispered into her mind like a caress as he kissed the tip of her nose.

Tatiana popped up onto her toes and captured his lips, gently at first, savoring the feel of them. Her hands curled against his chest as he held her closer, and the kiss quickly grew in intensity. She linked her arms around his neck and deepened the kiss as the now familiar fire flickered over her skin.

The sound of people clapping captured their attention. Dominic broke the kiss and laughed as he placed a kiss on top of her head and hugged her close. Tatiana, her head on Dominic's shoulder, caught a glimpse of Kerry and Dante, who stood behind them applauding loudly. She grinned at them before burying her face into Dominic's neck and giggling.

"Bravo," Dante said.

"Well played, kids." Kerry gave her them two thumbs up and laughed as Dante stood behind her and swept his mate into a sweet embrace. "Now, you two will have time to play doctor later, but don't we have funky psychic shit to take care of? Like creating a mental link with one of these gorgeous horses?"

"You ready?" Dominic asked. His hands slid down her back and rested at the top of her butt.

"As I'll ever be." Tatiana let out a shuddering breath and kissed the cheek with the scar. "I've got to get Obsidian. Don't go anywhere, okay?"

"Not a chance." Dominic smacked her butt playfully and released her from his strong embrace. "Let's do this."

Tatiana stood in the stall with Obsidian and whispered soothing sounds to the young mare while sending her gentle waves of reassuring energy. The doors of the stable were closed, and the other horses were out to graze. While it made the space thick with heat and humidity, Tatiana felt it could be distracting for both of them if there were too many equine energies in the immediate vicinity.

Kerry and Dante remained close by. If Tatiana had trouble making a firm connection, Kerry's psychic ability might solidify it. They gave Tatiana some space and observed from outside the stall. Dominic, however, stood inside with Tatiana, and even though she thought it might make Obsidian nervous, she knew there was no talking him out of it.

Tatiana closed her eyes and stood in front of Obsidian with both hands laid gently over the *jibbah* on her forehead. Her gorgeous black coat was pure midnight and shone almost blue when the light hit it. The mare's energy fluttered around Tatiana in pale lavender waves, calm and peaceful.

Sharpening her focus, Tatiana worked on finding that elusive tear in the ribbon of energy, the spot where she could slip inside and touch the carefully guarded soul of the gentle beast. As the connection deepened, Tatiana's body felt heavy and cumbersome. She concentrated on riding her own energy wave as it merged with Obsidian's. As the two swooped through the thick, summer atmosphere together, a crackle of bright, white light captured her attention.

Swimming within time and space, Tatiana whisked along, and with one final mental push, she slid through the crevice like a thread through the eye of a needle. Her body jolted, and her breath rushed from her lungs as the bond was formed.

Obsidian? Tatiana barely recognized her own voice as she linked her mind with the mare. *Can you tell me who killed, Spirit?*

Not who you think. The words surrounded Tatiana in a fog of muffled moaning sounds. *Bad man*. *Pretender*.

Who, Obsidian? The light around her faded, and the voice seemed farther away, but she was surrounded by a rushing noise. It reminded her of trying to hear the ocean in a conch shell—loud, white noise that was frustratingly indistinct. *Obsidian, what is his name?*

The light was sucked from her in a rush, like water swooshing abruptly down a drain. Blood pumped in her ears as her heart raced, and the mare's short, bristly hair rasped beneath her fingertips. Tatiana gasped for air as the connection was severed, and Obsidian whinnied loudly as she reared back. Tatiana lost her balance and was knocked backward, but instead of slamming into the wooden wall, she landed safely in Dominic's waiting arms.

Clinging to him, she fought to get her bearings as the psychic connection faded. It took her a moment to realize she was once again sitting in his lap in a pile of hay. Tatiana pushed her hair off her forehead as she caught her breath and saw that Obsidian seemed no worse for wear. The mare was in the opposite corner of the stall chewing on a carrot Kerry had given her.

"You okay?" Dominic asked. His face was etched with concern. "You were pretty out of it for a while. It's like you weren't here. I mean your body was, but your mind was somewhere else entirely. I tried to telepath to you, but there was nothing there. I have to be honest, that scared the shit out of me."

"Sorry," she said through a short laugh. Tatiana held her hand to her chest, reeling from the unusual experience. "That was nuts, but it worked."

"Dominic's right. You were in pretty deep, and I know those intense mental links can really take it out of a girl. Are you okay?" Kerry asked. She hung both arms over the stable door and tossed Obsidian another carrot. "What did she tell you?"

"Anything useful?" Dante asked. He stood next to Kerry and glanced from Tatiana to the horse. "Did she see who shot Spirit and wrote that message?"

Obsidian's words floated into her mind, haunting her. *Not who you think... bad man... pretender.*

"Tatiana?" Dominic's grip tightened as he sensed the shift in her energy signature. His fingers curled around her bicep, and he stroked the bare skin on her arm gently. "What is it?" he murmured.

Tatiana looked from him to Dante, and dread crept over her. One of the men on the ranch was a traitor. She shook her head as she stood up and extricated herself from his grasp.

"Nothing useful," she said without making eye contact. She brushed stray pieces of hay off her butt. "Just cryptic messages. I guess I'm not as good at it as I thought I was."

"Hold on." Dominic grabbed her arm and turned her to face him. "I can tell there's something else. What is it?"

"It doesn't make any sense." Tatiana held his stare and licked her lower lip, glancing from Dominic to Dante. "There's no way what she said could be correct."

"What did she say?" Dominic asked slowly.

"She said that one of the men is a pretender. *Not who you think he is*. That's what she said, but it doesn't make any sense. I can't believe that anyone on the ranch would do that."

"It wouldn't be the first time we've been betrayed." Dominic's expression darkened. "I never would have suspected my own sister of being a Purist."

"Or my father," Dante added quietly. Kerry rubbed his back with one hand as she leaned into him with a supportive smile. "We've all been betrayed at one point or another."

"I don't understand why she couldn't tell me his name." Tatiana let out a sigh of frustration and ran both hands along Obsidian's side. The horse made a snuffling sound and butted Tatiana with her nose. "You're really making me work for it, aren't you?"

"Maybe she doesn't know names," Kerry said as she handed a lead line to Tatiana. "She is a horse, after all."

"I guess," Tatiana murmured as she clicked the line to Obsidian's harness. Dominic opened the stall door, and they all stepped aside as she led the graceful animal out of the stable. "I wish I could get her to tell me who it was, but the connection was broken too quickly."

Tatiana patted Obsidian on the neck and unhooked her from the lead line, allowing her to roam freely in the field with the other horses. She smiled as four other mares trotted over to greet Obsidian, and a moment later, they galloped off together.

Dominic, Kerry, and Dante moved in on either side of Tatiana, and they all watched the animals in heavy silence. The one threat they'd truly feared had been confirmed. There was a traitor among them.

A cool breeze wafted over them, providing relief from the stuffy air of the barn, and Tatiana let out a sigh as she closed her eyes, reveling in the sensation.

"It may not be an Amoveo," Dominic said quietly.

"Really?" Tatiana sliced a look in his direction and let out a short laugh. "Who else could it be? One of the other horses? Other than Amoveo, that's all we've got on this ranch."

Dominic's brow furrowed, and he flicked a knowing glance to Kerry and Dante. The looks exchanged between them sent a chill up her spine because it gave her the distinct impression she was out of the loop. Tatiana stepped back with her hands on her hips and looked at each of them intently.

"What's going on?" Her voice wavered. "Why do I feel like there's inside info that I'm not privy to?"

Tatiana folded her arms over her breasts and arched an eyebrow at Dominic. He let out a slow breath, and his mouth set in a tight line. She could tell he was debating what to tell her, which pissed her off even more.

"You better start talking before I shift into my wolf and tear you a new asshole."

"Matt could be involved."

"What are you talking about?" Her voice rose with frustration. "Matt isn't even here. He left. Remember? Besides, Kerry read him and said he was clear."

"I'm not always right."

"Can I get that in writing?" Dante teased.

"Just listen." Dominic held up her hand to stop her from interrupting. "Last night they discovered another Purist energy signature on Matt's note and in your cabin. The energy pattern belonged to Savannah, and it looks as though the Purists abducted Matt."

"What?" she cried. "Why wouldn't you tell me about this."

"I didn't want to upset you before you tried to make contact with the horse."

"I'll deal with you later." She narrowed her eyes at him and turned to Kerry and Dante. "I don't get it." She shook her head as confusion washed through her. "Why would they want to abduct Matt? He's human."

"Our thinking was that they grabbed him as leverage to get to you and Dominic." Dante's mouth set in a tight line. "But there is another possibility."

"Matt could be conspiring with them," Dominic said.

"No way." Tatiana's hand went to her mouth, but she dropped it abruptly. "There's no chance he's involved. I refuse to believe that. If he's with them, it sure as hell isn't by choice. We have to get him back. I mean, we can't just let them have him."

"We already have a plan to do exactly that. Tonight I'm meeting with Moravian and performing a prisoner exchange—Daniella for Matt."

"When were you planning on sharing that with me?" Tatiana seethed. "More secrets?"

"I was going to talk to you about it this afternoon." Dominic kept his voice even. "However, given what Obsidian told you, we can't rule out the possibility that Matt is working with the Purists."

"Shit," Dante said. "He could have helped stage the whole thing."

"No way," Tatiana said adamantly. "If Matt is with these Purists, then he was taken against his will."

"Possibly." Dominic folded his arms over his chest and stared. "But given what we know now, we can't rule it out."

"Fine." Tatiana crossed her arms and stepped closer, so they were almost touching. She dropped her voice to a low, challenging tone. "Then you can't rule out the possibility that one of your so-called friends is in bed with the Purists, pretending to be on your side."

"She's not wrong," Kerry chimed in. "My money's on Eric or that Zachary guy."

"No way." Dominic's sharp gaze flew to Kerry's face, and his jaw set. "No fucking way is Eric involved, or Zachary. They are both Guardians."

"They're both unmated, Dominic," Kerry said gently. "You, Dante, Malcolm, and William are all mated to hybrid women, so it's obviously none of you. Oh, and not to be a bitch by bringing up a sore subject, but your sister was a Guardian too. At least, before she declared herself a Purist."

"I know," Dominic growled, his eyes glowing brightly. He swore under his breath and faced the mountains, his energy waves flickering with agitation. "If either were Purists, why wouldn't they have come out and sided with the rest of them publicly?"

"We assumed all the Purists came out and declared a side," Dante added. "But it would make sense, strategically speaking, to keep some people under wraps as spies. Think about it. Steven was a spy for Richard. Why wouldn't the Purists do the same?"

"I'll notify Malcolm and William about what we discovered," Dominic said. "Dante, I want you to keep an eye on Zachary, and I'll have Malcolm keep tabs on Eric. Under no circumstances will either of them be left alone with Richard. He'll be back in a few hours, and I don't want him unprotected when he returns."

"Dominic," Kerry interjected. "What about the prisoner exchange tonight? If Matt is with the Purists by choice and is part of some larger plan, I don't think you should be the one to go. He wasn't your biggest fan. Aside from the fact that you stole his girl."

"It wasn't like that," Tatiana said.

"Not for you, but you can bet your bottom dollar that kid had the hots for you somethin' fierce. The sexual chemistry between you and Dominic is off the charts." Tatiana blushed, but Kerry waved her hand dismissively. "Don't freak out, girl. The sexplosions are part of being mates, and even though Matt was human, you'd have to be deaf, blind, and dumb not to notice what's going on with you two crazy kids."

"Kerry's right, Dom." Dante linked his arm around Kerry's waist. "The more I think about it, the worse this whole prisoner swap feels. At the very least, you shouldn't do it alone."

"It's not up for debate. I need you and the others here to protect the prince," Dominic said firmly. "I'll do the exchange and deal with whatever consequences come of it."

"Oh really?" Anger, resentment, and fear flooded Tatiana. She shoved at Dominic with both hands and growled in frustration. "You're a macho butt-head. Do you know that?"

"That's our cue." Kerry stifled a giggle, grabbed Dante by the hand, and dragged him back into the stables. "We'll let you two talk, and in the meantime, I'm going to see if I can get a reading off Zachary or Eric. Getting a clear reading on pure-blood Amoveo isn't always a guarantee, but I'll give it a shot."

"You do that, but be subtle," Dominic said while he held Tatiana's furious gaze.

"Of course, kitten," Kerry purred.

Tatiana waited until Kerry and Dante left the barn, and then she let him have it. "You know something," she ground out. "You almost had me fooled into thinking you and I were a team, but that's obviously not the case."

Tatiana turned on her heels, stormed into the barn, and hung the lead line on the wall before turning to face him again. He'd followed her into the stables, and the confused look on his face stopped her in her tracks.

"You really don't get it, do you?"

Casanova, who had been sleeping on a bale of hay, was now whining at Tatiana's feet, but she ignored him.

"No." Dominic rested his hands on his narrow hips and shrugged. "I guess not. Why don't you explain it to me? I'm baffled as to why you're pissed at me for wanting to rescue your friend, even if there's a chance he's involved with the Purists."

"So, what?" She threw up her hands and glared. "You're willingly going into a volatile situation, one that could get you killed, and you don't think that requires discussion with me?"

"I'm sorry." He hung his head and ran one hand over his hair as he let out a slow breath before looking at her again. "I'm not cutting you out of decision-making, but there's really no decision to be made. I'm Head Guardian. Daniella is *my* sister, and Matt is *your* friend. All of these things add up to me making the exchange alone. I refuse to put anyone else in danger over this. This is *my* responsibility, Tatiana." He moved closer and cradled her face in his hand. "*Mine*."

"That's all true." Tears filled her eyes, and her

lower lip quivered as she held his glowing stare. "But *you* are also *mine*. You can't make me fall in love with you and then go off and get yourself killed. It's not fair, Dominic."

"I have no intention of getting killed," he said through a laugh. Dominic wiped a single tear from her cheek, the rough pad of his thumb grazing enticingly along her flesh. "I plan on spending the rest of my life finding out how many different ways I can piss you off."

"Is that so?" She giggled. "Why on earth do you want to fight and piss me off?"

"Are you kidding?" He wiggled his eyebrows. "For the make-up sex."

Tatiana laughed, but before she could tell him what an ass he was, he covered her mouth with his and swept her into his arms. He lifted her off the ground as he devoured her lips and tangled his tongue with hers. Still kissing her, he walked through the stable toward the doors with the puppy yapping at their heels.

Tatiana suckled his bottom lip and pulled back to look him in the eye.

"As much as I want to spend the afternoon having make-up sex," she said with a sigh and clasped her hands at the base of his neck, "I'd really like to check on Courtney."

Dominic stopped and let out a sound that hovered between a growl and a sigh as he placed her gently on her feet.

"Fine." He linked her fingers with his and walked with her toward the house. "But then we're going to have some major make-up sex."

"I would hope so." She bumped her hip into his

playfully before picking up the puppy. "I bet we could break more than the dishes."

Chapter 12

Dominic accompanied Tatiana to the medical suite while she tended to Courtney and Steven. He developed admiration for her over the past twenty-four hours. She was unshakable in a crisis and kept a cool head better than anyone he'd ever known. Male or female. Human or Amoveo. The woman was a rock.

Unfortunately, Courtney was still unconscious, and Steven was growing more concerned, along with everyone else. Tatiana, a healer and a naturally empathetic woman, was clearly disturbed, not only by Courtney's condition but by Steven's as well.

Casanova trotted into the room at Tatiana's heels and went immediately to Steven, attempting to soothe him. Tatiana was right about the little beagle being a good therapy dog. He definitely tuned into anyone who was hurting. Dominic's gaze landed on Steven.

"Nothing's working," Steven whispered. "I've never felt more helpless in my life. I can't heal her. I've tried everything, and she's not responding. Her body is healing, but mentally she's fading. She's getting worse, and I don't know how to fix it. I keep telling her to come back to me and our son."

"You have to eat something," Tatiana said gently as she pulled up a stool and sat next to a disheveled Steven. "Take care of yourself for her and the baby."

"I'm fine," he bit out. Steven leaned on the bed with

both elbows and held Courtney's limp hand. "I'm not leaving her."

"Alright." Tatiana looked at Dominic briefly before continuing, drawing strength from him. "What about the dream realm, Steven? Have you tried connecting with her there? The others told me that when Courtney was missing you stayed in a perpetual dream state so you could connect with her."

"I tried," he whispered as he kissed her fingers. "I looked for her, and I could feel her there in the mists, but I kept losing her. She slipped away time and again." A choking sob escaped his lips as he pressed them to her hand, and the sound of the heart monitor beeped loudly. "Even after Courtney came back, we never walked in the realm. She… she said the dream realm was too difficult to reach and that it had something to do with the pregnancy. I tried to help her, to guide her, but it never worked."

"I thought you said you did connect?" Dominic added.

"I lied," Steven rasped. "You think I wanted to admit I was a total failure as an Amoveo man? That I couldn't join my mate and walk in the dream realm with her?" His voice hovered above a whisper. "I couldn't save her at the Purist compound, and I can't save her now."

Dominic shifted his feet and adjusted the gun in his hands, feeling as if he'd spoken out of turn. It made him uncomfortable to hear Steven discussing his mating difficulties, but there was no way he would leave Tatiana alone, and she clearly wasn't going anywhere. He saw that determined look—the way her jaw set and lines between her eyes deepened as she processed what Steven told her. Oh yeah, the woman had a bee in her bonnet about something.

"Steven?" she began tentatively and dropped her voice to above a whisper. "I have to ask you something, but it's... personal."

"What?" He swiped at his eyes with the back of his hand but kept his gaze on Courtney.

"I know that your baby was conceived through non-traditional methods at the Purist compound. Right?" Steven stilled but gave a curt nod. "Well, have you and Courtney ever actually... *you know*?"

Steven gave her a sidelong glance and let out a long breath before answering. "No."

Now Dominic felt *really* uncomfortable, but Tatiana gave him a reassuring look that told her she had it under control.

"Okay, so then you never actually said the bonding rite, correct?"

"Correct." He turned his head and leveled a serious look at Tatiana. "She was afraid to make love. She wouldn't let me touch her, and I didn't blame her, especially after everything she'd been through. The pregnancy was touch and go at best, and neither of us wanted to do anything to jeopardize the baby's health or hers."

Steven straightened the sheet over Courtney's motionless body in a simple but loving gesture. "She'll be fine," he said adamantly. "She needs more time. That's all. I'd like to be alone with her if you don't mind."

"I understand." Tatiana rose from the stool and kissed the top of Steven's messy hair. "Call me if you need me, or if there's a change in her condition, okay?"

Steven nodded but said nothing.

Tatiana and Dominic opened the door to leave. She

called to Casanova to follow, but the puppy refused to move and stayed at Steven's feet.

"It's fine," Steven said without looking up as he absently scratched the beagle's head. "Courtney always liked dogs."

"Okay," Tatiana said hesitantly. "If he gets in the way, let me know, and I'll come get him."

Dominic followed Tatiana into the hallway and found Layla and William waiting.

"Do you two want a break?" Dominic asked.

"No, we're fine." Layla jutted a thumb toward the stairwell. "We took turns showering, and thanks to the whole mate thing, sleep is desired but not required. Any change in there, sis?"

"No." Tatiana sighed. "I can't be sure, but I think her condition is complicated by the fact they aren't officially mated. I guess all we can do is wait and see."

"Yes." William nodded, his expression grim. "We suspected that was the case, but obviously, no one wanted to inquire."

"Hey, what about the horses?" Layla tucked her long, curly red hair behind one ear and changed the subject. "Did you get more ideas about who killed Spirit?"

"It was a Purist," Dominic interjected. He sliced a glance in Tatiana's direction.

"As I suspected," William said haughtily.

"Not exactly." Tatiana sighed. "There's a traitor on the ranch."

As Tatiana explained their theory, William's face twisted into a mask of fury, and he pulled Layla into the shelter of his body. Dominic couldn't blame him. He felt pretty damn protective of everyone, but especially Tatiana.

"We need to be extra vigilant once the prince returns," Dominic said. "I don't want him left alone under any circumstances. Either me, you, Dante, or Malcolm should be with him at all times."

"Consider it done, but why don't we simply corner Eric and Zachary and confront them?" Layla asked.

"I don't want to rock the boat until after the prisoner swap tonight." Dominic slung the rifles over his shoulder. "If Matt really has been taken against his will, I don't want to do anything to put him in unnecessary danger. Besides, chances are the traitor in our midst will reveal himself during the exchange. Which is precisely why I need all of you to stay here with Richard while I do the swap with Moravian."

The four of them confirmed their plans, determining when and where to meet that evening.

When Dominic and Tatiana reached the main floor of the house, a crashing sound came from the kitchen. They ran in to find a mess of cereal and milk on the floor along with a broken bowl.

"I'm not eating that shit," Daniella seethed.

"Fine by me," Zachary said through a mouthful of Lucky Charms. "But you're missing out."

Daniella sat at the kitchen table with her arms folded over her chest. Zachary sat at the other end, eating an enormous bowl of cereal with his gun in his lap. Kerry and Dante sat across from Daniella, but neither of them were eating. Dante, however, had his gun firmly in his hands.

"What's going on in here?" Dominic asked in a calm, serious tone.

Daniella's eyes widened with surprise when she saw

Dominic standing in the doorway, but she quickly recovered and shot Zachary a look of contempt.

"I'm not eating that crap." She stuck her nose in the air. "I'm on a hunger strike."

"No one cares," Zachary snorted.

"Zachary," Dominic snapped. "She may be a Purist and a traitorous wretch, but she is still my sister. As much as I loathe what she's done, she is my family."

"Sucks to be you, dude."

"Dominic." Daniella turned her steely glare to him. "When is this prisoner exchange? I want to get the hell out of here. I don't want to be around any of you or your half-breed whores."

"The feeling's mutual, sweetheart," Kerry said sweetly.

Dominic growled as his eyes snapped to their clan form, and he walked slowly around the table, keeping his sister in his sights. He moved toward her with the purposeful steps of the tiger. Grabbing her chair, he spun it so she was forced to look him in the eye. Dominic leaned close, so his face was inches from hers.

"In spite of the fact that you are a Purist, I would not let them hurt you." His voice rumbled through the room, and sweat broke out on Daniella's forehead as he spoke. "However, if you refer to my mate as a whore ever again, make no mistake, I will think twice about keeping you safe. I don't know what happened to you, Daniella, or how you became so full of venomous hatred. All I can do is hope that *someday*, you will find someone who helps you dig your way out of the darkness."

Dominic pushed himself away from her chair and loomed over her.

"To be sure you don't cause any trouble until the

exchange, Dante and Kerry will stick close to you and Zachary." He flicked his eyes to Zachary, wanting to see his reaction. "I'm sure you wouldn't mind the help."

"Fine by me, brother." Zachary wiped his mouth with the back of his hand and let out a loud belch. "She's a pain in the ass, so I'm happy to share her sparkling personality with these two."

"You're a pig." Daniella rolled her eyes and turned her chair back to the table.

"Sorry, baby." He winked. "I'm all Lion Clan."

Daniella made a sound of disgust, but Dominic didn't miss the amused look on Tatiana's face.

"I have to go back to my cabin for a little while," Dominic said, ignoring his sister's attitude and focusing on his mate. "Tatiana and I have some things to take care of before I leave for the exchange this evening. We'll see you in the Council meeting later."

Keep an eye on him. Dominic telepathed to Dante through a protected mental link. *I still have a hard time believing he's involved with the Purists, but...* He didn't need to finish the thought because Dante knew as well as he did—it could be anyone.

I'm on it. By the way, I filled Malcolm in on the situation, and he's patrolling with Eric as we speak. They're still picking up a phantom energy signature around the edges of the ranch, but he can't nail it down.

Understood.

As Dominic and Tatiana left the house and headed to his cabin, he couldn't get his sister's face out of his mind. He had gotten good at hating her for what she did. However, seeing her again brought back a multitude of conflicting emotions. Daniella may be a traitor, but underneath it all, she was still his baby sister. As the dark emotions threatened to swallow him, he knew there was only one thing that could ease his pain.

As they walked down the gravel drive toward the cabins, Dominic stole a glance at Tatiana, and a funny feeling settled in his chest. He reached out and tangled her hand in his, linking their fingers and squeezing her palm tightly. It wasn't simply that he wanted to touch her—he *had* to.

Suddenly, he had an urgent, all consuming need to feel her skin rushing along his, to blaze a trail of kisses down her throat, to bury himself inside her, and to lose himself in the calm, natural beauty of her.

Tatiana smiled at him and squinted against the sun. Her eyes crinkled at the corners, making her even more gorgeous. Images of her naked body writhing beneath him filled his mind, igniting the carnal desire that always smoldered just beneath the surface. The craving slammed into him hard and fast, and in that instant he knew he couldn't wait until they got back to the cabin.

Dominic stopped and tugged her to him. He cradled her face with both hands, and as he stared into those gorgeous brown eyes, he knew he was lost.

"I have to have you, Tatiana." He dragged one hand down her back and held her against him, his erection pressing into her belly. "Right now."

Tatiana's eyes snapped to their clan form, and her lips parted on a sigh. She hooked her thumbs in the waistband of his pants, and her eyes twinkled with mischief as she ground herself against him. She wanted him too and not just for the physical connection. Ever since Steven's revelation, she'd felt uneasy, and she needed Dominic's soothing caress—the whisper of flesh brushing against flesh that made her feel safe.

"Then I suggest you use that blinky thing, and get us somewhere private." Tatiana licked and nipped at his lower lip. "I'm sure if I get nauseous you can figure out something that will make me feel better."

"*Verto*," Dominic growled as he scooped her into his arms and kissed her.

The funny feeling of displacement and a rush of static were barely felt as his lips melded with hers, and their tongues collided. Tatiana held him close as she dove deep and took all that he had to offer. When he broke the kiss and came up for air, Tatiana looked around and saw they stood next to the freshwater pool in the field behind their cabins.

"I thought you might like to go for swim," Dominic murmured between kisses along her throat. "Besides, I've been thinking about making love to you in the pool ever since you asked me about it the other day on the deck."

Dominic placed her on her feet but didn't release her. Tatiana untucked his shirt while she held his gaze.

"It's right out in the open," she whispered as she pushed the fabric up, exposing his gorgeous washboard abs. "Someone could see us."

Dominic grinned as he tore off his shirt and tossed it aside. He whispered the ancient language again, and in a burst of warm, prickling static, an enormous glass dome appeared. Tatiana gasped and spun around in awe.

"Okay." She giggled as she leaned back in his

embrace. "That's totally awesome, but since its see-through, doesn't that defeat the purpose?"

"No."

Dominic snagged her tank top and whisked it from her body in one fluid motion. She sighed with pleasure as the heated skin of his chest pressed enticingly against her back. Dominic kissed her cheek and splayed both hands over her flat belly, which quivered in anticipation.

"We can see out." He released the button on her shorts and drew the zipper down. "But no one can see in." Dominic pushed her shorts and undies down past her hips, and she moaned as the fabric skimmed over her sensitized skin. "In fact, if anyone were to walk by, they would see only an empty pool."

"Oh, that's cool." She was having trouble concentrating as Dominic's hands traveled up her sides and trailed slowly along the curve of her rib cage. "Dominic," Tatiana growled his name as his hands cupped her breasts.

"Yeah, Doc?" He licked her ear and squeezed her nipples as she arched into his touch.

"Shut up," she rasped.

Tatiana spun around and captured his lips with hers as her fingers fumbled with his fly. She made quick work of undoing it and pushing his pants and boxers off. Dominic kicked the offending garments aside, leaving them naked and tangled up in skin.

Licking and suckling her lips, he lifted her into his arms and carried her into the pool. The warm water enveloped them, and as he paid thorough attention to her mouth, he dunked under the surface, dousing them both. Tatiana laughed as they came up for air and tilted her head back, wiping the water from her face.

Dominic tightened his grip, and the hungry look in his eye almost made her come. She shivered and cradled his scarred cheek in one hand as he watched her through the glowing eyes of his tiger.

Tatiana brushed her lips over his, gently at first, almost reverently. She adjusted her position in his arms and wrapped her legs around his waist as she kissed him. With the help of weightlessness in the water, she hoisted herself enough so the head of his thick erection was poised at her swollen entrance.

Tatiana broke the kiss but held his stare as inch by delicious inch she impaled herself on his thick shaft. They gasped in unison as her hot sheath covered him completely. Dominic braced himself against the edge of the pool with one hand as she rode him in long, unhurried passes. Her fingers linked behind his neck and her ankles hooked against his lower back, as she took him in and drew him out, again and again, in a slow, languid motion.

It was highly erotic to have this kind of control, to see the hungry, almost desperate look as she engulfed him time after time. She increased the tempo, riding him faster, but as they approached climax, he kissed her and lifted her off him, disengaging himself from the shelter of her body.

"Not yet, Tatiana." He grinned, and his hands encircled her small waist as he hoisted her onto the edge of the pool.

The smooth stones were slippery beneath her wet bottom, and she looked around self-consciously. "Are you sure no one can see us?"

There didn't seem to be anyone in the area, but that didn't mean much. The Amoveo were good at hiding and sneaking around, especially in their clan form. She knew that better than anyone. That's how she'd avoided Dominic for so long, but as she stared into his handsome face, she could barely remember why.

"Not a chance." He stood in front of her and spread her legs as he ran his hands up and down the wet skin of her inner thighs. With every pass, Dominic's fingertips slipped closer and closer to her most sensitive spot. "Do you think I'd ever want anyone else to see you like this?"

Tatiana, taut with desire, was unable to utter a word. She bit her lip and shook her head. Grinning, he pulled her closer, and she moved with him so that her butt was on the edge of the pool.

"Will you lie down for me?" Dominic's voice was quiet but commanding. He ran one hand up her side and kissed her breast, flicking the sensitive nipple with his tongue. "I want to see you naked and spread wide."

Tatiana lay back and stretched her arms behind her head, anticipating what was coming next. She shivered as his arms hooked around her thighs. Dominic leaned in and kissed the tender flesh of her inner thigh, trailing butterfly kisses and licking beads of water away. He parted her lips and blew gently on the highly sensitized flesh.

Tatiana gasped and moaned as he teased, and just when she thought she'd scream with need, Dominic took a long, loving taste of her. She arched back and cried out as he licked and suckled the little bundle of nerves furiously. Sounds of pure pleasure escaped on breathy sighs, and she grabbed his head as his talented tongue fondled her to the brink. Her hips writhed, and she bucked beneath his assault, but Dominic held her down beneath his erotic assault.

I want you to come for me, Tatiana. His mind touched hers as his tongue dove inside her. Lights exploded behind her eyes, and the world shattered as the explosive orgasm rocked her to the core. Tatiana screamed his name as a second wave of pleasure ripped through her, and her body shuddered until the sensations finally ebbed, leaving her with a weak, boneless feeling.

As the fog of bliss lifted, ragged breaths wracked her as she pushed herself onto her elbows and locked eyes with Dominic. He was floating in the water, resting his chin on her thigh as he wiped beads of moisture from her hip, all while looking rather pleased with himself.

"You think you're quite a stud, don't you?" she teased as she attempted to catch her breath.

"I have my moments." Dominic pushed himself away and drifted backwards, evidence of his own unsatisfied desire glaringly obvious.

"Well, you're not the only one," she said playfully as she hoisted herself into the water and swam after him. "It's my turn to make you scream, but I'm getting all shriveled from being in this water." She flicked a glance at his erection. "Although, you clearly aren't having that problem."

Tatiana launched herself into his arms, ready and willing to do what she promised, but his body tensed as he looked to the sky. She looked up to see what had captured his attention and swooping overhead was an enormous eagle—Malcolm.

"Is something wrong?" Tatiana asked as her fingers trailed along the back of his neck. "Did they find something else?"

"No." His jaw clenched, and his body tensed beneath her touch. "He's still chasing that weird energy pattern. I should really patrol the property with them."

"Not now. You've done your duty, and tonight you're going to do it again. Right now, I simply want you all to myself." Tatiana swam around him and climbed on his back like a monkey. She wrapped her limbs around him and nibbled his ear. "Let's take this inside."

"Your wish is my command." Dominic hooked his hands beneath her thighs and started walking toward the edge of the pool with her still on his back. She wiggled enticingly, the heat of her feminine core pressing against his back.

"I'll even agree to taking the blinky way there."

"You've got a deal," he growled.

Dominic uttered the ancient language, and in a rush of static they vanished and reappeared in Dominic's bedroom. Her head spun, and she clung to him as she waited for the dizziness to pass. She slid from his back and let out a sound of relief as her feet hit the cool, wood floor. Before she even had time to say anything, he spun around and kissed her.

It wasn't the ravishing, urgent kisses he usually gave her. It was slow and tender. His mouth moved over hers reverently, and his tongue explored her mouth in unhurried strokes, as if he wanted to memorize every bit of her.

Tatiana sighed and hooked her arms around his waist as he kissed, licked, and suckled her lips in the most tender, loving way. Still kissing her, he lifted her off her feet and placed her on the bed with heart-shattering tenderness. He ran his fingertips up her arms, over the curve of her shoulder blade and dragged them along the swell of her breast, while paying thorough attention to her mouth.

They spent the next hour simply touching and kissing one another. Exploring every inch of skin and swath of flesh, and it was the most erotic, intimate experience of Tatiana's life. Through it all, Dominic said nothing. Not a word. Her gut feeling was that his emotions were too strong. Words would cheapen it, but that was just fine, she didn't need him to say a thing. Every touch, stroke, and caress revealed more about his heart than any single word could.

For the first time, Tatiana understood why it was called *making love*.

As darkness fell, and the impending event of the night crept closer, the cold finger of dread tripped up her spine. She and Dominic showered and dressed quickly, but try as she might, the dark thoughts and fears drifted into her mind. Tatiana knew that even though Dominic would never admit it, he was scared. He was as scared of losing her as she was of losing him.

Tatiana's heart sank as the reality of what was to come settled over her. She'd allowed herself to forget, for a little while, what Dominic was about to do. However, as they walked toward the house, and the other Amoveo came into sight with guns at the ready, reality came crashing back.

Dominic squeezed her hand, and even though that tiny gesture steeled her strength, she couldn't drown out the voice of doubt. Their little afternoon together may well have been their last. If the Purists had their way, Dominic would never survive the exchange.

Chapter 13

Malcolm said he and Eric had been chasing the same phantom energy signature all day, but every time they got close, it vanished. They all met in the Council meeting hall to regroup before the exchange, but a couple of people were notably absent.

They wanted to move Courtney to New York with the others, but Steven wouldn't hear of it. He felt her condition was too fragile, so they left Layla and William in the medical suite with them and armed to the teeth. If a Purist came anywhere near that room, they would get a face full of bullets as Steven visualized Courtney out of there, but he only agreed to do it as a last resort.

At least, that was the plan.

Dominic breathed deeply and savored the familiar scent of pine as it filled his head. They stood in the cavernous space of the Council meeting hall awaiting Richard's arrival, but no one spoke. They were all wound too tight. Dante and Kerry were sticking close to Zachary as Dominic instructed. Kerry had tried to get a reading off both men but had been unsuccessful.

Daniella seemed more uncomfortable in the meeting hall than she did in the house. Dominic wanted to talk to her, to try one last time to bring her to her senses, but she wouldn't look at him. He even tried to telepath, but she kept her mind closed to him.

Heavy silence blanketed the group. Dominic adjusted the ammo and knife belt he wore around his waist and checked his handgun one more time before slipping it into the holster. Tatiana's nervous energy waves flickered in skittish ripples, and it took every ounce of self-control to keep from grabbing her and getting the hell out of there.

Tatiana kept her large, dark eyes on him and even offered a supportive smile, but there was no hiding her concern. To her credit, she remained calm and focused, but she'd said little since they left the cabin. She wasn't angry, but she seemed distant, as though she was slipping away from him somehow. He knew it was probably her fear, concern over what might happen to him, but any barrier between them felt unacceptable.

Dominic was about to broach the subject with her when a crackling rush of static filled the space, and Richard appeared. He stood on the platform at the end of the arena, his eyes glowing bright blue and his face stamped with concern. Richard jumped from the platform and stalked toward the group, his gaze fixed on Eric and Zachary.

Dominic telepathed to him earlier and told him their suspicions about Eric and Zachary. Needless to say, Richard was not taking it well. Dominic couldn't blame him because it was yet another betrayal, another brother at arms who threatened their mates and brought violence to the ranch.

"We end this tonight," Richard said tightly. He scanned the room, looking at each of them individually, but stopping on Dominic. "Chances are the Purists have others prepared to strike while we make the exchange with Moravian. Ladies, you will go back to New York City and wait at the vampire stronghold until this is finished."

Kerry and Tatiana started speaking at once, but Richard raised one hand, silencing them.

"I know you feel this is a sexist decision, especially given what I said before, but things have changed." A sad smile played at his lips, and Dominic knew he was referring to the issue with either Eric or Zachary. "I've already spoken with Layla, and she gave me an earful. However, she has done as I requested and left for New York with Salinda."

Dominic linked his arm around Tatiana's waist and pulled her into the shelter of his body, needing to feel the weight of her and the warmth of her skin against his. He kissed the top of her head and inhaled her sweet cherry scent. His heart beat in perfect sync with hers as their energy signatures merged as one and swirled through the air.

"I am also fully aware of the difficulties that can arise when mates are separated, but we cannot risk your safety." Richard looked from Kerry to Tatiana. "You are far too important to us and to the future of our race. The Purists have made it clear that hybrid mates are the focus of their hatred and their wrath. Therefore, we need to remove you from imminent danger. If and when they attack, you will be the first ones they go after."

Richard's word was resolute, and while Dominic sensed the frustration from the women, Tatiana in particular, he was enormously relieved by the prince's decision. He wanted Tatiana out of harm's way more than anyone, but he knew if he had been the one to insist on it, she would resist. However, since the prince was commanding it, no one would argue.

"What about Courtney?" Tatiana spoke up.

So much for no one arguing the point, Dominic thought on a sigh.

"I'm the only person, other than Steven, who is even remotely qualified to help her. With all due respect, Richard, I feel that I should stay behind with Steven and Courtney."

"No." Dominic's eyes glowed, and his fingers dug into her waist. "You will do as Richard says and go to New York with the others."

"No, I won't. You might be my mate, Dominic, but you're not my father or my boss." Tatiana slipped out of his arms and crossed to Richard. "Look, I know the risks, but I can't leave Courtney here. Steven is a hot mess, and the guy isn't thinking straight. If something goes down, I don't know if he'll to be able to handle it on his own." Hands on her hips, she jutted a thumb at Dante. "If you're so worried, then leave Dante *and* William with us in the medical suite. They have enough firepower to take out half the state."

Richard's eyes narrowed as he stared at Tatiana, clearly weighing his options.

"Your highness," Dominic said. "You can't seriously be entertaining this idea?"

"Wait a minute!" Tatiana snapped her fingers and pointed at Richard as an idea bloomed. "I know Steven doesn't want to move Courtney, and he's only doing it if he absolutely has to, right?"

"True," Richard said slowly. "He said he would if danger was imminent."

"Well, if things get really hairy around here, we will use that blinky thing to get out of here. I mean, they'd find us eventually, but it could buy us time."

If need be, Tatiana touched her mind to Richard's and Dominic's using a protected path, *we could go to my home in Oregon, Richard. None of the others know where it is, and we would be safe there, at least for a while.*

Hands clasped behind his back, Richard nodded and looked from Tatiana to Dominic.

"Your highness," Dominic said. "Please don't listen to this nonsense. She doesn't know how to use her visualization abilities yet."

Dominic regretted the words before they were even out of his mouth.

"I'm a quick learner," Tatiana bit out. She shot him a dirty look and turned her attention back to the prince. "I could do it if I had to. Besides, I won't be alone. Dante and William would be there too."

Dominic's jaw clenched, and his hands balled into fists at his side as held his breath and waited for the prince to make his decision. The others stood in stunned silence, and all eyes were on Richard as he kept his gaze on Tatiana.

"Fine." Richard flicked his glowing eyes to Dominic. "You have a brave mate, Dominic. You should be proud." Richard looked at his watch. "Kerry, you should go now and join Salinda."

"Yeah, about that," Kerry said on a sigh. "I'll be with Tatiana. She might need psychic backup, so since none of you have that particular ability, I'll be sticking around too."

Richard let out a weary sigh and ran one hand through his hair as he held Kerry's gaze briefly before looking to Dante for help.

"She's not wrong, Richard." Dante wrapped his arm around Kerry's waist. "We might need her help. Besides, I learned a long time ago that arguing with Kerry is pointless. Once she has made up her mind about something, that's it."

"Fine." Richard's face grew serious. "Dante, you and Kerry will go with Tatiana to the medical suite, but if you get even a whiff of a Purist, then you get the hell out of there. I don't care how much Steven protests. You leave and take him and Courtney with you."

"We better get this show on the road, Richard," Zachary said. He nudged Daniella toward Dominic. "She's all yours, dude. Bye, sweetheart. It's been real."

"Shut up," Daniella seethed.

"Hold on." Dominic extended one arm but didn't take his eyes off Tatiana. "I need a minute."

"Oh Christ," Daniella groaned. "Spare us the sappy good-bye."

Dominic's eyes shifted to the glowing amber eyes of his tiger, and he growled a warning over his shoulder to his sister, silencing further comments. He took Tatiana's hand and led her to the other end of the arena, which was the most private spot he could find given the circumstances.

Looking into her eyes, his heart hammered in his chest as his worst fears bubbled to the surface. What if she was hurt or needed him, and he couldn't be with her? What if she was in danger, and he couldn't get to her in time? Dominic rested his forehead against hers as he cradled her face in both hands.

"You're a pigheaded woman, do you know that?" he whispered.

"So I've heard… but I can't leave Courtney, Dominic." Tatiana clasped her hands over his and pressed her lips to his cheek. "So you better come back to me."

"Does that mean you'll stay with me, Tatiana?" He pulled back and looked her in the face, and his voice dropped low. "When this is all over, will you commit your life to mine?"

"I guess you'll have to survive this mess in order to find out," she said with a smile.

Tatiana pressed her lips to his and kissed him tenderly as one tear rolled down her cheek. The warm liquid trickled over his fingers, and her sweet fragrance filled his head. Dominic suckled her lip and broke the kiss as his mind grazed hers. *I'll come back to you, Tatiana.*

Tatiana's hands curled against his chest and pressed the cool metal of his dog tags against his skin. Dominic linked his fingers around the chain at the back of his neck, removed the precious amulet, and pressed it into Tatiana's hands. He closed her fingers around it and pulled her hands to his chest as he held her gaze.

"Keep these for me," he said quietly. "If anything happens to me, then I want to be sure you have them."

"No." Tatiana shook her head and tried to give them back. "You always wear these."

"Now, you do." Dominic took the chain from her hands and placed it around her neck. He adjusted the shiny tags, nestling them in between her breasts. "They have my energy signature imprinted on them. Just wear them. It will make me feel better, okay? Like a part of me is here with you."

"Time to go," Richard said.

Dominic nodded and placed a tender kiss on Tatiana's

lips before turning on his heels and crossing to Daniella and the others.

"I'll take care of her," Dante said firmly as he shook Dominic's hand. "Just make sure you get your ass back here in one piece."

"Thank you."

Dominic locked gazes with Tatiana as she stood between Dante and Kerry. Dante uttered the ancient language. In a blast of static, they vanished, but as Tatiana disappeared, her voice touched his mind. *I love you, Dominic.*

The meeting hall felt far emptier without his mate, but Dominic shoved aside the self-defeating thoughts that threatened his composure and turned his attention to the others.

"We should leave now," Richard said.

Dominic stilled. "We?"

"Yes." Richard took one of the guns from Malcolm and checked the chamber for ammunition. "We. You, me, and Daniella."

"Your Highness," Dominic began, "I don't think it's wise for you to come with me. We all know this could be an ambush, and risking your safety is unacceptable."

"Dominic," Richard said with measured patience. "I am almost three times your age, and I possess certain powers you do not. Now, while I know you are an exceptional soldier, I am the leader of the Amoveo. I *cannot* and *will not* send one of my men into a situation like this alone. We go together or not at all."

Dominic flicked a sidelong glance toward Malcolm, who stood between Eric and Zachary.

"Your Highness," Eric interjected. "I agree with

Dominic. If you insist on going, then you should have two Guardians with you."

"No." Richard turned his glowing eyes to Eric. "You and Zachary will patrol the property around the main house with Malcolm. The energy signature that's been detected along the outskirts of the ranch troubles me. My one consolation is that it has not been picked up on the main property. I have placed another shield around the house, which should prevent anyone other than Dominic or myself from visualizing themselves inside. I used a different spell, so if they are capable of breaking through, it should take them awhile to figure it out. So I want you three posted outside just in case." His eyes glowed brightly. "Are we clear?"

"You got it, chief," Zachary said as he popped a stick of gum in his mouth. Malcolm gave him a look of disapproval, but Zachary's eyebrows flew up in surprise. "What?"

"Let's do this." Dominic grabbed Daniella by the arm and pulled her next to him. He removed his gun from the holster and flipped the safety off as he pointed at her. "Don't try anything funny. I don't have any desire to see you harmed, but make no mistake, I will kill to protect the prince."

Daniella stiffened but said nothing, and though guilt tugged at him for threatening his sister, he meant what he said.

"Take care of the others." Richard stood on the other side of Daniella with his gun drawn.

"Be careful," Malcolm said.

"Yes." Richard glanced at Eric and Zachary briefly before looking back at Malcolm. "You too."

Dominic closed his eyes and pictured the cool, crisp air of Trapper's Summit. In his mind's eye, he imagined the wide-open sky and the bird's-eye view of the world from the eastern ridge. The smell of dirt, pine, and fresh air filled his head, and as he uttered the ancient language, the three of them slipped through space on a wave of static. Seconds later they materialized on the ridge overlooking the mountains.

With guns drawn and Daniella pinned between them, Dominic and Richard took immediate stock of their surroundings. The mountaintop was bathed in the gentle light of the moon and stars. Dominic gripped the gun tighter and held his sister with his other hand as the sounds of an owl hooting captured his attention.

They're here. Richard's voice rumbled into Dominic's mind. He glanced over his shoulder to see the prince slowly pivot with his gun pointed at the wooded area. His blue eyes glowed brightly in the summer evening as he moved almost imperceptibly. *At least three—possibly four*.

The sound of twigs cracking and gravel skittering down the edge of the mountain made both men freeze. Even Daniella, usually full of piss and vinegar, didn't make a sound, and she clung tighter to her brother. As her fingers curled around his arm, a thick, dark energy signature snaked through the air like smoke.

"Moravian's here." Dominic stood stone-still and waited, his body rigid with anticipation. He reached out with his mind in search of the source, and there was no mistaking it when his energy signature brushed Moravian's. "There."

Dominic swung his gun to the right, where he sensed

movement, and a moment later, two pairs of glowing yellow eyes peered down at them from the cover of the trees.

He's in his clan form, Richard. It's Moravian and another member of the Falcon Clan. They're in the tree to my right. I don't sense any sign of Matt.

There's another to my left. Richard's voice was tight and controlled. *Bear Clan. Male. Be ready for anything, Dominic. No matter what happens, Moravian doesn't leave here alive.*

"Dr. Moravian," Richard called out calmly. "I can't imagine you're afraid to show yourself in your human form. Hiding in the treetops seems so… sophomoric."

A blast of static-filled air blew from the tree line, and Dominic sharpened his focus with his gun trained on the ones who approached. Daniella whimpered and shrunk behind Dominic, her body shivering with fear as seconds of silence ticked by.

I can't believe you're afraid of him. Dominic touched his sister's mind sharply. *I thought you wanted to get away from us and back with your people.*

I don't have my powers, Dominic. Her voice wavered with fear. *I saw what he did to some of the other girls.*

Moments later, two men walked out of the trees, revealing themselves in the pale moonlight, and the look of hatred carved into Moravian's face was nothing short of evil. His bright yellow falcon eyes narrowed as he and the other man, a younger member of the Falcon Clan, took cautious steps forward.

The two stood face-to-face with Richard and Dominic, but Daniella cowered behind her brother. What she said gave him pause, and he wondered if she was as devout a Purist as she claimed to be. Was she really hateful, or was it an act? Did she simply think there was no way to redeem herself?

Dominic's gut clenched, and he reached back with one hand, keeping her protectively behind him. As he got a clear view of Moravian, it was painfully obvious he was of little threat. Dominic took a closer look and was surprised to see both men looked ill. The doctor most definitely had lost weight, and the boy was clearly undernourished.

They reminded him of fugitives, men on the run with nowhere to turn and few resources. Perhaps the Purist movement really was dying.

You don't have to go with him if you don't want to, Daniella. We can figure something out.

Yes, I do. Her voice quivered as it brushed his mind with heartbreaking familiarity. *It's my only option.*

"I thought we agreed to no weapons," Moravian said with a sneer. "And I only expected to have your Guardian here, Richard. Not you."

"Yes, well, you didn't come alone either. Your friend from the Falcon Clan is armed, and I'd bet the fellow from the Bear Clan, the one hiding in the woods to my left, is also armed." Richard shrugged. "I guess we both broke the rules, but given what you've been up to, I'd say it's par for the course."

"Where is she, Richard?" Moravian barked.

"Looking a bit under the weather, Moravian." Richard inched closer to Dominic. "What's the matter, are you and the other Purists having a hard time fending for yourselves since your leader was killed?"

Sweat broke out on Moravian's brow, and the other

man inched behind him bit by bit, but he was still in Dominic's sights. Fear rippled from their energy signatures, although both tendrils were far weaker than a typical Amoveo pure-blood.

"You don't care about us or how we're doing," Moravian snapped. "Just show her to me now, Richard, or this meeting ends before it gets started."

Richard and Dominic exchanged looks. He may not have been able to see Daniella completely, but unless the guy was blind, it was relatively obvious she was hiding behind Dominic.

"Where's Matt?" Dominic asked. He kept his eye on the man with the gun in his hand standing next to Moravian because it was pointed at the prince. "The human. Did you really take him, or is he one of your puppets too?"

Movement to the left caught Richard's eye, and with the lightning fast reflexes of an elder and a royal Amoveo, he whipped out another gun from the back waistband of his pants and shot into the tree line without looking. A growl and a loud crashing sound followed as the Purist hiding in the woods was shot and killed.

Static crackled in the air as Moravian bellowed his outrage, but Richard swung his guns at the two men. "I suggest you tell your comrade next to you to stand down, Moravian, or I'll put two bullets in his head." Richard grinned and cocked both guns. "Or yours."

"Do as he says, Samuel," Moravian snapped.

"No, Uncle." Samuel, his eyes wild with fear, kept his gun on the prince. "I—I won't leave you unprotected."

"Do as he says, boy," Dominic growled. "Or you'll end up like your friend from the Bear Clan."

Samuel licked his dry, cracked lips and flicked his gaze between the two men, but eventually, he tossed his gun on the ground and put both hands in the air.

"I'm—I'm right here," Daniella said in a shaking voice as she stepped out from behind Dominic.

"What the hell is going on?" Moravian seethed. His eyes glowed brighter, and his energy signature whipped around them like a storm. "Where's my daughter? Where's Savannah?"

Tension filled the air along with a good amount of confusion.

"What are you talking about?" Dominic asked as he glanced at Daniella. "We brought you Daniella, like we said we would."

"No." Moravian shook with fury as he clenched his hands into fists. "You have my daughter. I know you do, you son of a bitch. You took her when you and your filthy Loyalists stole that pregnant girl from me."

"Actually," Richard said slowly, "I told you we had the traitor, and we would give her to you in exchange for Matt. Come to think of it, I never referred to her by name. I only said we had the girl." Richard's energy waves rippled faster. "Where is Matt—the human?"

"I don't have any human," he sputtered. "I don't even know who you're talking about, but I want my daughter back." Moravian's eyes glowed as he bellowed with blind outrage. "I know you took her. Where's Savannah?"

Moravian rushed forward, charging the prince, and at the same instant, a large grizzly burst out of the woods to the left. Richard spun and shot several rounds into the enormous bear, killing him once and for all. Dominic aimed his gun at Moravian, knocked Daniella backward, and squeezed the trigger twice, hitting the good doctor in the chest.

Moravian and the Bear Clan Purist tumbled to the ground, and their bodies skidded to a stop at Richard's feet. The bear shifted into his human form as the life faded from his body. His head settled next to Moravian's, and two sets of lifeless eyes stared up at them blankly.

"No," Daniella screamed as more gunfire tore through the night sky.

In that moment, time seemed to stand still.

When Dominic looked up, Samuel's rage-filled gaze was all he saw as Daniella launched herself in front of her brother. The bullet slammed into her chest, and the force of the blow sent her flying into Dominic's arms. He cradled her against his chest and barely registered the second shot as Richard killed Samuel, and the woods fell silent once again.

A gurgling sound escaped her lips as her energy signature sputtered and waned. Dominic pressed his hand against the wound in her chest, like Tatiana taught him, but the blood continued to pump, and he watched helplessly as it seeped through his fingers. Daniella clutched his hand, gasping for air, and winced as pain wracked her body.

"I'm sorry, Dominic," she whispered through ragged breaths. "I—"

"Don't talk, Daniella." He bit back the tears and held her close, but blood poured from her, taking her life force with it. "We'll get you back to the ranch, and Tatiana will help you."

"She's at the ranch," Daniella wheezed between short

sporadic breaths. Her eyes rolled back in her head as her body convulsed.

"Yes," he murmured. "We'll take you to the ranch."

"No." She choked on the word, and blood ran from her nose. As her body went limp in Dominic's arms and the life faded from her eyes, one final word escaped her lips. "Savannah."

Chapter 14

MALCOLM SWOOPED OVER THE HOUSE, USING THE binocular vision of his golden eagle to survey the property. He still detected the phantom energy signature but couldn't pinpoint where it was. Richard and Dominic hadn't been gone long, but Malcolm couldn't shake the growing sense of impending doom.

The thick atmosphere of the summer night washed over his bronze- and gold-feathered body as he circled above the stables, but it did little to ease the tension. Whoever was lurking nearby was frighteningly good at disguising his or her presence, and he found it infuriating and unsettling.

Soaring on a thick current of air, he reached out to touch Zachary's mind, wondering if perhaps he picked up on it as well. However, instead of finding the familiar zap of a mental link, he was met with an unsettling void.

Landing silently on the weather vane at the peak of the stable roof, his yellow talons gripped the metal tightly, and he sharpened his focus. He thought that perhaps the shield Richard placed around the house was somehow impacting his ability to connect with the others. He shook his feathered head and let out a low screech.

If Samantha were here, she would tell him he was being impatient and give him one of those smiles that made his heart melt. Malcolm bobbed his head as movement in the shadows to the left of the house caught his attention. *Zachary? Eric?*

Malcolm extended his energy signature in search of the source as a muffled, whooshing sound sliced through the air. An instant later, white-hot pain bloomed in his chest as the force of the blow knocked him from his perch. He fought through the searing ache and struggled to fly, but the wound was too severe.

Unable to take flight, Malcolm tumbled over the side of the barn, shifted midair, and landed with an audible grunt on the grass below. He wrestled with consciousness and nausea as he attempted to push himself onto his knees, but the pain was overwhelming. Something warm and wet seeped down his belly, and he knew beyond a shadow of a doubt it was blood. As he rolled onto his back and covered the weeping wound with his hand, he caught movement out of the corner of his eye.

A split second later something slammed into the side of his head, and as the world went dark, he heard a voice whisper, "Two down, and several more to go."

"How did you get in here?" A crashing sound from the recovery room captured their attention in the hallway as Steven's angry voice filled the space, along with the sound of the puppy barking frantically. "You stay the hell away."

"Tatiana and Kerry, stay here with Dante," William shouted.

"Are you kidding?" Kerry yelled as the four of them ran into the medical suite.

William and Dante, with their guns drawn, pushed

open the door and found Steven standing protectively in front of Courtney's bed in his coyote form. Growling and snarling, hackles raised, he was ready to pounce as he glared at the young woman through bright green eyes.

A young blonde Amoveo girl stood at the far end of the room looking terrified. Her clothes were torn and bloodied, and she looked as though she hadn't bathed in weeks. Her energy waves rippled with anxiety, her large green eyes were wide with fear, and she twisted her fingers nervously.

Dropping to her knees, she raised her hands in a clear sign of surrender.

"Please don't hurt me," she whimpered, as long hair fell over her face.

"Holy shit," Kerry breathed. "It's Savannah."

Dante and William kept their guns trained on her, and tension in the room was so thick, Tatiana thought she might choke on it.

Static flickered, and Steven shifted back to his human form.

"I should rip your fucking throat out," Steven seethed. "After what you and your father did to her, you have the nerve to show yourself here?"

"You're all in danger." Savannah's voice was small and shook with fear as she cowered on the floor. "You have to believe me."

"I'll be the judge of that." Kerry pushed past the others before squatting down in front of the girl.

"Be careful, princess," Dante said evenly. He stayed close with his gun aimed at Savannah's head.

"I think I'll be just fine." Kerry extended her hand

and grinned. "Given your pathetic state, I shouldn't have too much trouble reading you. Should I?"

Savannah shook her head furiously and placed her hand in Kerry's. Their bodies jolted as the connection was made, and the room filled with a familiar humming as everyone watched in riveting silence. After what felt like forever, Kerry dropped the girl's hand and rose to her feet.

"You've been hanging around here?" Kerry said in disbelief. "In your clan form. You've been hiding in the mountains ever since you brought Courtney back here. Haven't you?"

"Yes." She nodded and wiped tears away with the back of her hand. "I couldn't go back. Not after getting Courtney out. My father's resources were dwindling, and there were so few Purists left, I was worried he wouldn't be able to care for her or the baby, and her condition was getting worse. I knew she'd be safe here with all of you." Savannah lifted one shoulder and gave Steven a sidelong look. "And I knew Steven would care for her, but… I—"

"You couldn't just leave her here, could you?" Tatiana asked quietly. She pushed past the two men and stood next to Kerry. "You stayed close so that you could keep an eye on her and make sure she would be okay."

"Yes," she whispered. "And besides, I had nowhere else to go."

"She didn't have anything to do with Matt's disappearance either," Kerry added. "She's been skulking in the mountains, but far as I can tell, she hasn't hurt anyone."

"If you didn't take Matt, then who did?" Tatiana

asked, almost not wanting to know the answer. "Where is he?"

"I'm sorry." Savannah's green eyes filled with tears. "He's dead—he's—"

When Tatiana heard the words, it was like getting punched in the gut. Matt was dead. Her friend was dead because of her.

Savannah's jaw went slack, and a funny, glazed look came over her face as she wavered on her feet. Tatiana and Kerry grabbed her arms to prevent her from falling, and a moment later, she blinked as she gasped for air, holding onto the two women for dear life.

"You get visions too?" Kerry asked with surprise, and she locked eyes with Tatiana. "I've never met a pure-blood who can do that."

"Oh my God. He—he shot Zachary and Malcolm." Savannah looked from Steven to Courtney and tugged on Tatiana's arms. "Please, we have to get her out of here now. He's not stopping until all of you are dead."

"It's Eric. Son of a bitch," Dante seethed as his amber eyes gleamed brighter. "I can't reach Malcolm or Zachary. Something's definitely wrong. God damn it. Eric's a fucking Purist."

"No." Savannah shook her head and flicked her frightened gaze toward the door. "He's not a Purist. At least, he's not working with my father and the others."

"Then what the hell is his problem?" Kerry asked in complete exasperation.

"How do we know she didn't do something to them?" Steven seethed. "I'm not going anywhere with her. She could be working with Eric or the others and this could be a trick."

"I read her memories, Steven," Kerry said urgently. "She hasn't been with Moravian or the other Purists in months, not since she brought Courtney here. She's not lying."

"Please," Savannah whimpered and looked around wildly. "There's no time to argue. We have to get out now. Eric is Guardian of the ranch, and he knows this place better than any of you. There's nowhere to hide. He waited until Dominic and the prince left. *Please*."

"She's right," William said. His eyes glowed black in the eyes of his falcon. "We can't stay here. We should take everyone to the vampire stronghold in New York."

"No." Steven shook his head furiously. "Courtney has expressed her dislike of vampires in the past, and I won't take her anywhere that could impede her healing process."

"Steven, you're being unreasonable," William chided.

"Fuck you, Willie."

"Oh, that's quite mature."

"We can go to my place in Oregon," Tatiana said quickly. "It can buy us time. Eric isn't mated with any of us, so he didn't imprint on us, and he has never been to my home. He can't just blink himself there. Right? I mean, he might figure out where we went, but he'd have to drive or take a plane. Right?"

Tatiana held her breath as the seconds ticked by, and she glanced at the door, worried that any second Eric would burst through and shoot them. Great, the bad guy was armed to the teeth too.

"Go." Kerry grabbed Tatiana and Savannah by the arms, pulling them over to William. "William, you keep that big fucking gun on Savannah, and if she looks at anyone funny, you blow her head off."

"I won't do anything," Savannah whimpered. "I swear to God."

"Ah yes," William simpered and pointed the gun at Savannah. "The promises of a Purist are so reliable."

"What about you?" Tatiana looked from Kerry to Dante as Savannah clung to her like a frightened child.

"We'll stay behind and make sure you get out." Kerry gave them a nervous smile. "Close your minds. No telepathic communication. We can't risk it. We'll get in touch with you once we're settled."

"We have to find Malcolm and Zachary." Dante's face was a mask of fury. "If they're not already dead."

"What about Dominic?" Tatiana asked. Panic gripped her as she realized she might never see him again. For all she knew, he and Richard were dead.

"Dominic's your mate. Believe me, he'll find you," Dante said tightly. "Now go."

Tatiana nodded her understanding and prayed Dante was right. Dominic was her mate, and after everything they'd been through, all that they'd shared, she had to believe she would know if he was harmed. He was okay—he had to be.

Tatiana picked up Casanova and handed him to Savannah, which instantly calmed the girl. Then she made quick work of removing the heart monitor pads from Courtney's chest and grabbed two more bags of IV fluid from the cabinet. She placed them on the bed next to Courtney and prayed her friend would survive whatever would come next.

"Okay." Tatiana shoved her hair off her face, wishing

she could wipe away her anxiety as easily. "What do I do?"

"Place one hand on Courtney. Now, picture your house in your mind, Tatiana." William's voice, edged with tension, filled the room as he stood next to Tatiana with one hand on her shoulder. "The sounds and smells that distinctly remind you of home."

Steven clasped Courtney's hands and the IV pole as he leveled a glare at Savannah, whose shaking hand clung to Tatiana. Tatiana laid one hand on Courtney's arm and closed her eyes, doing as William instructed.

The thick green line of trees filled her head. The fresh smell of pine mixed with vanilla from scented candles wafted through her head. A smile played at her lips as she remembered the beautiful solitude of her cabin in the woods. *Home*.

Static flickered in a pulsing blanket of prickling heat, and with a flash of light, they whisked along a surge of psychic energy. Tatiana held the picture of her log cabin–style home at the forefront of her mind, and like water swirling down a drain they swept through time and space. Minutes later, they landed with a dizzying snap in the living room of Tatiana's home.

As she steadied herself and the fuzziness cleared from her head, the scene around her slowly came into focus. Courtney lay on the gurney with Steven at her side and once again totally tuned into her. The IV drip and the pole it hung on had even come along for the ride. William already stood guard in front of the stone fireplace with his weapon trained on Savannah who stood next to Tatiana. Cass was snuggled to within an inch of his life, and Savannah had her eyes fixed on Steven.

Tatiana sucked in a deep breath and looked around her home. The one place she swore she'd never soil with the Amoveo and their world was now bursting at the seams with them. Yet, instead of feeling intrusion, all she felt was empathy. These people were her friends, her new extended family, and she had no doubt they would shelter her the same way if she needed it.

As Tatiana launched into action and worked with the others to get Courtney settled in the guest room upstairs, there was only one person on her mind.

Dominic.

Tatiana had no idea where he was or if he was alive or dead, and without telepathing to him, she would remain in the dark. She prayed that this whole mate thing worked, and he'd be able to find her. The idea of facing this without him was more terrifying than anything else.

When Dominic's attempt to telepath Malcolm didn't work, he connected with Dante, who filled them in on the latest shit storm. His only consolation was that Tatiana was safe—for the moment. Dante and Kerry found Malcolm and Zachary—both men were badly wounded. Richard instructed them to take the two men to Pete at the vampire stronghold, and with any luck the vampire's healing blood would do what they hoped.

Tatiana and the others had fled the ranch, and Dominic knew where she'd taken everyone. However, when he'd heard what had happened, all he could think about was *her*. He had to see her, hold her in his arms, and breathe her in. As he worked with Richard, searching the property for Eric, he made a promise to himself that whatever happened, he would never leave her side again.

Duty could be damned. If she didn't want to move to the ranch, then he would resign his post as Guardian and live wherever the hell she wanted.

Dominic cut off communication with her and severed the connection between their energy signatures when he left for the meeting with Moravian, and the emptiness in his chest was nothing short of torment.

Standing alone in the cool, cavernous space of the Council meeting hall, Dominic opened his mind and extended his energy signature in search of Tatiana's. It took a few minutes, but finding her had been far easier than he thought. His lips curved as the familiar scent of cherries and vanilla filled his head.

Then again, he'd never been mated before.

As Tatiana's sweet tendril of energy merged with his, Dominic whispered the ancient language and threw his arms wide as the rush of static enveloped him and carried him away.

With an energizing surge of electricity, he materialized in the driveway of Tatiana's home. The sun was beginning to rise and cast soft golden rays of light over the A-frame log cabin. To the right was the barn, which she used for her veterinary practice.

Dominic raised his gun and surveyed the area, but the only energy patterns he picked up were of his friends inside the house—and Savannah.

As he lowered his gun and holstered it, the front door of the cabin swung open, and Tatiana came bursting through. His heart thundered in his chest at the sight of her. With a wide smile and open arms, she ran down the steps and leapt into his arms, and the force of it almost knocked him over.

Clinging to him, she rained kisses all over his face before nuzzling his neck and breathing him in. Dominic held Tatiana, her feet dangling off the ground as she pressed her warm lips to his throat.

"I thought I'd never see you again," she whispered, her voice thick with tears.

"It's okay, baby," Dominic growled as a tsunami of feelings washed over him. Joy. Relief. Home. This woman, wherever she was, that was home. He placed her on her feet, cradled her face in his hands, and brushed his lips over hers. "I'm not going anywhere."

"You better not." She sniffled and kissed him again. "Since you scared the shit out of me, you do realize this means lots and lots of make-up sex."

Dominic grinned and murmured against her lips, "I'm counting on it."

"Wait a minute." Tatiana's smile faded, and she looked around as concern and reality crept in to steal their moment. "Where's Richard?"

"He's in New York with the others."

"Daniella?"

"She's gone." Dominic shook his head curtly.

"I'm sorry," she murmured.

Dominic kissed her forehead and draped his arm over her shoulders as he walked toward the house. "Let's go inside so I can fill everyone in at once."

As they climbed the steps, Dominic took one more scan of the property. He knew Eric would eventually find them. He was smart and would figure out where they were holing up, but it was over a twenty-four-hour drive.

Thank God he couldn't imprint on anyone here. That bought them time to prepare for the battle that would inevitably come. At least Tatiana's house was hidden in the hills, and there didn't seem to be neighbors in sight. Let him come, Dominic thought. No more hiding. The man he once thought was his friend, his brother in arms, was now his enemy.

Dominic followed Tatiana into the cabin and was immediately hit with her familiar, comforting fragrance. The space was cozy with an open floor plan and carried her scent throughout, but nothing could mask the tense, fluttering energy waves of Savannah and William.

William stood guard in front of the massive stone fireplace with his gun pointed at a young woman. Dominic knew in an instant this was Savannah. She sat on the couch, with her feet tucked underneath her, and looked as though she didn't have a friend in the world, except for the dog, which was curled up contentedly in her lap. Based on the way William looked at her, she certainly didn't have one in him.

"Good to see you still in one piece," William said without taking his sharp gaze off Savannah.

"You too." Dominic flicked his glowing eyes to Savannah. "You have some explaining to do." She shrunk further into the couch when she set eyes on Dominic. He turned to Tatiana as she shut the door. "How's Courtney? I can sense Steven with her upstairs."

"She's the same as she was before. I set them up in the guest room."

Tatiana moved into the room and sat on the arm of the sofa. Wearing yoga pants and a tank top, she was more beautiful than ever. Although her face was weary and reflected the stress of the past twenty-four hours, she radiated pure light, and all he wanted was to wrap her in his arms and bathe in it.

"What happened, Dominic?"

"Moravian, and the Purists he brought with him to the exchange, are all dead. He didn't have Matt. Never did. He agreed to the meeting to get *her* back." Dominic moved around the couch and leveled a serious glare at Savannah, who wept quietly. "Your father was under the impression that you and Courtney were abducted by *us*, and he thought *you* were the one we wanted to trade."

"Tears for your father?" William murmured. "How touching."

"He was a bastard," Savannah said through her tears, "but he was still my father."

Dominic nodded. He understood the conflicting emotions the girl felt because he had the same experience regarding the loss of his sister. She'd betrayed their people and allowed her hatred to rule her, but in the end, she was still his sister.

"But the note?" Tatiana said with confusion. She looked at Savannah. "Kerry found your energy signature on Matt's note and in the cabin."

"I know." Savannah swiped at her eyes but looked down at her hands as she spoke. "I'd been hiding on the property in my clan form, using my psychic abilities to mask my energy signature. I saw Eric and Matt outside your cabin." She took a shuddering breath and looked at Tatiana. "He followed Matt inside, and it looked like they were arguing. Then Eric put him in a headlock and broke Matt's neck. I read the fake note he left on the porch but got back to the mountains before anyone saw me. That's why my energy pattern was on it."

"Why the hell would he kill Matt?" Dominic murmured. "That kid couldn't hurt a fly."

"Maybe he got wind of what Eric was up to?" William's eyes narrowed.

"Possibly." Dominic rested his hands on his hips, and that hinky feeling crawled up his back again. He turned his attention to Savannah. "Was Eric involved with your father?"

"No." Savannah shook her head and clung to the puppy like her life depended on it.

"What the fuck is his deal?" Dominic said tersely. "If Eric's not a Purist then what the hell is he doing?"

"Why wouldn't you come to us sooner?" Tatiana asked, her voice wracked with grief for the loss of her friend. She folded her arms over her breasts, hugging herself. Dominic closed the distance between them and pulled her into his arms. She leaned into him for support but looked at Savannah. "When you saw him hurt Matt, why wouldn't you tell us?"

"I was scared," Savannah whispered. "I—I didn't think you'd believe me. It would be my word against his. As far as all of you are concerned, I was some nasty Purist, and he was a Guardian."

"But why even hide?" Dominic asked. "You brought Courtney back. Why wouldn't you ask for amnesty from the prince?"

"Does it matter?" She sniffled and flicked her teary eyes to William. "I wanted Courtney and the baby to be alright. I didn't want that child born anywhere near my father or the others. Although after the last couple of days, I don't think there's anyone left."

"That may well be the case," Dominic said. "However, Eric is still out there. He's already tried to kill Malcolm and Zachary."

"Are they okay?" Savannah asked.

"Yes." Dominic nodded. "They're on the mend, but it will be awhile before they're up and running."

"He's going to find us eventually," William murmured. "If he's not in bed with the Purists, I can't imagine why on earth he's trying to kill everyone. Regardless of how baffling it is, that clearly seems to be his mission in life. I do *hope* I have the pleasure of killing him."

"Not if I get him first," Dominic said evenly.

"Will you at least let me watch?" William quipped.

The room hummed with silence for a beat or two.

"He's going to find us no matter where we go." Dominic's voice was edged with anger. "I've known Eric a long time, and he won't stop until he's finished the job he's set out to do. Richard and Dante will be here before sundown. I've kept my mind open to the two of them, so they'll be able to follow the path."

"How much time do you think we have?" William asked.

"Eric will wait until nightfall to try something. That should give us at least a day to prepare. Maybe two."

"How can you be so sure he'll find us that quickly?" Tatiana asked. "He can't use visualization to come here. He hasn't been here before, and he's not imprinted on any of us."

"He can still drive, Doc." Dominic smirked and kissed the top of her head. "Besides, he knows Steven wouldn't bring Courtney to the vampire stronghold. The next logical place to hide would be at the home of a woman who had no plan to be part of our world."

"Right," Tatiana said through a wry laugh. "Well, like my aunt Rosie always says... *while you make plans, God laughs*."

Dominic and Tatiana left William downstairs with Savannah as they checked in on Steven and Courtney. Unfortunately, she was still unconscious, and he continued to be the immovable force at her side. Dominic wanted to scout the property and get a better bead on their surroundings, but Tatiana wouldn't hear of it.

"Oh no, you don't." She grabbed his hand and pulled him down the hallway to her bedroom. "You need to rest—at least for a little while."

"Normally, I'd argue with you, but I don't think I have enough energy left."

Dominic followed her into the bedroom. It was a bright, clean space, mostly white with accents of aqua blue, and it reminded him of the beach. His body felt heavy and cumbersome. He couldn't remember the last time he had any sleep. In that moment, the weight of everything that had transpired hung over Dominic like a lead blanket. Eric's betrayal. Daniella's sacrifice.

Yet through it all, there was one thing that remained constant and kept him from feeling lost. Tatiana. His love for her held him, kept him grounded, and stopped him from tumbling over the edge into the abyss of revenge. Before Tatiana, he would have allowed bitterness and anger to take over and consume him. Now, the only thing that consumed him was his love for her and the driving need to protect her.

The king-size bed looked ridiculously inviting. Tatiana sidled up behind him and slid her warm hands beneath his T-shirt. Her fingers grazed up his back, and he lifted his arms as she pulled his shirt off and tossed it aside.

Dominic grasped her hands and held them to his belly, closing his eyes as he allowed himself a moment to simply feel her. Tatiana's silky, soft fingers linked with his, her warm lips grazing his back. The heat from her gorgeous body as it pressed against him made him stir, but before he could do anything, she nudged him toward the bed.

Without a word, she pushed him down and lay quietly next to him. He wrapped his arm around her as she snuggled up. She laid her head on his shoulder while her fingers trailed little circles on his stomach, and she draped one leg over his.

"We can have make-up sex later," she whispered. "Right now, even though I want to maul you, I insist you sleep." She kissed the scar on his cheek. "Doctor's orders."

"You're not a people doctor," he said in a sleepy voice. His eyelids felt heavy, and he struggled to keep them open. "You take care of animals."

"Yeah." She giggled. "Then I guess I can take care of you since you're half tiger. Now stop arguing, and get some rest."

"Yes, ma'am," he murmured.

As the welcoming arms of sleep claimed him with the love of his life wrapped around him, Dominic knew he was home.

Chapter 15

TATIANA LANGUIDLY EMERGED FROM THE CLOUD OF sleep. Dominic's butterfly kisses fluttered down her arm, and his strong hand traveled up her bare thigh. The rough, calloused skin of his palm rasped over her enticingly as he nibbled her ear. He curled up, spooning her, and his erection pressed into her back insistently.

Sighing, she rolled onto her back as she stretched her arms over her head, arching as Dominic pushed her shirt up and nuzzled her breast. His hot breath washed over her skin as he flicked aside the lacy fabric of her bra and took her nipple in his mouth. Tatiana moaned as white-hot pleasure zipped to her core.

One hand tangled with hers above her head as the other slipped beneath the waist of her yoga pants. She was already wet as he slid two fingers inside her, and his thumb massaged the tiny nub. Tatiana bit her lip and held back the cry of desire as he took her to the brink of orgasm.

Tatiana tore her hands free and pulled his face to hers, devouring his lips and sweeping her tongue into the hot cavern of his mouth. Dominic growled, and in a tangle of limbs they cast the rest of their clothing aside, leaving them naked with skin brushing along skin.

Dominic covered her body with his and lifted her leg over his hip as he drove his thick shaft deep inside. Tatiana clung to him, kissing him as he pumped into her, filling her deeper each time, and taking all she had to give.

There was a feverish pitch to their lovemaking, as though both secretly feared this could be the last time, needing to take everything, absorb it all, afraid the memory of this moment alone would be all they had left.

Growling, with muscles straining, Dominic pushed forward in one final thrust and arched back as the orgasm rocked them both to the core. He fell forward, bracing his hands on either side of her head and stayed there, his face hovering inches from hers. His body locked inside hers, and she never wanted him to leave. She wanted to keep him there forever, to savor the intimate moment of perfection, and hide from the world in a cloud of bliss. As the effects of the orgasm faded, the sounds of the others talking downstairs brought them back to reality.

Dominic withdrew and rolled over so he was stretched out next to her. He pulled her into his sweaty embrace, and she felt his heart beneath the surface. Tatiana smiled as she noted the comforting way it beat rapidly in sync with hers.

Tatiana's thoughts were interrupted as she picked up two new energy signatures in the house.

"Dante and Richard are downstairs," she said quietly as she looked at their intertwined fingers.

"You can pick up on each of them individually?" Dominic asked, pulling back and adjusting the pillow so he could look her in the face. "That's good. Your abilities are getting stronger, and when Eric shows up you'll need every bit of power you have."

"Maybe he won't come."

"Yes, he will." Dominic played with her hair and let out a slow breath. "It's not a matter of if, but when."

Panic swamped her. There would be an Amoveo battle on her property. The world she'd tried to avoid had infiltrated every part of her world, and there was no going back.

"I'm going to hop in the shower." She glanced at the digital clock on the dresser and extricated herself from his embrace. She didn't want to think about Eric or what he might do. "It's almost two o'clock. We should really go downstairs."

"Hey." Dominic grabbed her wrist and propped himself up on one elbow as he gave her a concerned look. "It's going to be okay."

"No, it's not."

Tatiana pulled her arm from his grasp and walked to the bathroom door, practically forgetting that she was naked as a jaybird. Funny. She'd never been comfortable walking around naked in front of anyone, not even herself, but somehow, being naked with Dominic seemed… natural.

However, there was nothing *natural* about the situation they were faced with.

"No." Her hand lingered on the bathroom door, and she leveled a serious stare at him. "Nothing is going to be okay again." Tatiana shivered as the reality of what her life could be like swiveled vividly into focus. "I don't think I can live like this, Dominic."

"Like what?" He swung his legs over the edge of the bed and smirked at her. "Waking up to hot sex every day?"

"Be serious, would you please?"

"I am." He strode toward her, evidence of his renewed desire rearing to life. He linked his hands around her biceps, his fingertips pressing gently into her arms as he pulled her to him. "Tatiana, talk to me. Don't shut me out."

"I'm not a fighter." Her voice quivered, and she fought the tears that threatened to spill over. "I'm not good at this. I spent my life healing animals and curing them. I can't spend the rest of it running from people who want to kill me, or fighting for my life at every turn. It's terrifying. It's cruel, you know. I was fooled for a little while into thinking I was safe."

"You will feel safe again. I promise, your life will not be like this all the time." He wrapped her in his arms, his hands splayed across her back, searing her and branding her as his with every touch. "After this is over, and I put Eric down like the fucking traitor he is, I'm leaving my position as Guardian."

"What?" Tatiana sniffled and pulled back to look him in the face. Her eyes searched his and found nothing but his typical resolute stubbornness. "But—but you love being Guardian, Dominic. I can't let you do that."

"Tatiana," he said on a sigh as he cradled her face in his hands. "I love *you*. Don't you get it?" His voice, gruff and serious, surrounded her. "My place, my home… *my life* is with you. I already told Richard, and while he wasn't happy, he understands my decision."

Tatiana was speechless. However, before she could say anything else, Dominic slapped her naked butt playfully, scooped her up, and carried her into the shower. He kissed the argument right out of her.

They made love again under a cleansing spray of

water, and afterwards, when they dressed to go downstairs, Tatiana caught sight of Dominic's formidable silhouette in the light of the window. He was a soldier in every sense of the word, and his presence filled her tiny bedroom the same way it filled her heart.

Taking over, totally and completely.

As she followed him downstairs, she couldn't help but wonder if he would do what he said. Could he really give up the life of a Guardian and be happy here, or would the life of a warrior always call him back?

After Dante and Richard arrived, William took a turn catching up on much-needed sleep. The others took a survey of the property, imprinting on the area. The sun was setting, and as it sank deeper into the horizon, Tatiana's anxiety ratcheted up, bit by bit. The darkness approached, and more than likely, Eric along with it.

Tatiana's nearest neighbor was almost a quarter of a mile away, and her property backed a nature preserve. So while there was minimal chance of human involvement, it didn't stop her from worrying about what might happen. Her thoughts went to Matt, and tears stung her eyes, but she willed them away. Crying wasn't going to solve anything, and the best thing she could do was to help stop the man who killed him.

However, since she wasn't much of a soldier, she did what Rosie always did in a crisis when Tatiana was growing up. She made food. Lots and lots of food. Normally, she'd make one of Rosie's pies, but given time constraints, they would have to settle on sandwiches.

Tatiana worked on an assortment of turkey, ham,

and roast beef sandwiches for the men and enlisted Savannah's help. The girl seemed happy to be doing something other than sitting around with a gun in her face. Savannah had showered and was wearing a pair of Tatiana's pajamas. She was a beautiful woman, but weariness rimmed her eyes, evidence that the ghosts of her past clearly haunted her.

Everyone had agreed that Savannah wasn't an immediate threat, and if she'd wanted to do something, she would have done it by now. It was a guarded trust, but Tatiana was grateful for the modicum of peace in an otherwise volatile situation.

She avoided scolding Savannah when she fed Cass some lunch meat. Tatiana smiled as she watched the puppy work his soothing magic on Savannah.

"I'm not sure where you'll go after this whole mess is finished," Tatiana said as she put the lid on the mustard, "but why don't you keep Casanova for a while?"

"Really?" Savannah's green eyes lit up as the puppy licked her face. "I always wanted a dog, but my father wouldn't hear of it."

An awkward silence fell between them at the mention of Moravian. Tatiana didn't push. With everything else going on, an awkward silence was the least of their problems.

"We—we should probably bring something up to Steven," Savannah said with a little smile. "He hasn't been taking care of himself, and he needs all of his strength." She lifted one shoulder and looked back at the tray of food. "You know, for Courtney."

"Mm-hmm."

Tatiana nodded as she spread mayonnaise on several

slices of whole wheat bread. Something about the way Savannah talked about Steven gave her pause. She seemed more in tune with him than anyone else, and while she was clearly concerned for Courtney, she seemed more worried about Steven.

"Tatiana!" Steven's voice filled the house. "She's waking up. Come quickly, please."

Tatiana wiped her hands on her jeans and ran upstairs with Savannah close behind. *Dominic, Courtney's waking up*. Taking the stairs two at a time, she ran down the hall and burst into Courtney's room as Dominic materialized next to her.

Courtney's eyes fluttered open, and Steven sat on the edge of the bed, holding her hands. He kissed her fingers and brushed her blonde hair from her forehead.

"Courtney, honey?" He spoke softly and smiled through his tears. "Can you hear me? It's me, Steven. You know, you really shouldn't scare your mate that way."

"No." Courtney licked her dry lips and squinted against the light as she winced in pain and tossed her head back and forth. "You're not. I'm so sorry, Steven, but I'm not your mate."

Stunned silence fell over the room, and they all stared at the beleaguered couple, but Tatiana glanced over her shoulder at Savannah. The look on her face said it all, and when she locked eyes with Savannah, everything fell into place. The girl backed into the corner of the room with Cass clutched tightly in her arms and sat in a small wooden chair.

Courtney wasn't Steven's mate—*Savannah* was.

"What are you talking about?" Steven let out a sound of disbelief and gave Tatiana a frantic look before turning back to Courtney. "Sweetheart, yes, of course I am. You had the baby. It's a boy. Our son is healthy and gorgeous. Don't you remember how excited we were and the name we picked out for him? For our son."

"It was all a lie," Courtney whimpered and pleaded through red-rimmed eyes. "I'm sorry. He—" The words came between short, gasping breaths. "Moravian used me as a host. A surrogate."

"This is crazy," Steven rasped as he turned his furious eyes to Savannah. "What is she talking about?" His eyes glowed brightly, and a growl rumbled in his chest as he rose from Courtney's bedside. "What did you do?"

"Don't," Courtney sputtered. She reached blindly and grabbed Steven by the arm, pulling him toward her. She grit her teeth, using her last bit of life to set things straight. "It's not her fault, Steven… take care of your son… the same way you took care of me."

Courtney lifted a pale, quivering hand and laid it against Steven's cheek. As her eyes fluttered closed, her arm fell limply to her chest as the last breath escaped her broken body.

Steven dropped to his knees and sobbed over her, clinging to her as deep, grief-stricken cries wracked him. He pleaded for her to come back to him, but it was no use.

Courtney was gone.

Tears fell down Tatiana's cheeks in a steady stream as Steven's grief filled the room. Dominic moved in next to her, linking one arm around her waist and holding her close, needing to feel her as much as she needed him. That deep, innate connection, the one that Courtney never had with Steven, drove him to pull her into his arms and comfort her.

That realization only made Tatiana's tears fall faster.

Swiping at the tears, her heart broke—for all of them. Steven, Courtney, and even Savannah. Tatiana sniffled and looked back at Savannah. Weeping quietly, she sat in the far corner of the room with Cass licking away her tears.

"I'm—I'm so sorry," Savannah whispered in a tear-strained voice. She rose from the chair but stopped short when Steven turned his fierce, glowing gaze on her. "Something in the rock of the mountains at the Purist compound stifled our powers. You thought Courtney was your mate, but it wasn't her. It was me. It *is* me. I am your mate, Steven."

Tatiana looked from Savannah to Courtney and couldn't believe she didn't see the resemblance before. *They do look alike. Both blonde, similar build, and large green eyes.* She touched Dominic's mind. *If there was some weird, whammy thing blocking the Amoveo abilities, it's easy to see how wires could get crossed.*

"I saw you in the dream realm once you arrived at the compound, but you slipped away, like a radio station with heavy static." Savannah moved cautiously toward Steven, her voice gentle and soothing. "When the guards captured you trying to break into Courtney's room, I confessed to my father. I thought if he knew you were my mate, he would spare you… but instead, he did something unthinkable."

Steven growled, and Savannah stopped a foot from the bed.

"My father harvested my eggs and implanted them with your sperm." Savannah's voice wavered, and she paused, squeezing her eyes shut as though saying it out loud was too much to bear. "So many of the women in the breeding program were dying. He didn't want to risk my safety. He used Courtney as a surrogate because you are both from the same clan and had her carry the pregnancy. You are my mate, Steven, and the baby is *our* son."

"That's not possible." Steven looked from Courtney to Savannah, his brow furrowed, his face carved with anger. "You are not my mate. My mate, the mother of my son, is dead because of you and your psychotic father," he shouted.

Steven lifted Courtney's lifeless body from the bed and cradled her against his chest before turning his glowing coyote eyes to Savannah.

"Steven?" Tatiana asked gently. "What are you doing?"

"I'm taking my wife to have a proper Amoveo burial." He leveled a deadly glare at Savannah. "Savannah—you will come nowhere near me or *my* son ever again." His voice cracked with emotion. "*Courtney's* son."

Steven growled the ancient language, and in an eruption of static electricity, they were gone. Savannah broke into hysterical sobs and dropped to her knees on the floor, weeping uncontrollably. Tatiana looked at Dominic before crossing to Savannah, squatting down next to her, and wrapping her arms around her.

"It's not your fault, Savannah." She pulled Savannah to her feet and looked at Dominic as she comforted the inconsolable girl. "You are as much a victim of your father's actions as the rest."

"It doesn't matter." Savannah pushed Tatiana away as her eyes glowed yellow, the eyes of her clan, with hurt and frustration edging each word. "Everything I did to protect Courtney and the baby, to keep Steven happy—it failed. Now, the woman he loves is dead." Her voice dropped to a ragged whisper. "And I'll never see my son… but then again, I don't deserve him, do I?"

Savannah put the puppy on the floor.

"I don't deserve you either."

Dominic edged closer to Tatiana, clearly unnerved by Savannah's outburst, and held his weapon at the ready. Tatiana made a face and pushed the end of the gun toward the floor.

"Can you blame Dominic for being cautious, Tatiana?" Savannah asked through a slightly hysterical laugh. "I no longer have a place among the Amoveo. I am, and always will be, the daughter of Dr. Moravian." Her shoulders sagged, and a complete air of defeat washed over her. "Tell my son, and Steven, that I love them… and… I'm sorry."

Savannah uttered the ancient language, and in a violent rush of static, she vanished.

Standing alone with Tatiana, Dominic wrapped her in his arms. She buried her face in his chest as the tears continued to fall. He stroked the back of her hair and murmured to her softly as he kissed her head.

"I knew something wasn't right," Tatiana said through a sniffle. She rested her cheek against his chest and took a shuddering breath as the beat of his heart thrummed strong and steady beneath his chest. "That's why Courtney jumped in between me and that Purist. She wanted to die. I should have known—after all the crazy things she was saying. I should've known."

"Tatiana," he whispered gruffly and squeezed her tighter. "How could you possibly have known any of this?"

"I don't know. All I do know is that I feel responsible." She wiped her tears and pulled back, looking him in the face. "Courtney's dead because she tried to save me, and Matt's dead because of me too."

"Don't say that." His eyes glowed brightly, and the line between his brows deepened. "That's not true, Tatiana. Courtney chose to step in the middle of that battle. No one made her do it or asked her to. *She* put her life and the life of the baby at risk, not you. And you didn't kill Matt—Eric did."

"Maybe," she said slowly, "but he wouldn't have been there if it weren't for me. Matt's dead, all because I brought him to that ranch, just to try and keep all of the Amoveo in line. Not to mention, trying to keep you away from me." Her voice caught in her throat as shame washed over her. "I *used him,* and now, he's dead. It was all for nothing because we're together anyway. Aren't we?"

Tatiana's voice rose with anger, and her eyes snapped to their clan form as her grief, frustration, and helplessness boiled over.

"Fate stepped in," she shouted, "taking all choices away. It moved us around like pawns on a chessboard, doing its bidding, and making us dance like puppets."

Dominic's face fell, and it looked as though she'd smacked him. He dropped his hands as a wounded expression came over him and stepped back, increasing the distance between them.

"I see." His voice was barely audible, and his jaw

set. "Well, you can have your life and your choices back, Tatiana. As soon as we've eliminated Eric and the immediate threat, I will leave you to whatever fate you choose. I wouldn't want to think you were with me against your will."

Tatiana's head spun as she watched him walk out of the room, and as he left, his energy signature severed from hers. The door slammed behind him, and she was left in an empty room with a gut-wrenching void. Dominic left her truly alone, and she didn't blame him one damn bit.

Crumpling onto the edge of the bed, she put her face in her hands and wept. In a matter of seconds, Tatiana had managed to alienate and insult the only man she'd ever loved. Confusion, frustration, and fear clawed at her from the inside, scraping at everything she thought was real.

Tatiana cried until she didn't have anything left. She shed tears for everything and everyone they'd lost. She wept for the loss of her friends and the undeniable forfeiture of stability or safety. And no matter how many puppy licks Casanova doled out, nothing could make it better.

This time, she couldn't blame the Purists, Eric, the Amoveo, or the almighty hand of fate for the loss she suffered. They weren't the ones who said impulsive, hurtful things to Dominic. Just as no one had made Courtney sacrifice herself, no one had made Tatiana utter such thoughtless words to someone who'd only tried to take care of her.

This time, the only person Tatiana had to blame was herself.

Chapter 16

NIGHT SEEMED LONGER THAN USUAL. TATIANA SAT AT the picture window sipping a cup of coffee as she looked out over the moonlit woods the way she had so many times through the years. She wasn't alone in her home, but she'd never been this lonely in her life. Casanova snuggled with her, doing his best to make her feel better. Dominic hadn't said a word to her since he left her in the bedroom, and the only telepathing he'd done was when he spoke with them collectively.

The man was pissed, and he had every right to be. Tatiana wanted to apologize and vow to set it straight as soon as he'd speak to her. She only hoped it would be sooner rather than later.

William, Dominic, and Richard patrolled outside. It was well after midnight, and so far, there was no sign of Eric or anyone else. Occasionally, she would catch a glimpse of Dominic's glowing eyes as he slipped in and out of the tree line, but only for a moment. She crushed him and had absolutely no idea how to fix it. Somehow, saying *I'm sorry* simply didn't seem like enough.

We're picking up human energy patterns on the outskirts of the property. Richard's voice touched their collective minds. *I suggest we shift. We'll cover more ground faster in our clan forms*.

Seems rather late for humans to be wandering in the woods. William's typically stuffy tone chimed in curtly.

People do camp in the reserve behind my property, Tatiana added. *So that's probably all it is.*

Confirmed. Dominic's voice cut in briefly. *Back here in ten.*

As his voice touched her mind, even for that brief moment, Tatiana was filled with an overwhelming sense of calm, and for an instant, the void was filled. Yet when he closed off communication, the darkness returned with a vengeance.

Tatiana squeezed her eyes shut and shook her head as if she could somehow clear her confusion about her own feelings. There had been no word from Steven since they'd left, and she doubted there would be anytime soon. Savannah hadn't been in touch since her hasty exit, and Tatiana couldn't help but worry about her. The girl didn't seem to have a friend in the world.

Dante stood at the other window with his gun in hand. He peered outside through glowing amber eyes, no doubt exploring the surrounding area with his keen Amoveo senses.

"He'll get over it," Dante said, breaking the unsettling silence. He sliced a glance at Tatiana over his shoulder and smirked. "Kerry didn't want much to do with me in the beginning either, but somehow, it all worked itself out. And William?" Dante let out a scoffing sound and shook his head as he looked back out the window. "Layla turned his world upside down. Poor bastard didn't know his ass from his elbow when he found your sister, and look at him now. He actually smiles. Shit, until he and Layla got together, I didn't think the guy had any teeth."

"I hurt him," she said quietly. Tatiana pulled her feet under her and sipped her coffee. "I said something shitty, and I can't take it back. Once it's out there, it's out there."

"What did you say?"

"Well." She sighed and laid her head back on the couch before glancing at Dante. "In a nutshell, I blamed our relationship for Matt's death and implied that what we have isn't real. It's merely a trick of fate. I mean, look at that mess with Steven and Courtney. Did he really love Courtney, or did he convince himself he did because he thought she was his mate? Did Savannah do what she did only because she believed he was her mate, or were her feelings genuine? So why should I believe our feelings for each other are real? What if they're just some side effect from this mate legend?"

"You're right." Dante nodded with his back to her. "That's shitty."

"Thanks." She sipped her coffee again and let out a short laugh. "If this is your idea of a pep talk, it sucks."

"Sorry." Dante lifted one shoulder. "I don't know if you've noticed, but the Amoveo men aren't great with subtlety."

"Yeah, I noticed."

"We're good at some stuff though."

Dante turned around and faced her, his brown eyes smiling at her. Tatiana's face heated with embarrassment, and she looked away because she had a feeling he was referring to the crazy, toe-curling sex.

"Well, yeah." He laughed and ran one hand through his thick auburn hair, embarrassed by the same thing. "But we're good at other stuff too." His expression grew serious. "Like taking care of the people we love, and make no mistake about it—Dominic loves you. Before you came along, the only thing that man could see was duty—his job as Guardian. Not so much anymore." He held up one hand. "Don't get me wrong. He's out there right now in full-on Tiger Clan mode ready to rip Eric's throat out, but it's different than it was before."

"How do you mean?" Tatiana sat up and put her mug on the wooden coffee table as she leaned both elbows on her knees, interested in any insight she could get on this mate thing. "How is he different now?"

"His motivation." Dante smiled and pointed at her. "You, Tatiana. Everything he does, every decision he makes, is made with your best interests at heart. He'll do whatever it is that he thinks will make you happy and keep you safe. So, if you told Dominic that you don't think your feelings are real and that all of this is some kind of trick, then my guess is he's going back to the ranch and will resume his position as Guardian… without you. Not because that's what *he wants,* but because he thinks it's what *you want*."

Tatiana's heart sank, and she let out a slow breath as she pressed her mouth against folded hands. Dante turned around and looked back out at the quiet forest as she let it all sink in. Maybe that's what she needed to do. Let him leave.

When this was all over, she would let Dominic go back to the ranch while she stayed here. Perhaps the only way to know if their love was real was to get some space from each other. What was that expression? If you love something, set it free. If it comes back to you, it's yours. And if not, it wasn't meant to be.

A high-pitched sound in conjunction with shattering glass made Tatiana jump. For a second, she wasn't sure which direction it came from until Dante wavered on his feet before falling in a heap to the ground. Seconds later a hail of bullets sprayed the windows from both sides.

Tatiana grabbed Cass and dove onto the floor. She crawled past the table and skittered along the floor on her belly to Dante's side as glass and wood shards rained over her. Cass hid under the table, whimpering.

With strength she didn't know she had, she dragged Dante away from the window and into the kitchen. He touched the wound on his chest as he winced in pain. "Motherfucker that hurts."

Tatiana! Dominic's panicked voice thundered into her mind.

I'm okay, but Dante's been shot. A large dark stain spread across his shirt, and she pressed her hand to the wound in an effort to stop the bleeding. *It's bad, Dominic. What the hell is going on?*

There were four individuals. Dominic sounded winded, and a growl rumbled. *I killed one, but Eric and the other two are heavily armed. William's been hit. Goddamn it. They waited until we were in our clan form to hit us. You get the fuck out of here, right now.*

I can't. She pulled Dante's shirt up and inspected the gunshot wound. He was hit just below his shoulder, and based on the blood seeping onto her legs, the bullet passed straight through. *I've got to stop this bleeding, or he's going to be in big trouble.*

Tatiana closed her eyes, and holding onto Dante, she shrunk against the cabinets as the hail of bullets continued. She reached out through space and did what they taught her. She pictured the inside of her office, the smell of antiseptic in the surgery suite, and the familiar scent of cats and dogs, which lingered.

As the sense-memory came rushing to the forefront of her mind, she visualized herself in the space. In a flurry of static electricity, she and Dante materialized on the cold tile floor in the exam room of her veterinary practice.

It was dark except for the silver ray of moonlight spilling from the tiny row of windows along the top of the walls. The gunfire stopped, and Dominic's mind disengaged from hers, which invoked a wave of panic. She bit it back and focused on helping Dante. She hurried to the cabinet of supplies and grabbed what she needed before diving back to the floor to help him.

Tatiana worked quickly to sop up the blood, but she stilled as the roar of a big cat rattled the air. She held her breath as it was followed by gunfire and the wailing scream of a man. Then silence. Tatiana's heart hammered in her chest. She tried to reach out to Richard and Dominic but was met with horrifying silence.

Were they dead or merely cutting off telepathic communication to keep her safe? She prayed it was the latter.

A split second later, static flickered in the room, and Kerry materialized in front of her. Tatiana let out a shuddering sob of relief and sat back on her heels. The statuesque beauty looked like a pissed-off Amazonian goddess. Her yellow panther eyes glowed brightly as she dropped to her knees and huddled next to her wounded mate.

"Oh, no you don't, Tarzan," Kerry said through trembling lips. She pulled him into her lap as he attempted a weak smile and placed a shaking hand over hers. "You can't go around getting shot and dying. That is not what I signed up for. No way. You are not allowed to die."

"Take him to the vampires," Tatiana whispered. "Go."

"You have to come with us." Kerry's long dark hair fell over her face as tears filled her eyes. "You can't stay here."

Tatiana placed her finger to her lips as the sound of someone walking outside caught her attention, and neither one moved. Tatiana's eyes shifted to the burning golden eyes of her wolf, and she captured Kerry's gaze. *You came here for Dante when you knew he was in trouble. I'm not going anywhere until I know Dominic is okay.*

I know better than anyone that it's pointless to argue with a hybrid Amoveo woman. Kerry squeezed her friend's hand. *Be careful. I'll send help as soon as I can, so don't do anything crazy, okay? Wait for Pete.*

Tatiana nodded and gave Kerry a tight smile as she and Dante vanished in a flurry of static, leaving her alone. She sucked in a shaky breath and grabbed the edge of the counter as she pulled herself to her feet. Tatiana winced at the stinging cuts on her face and arms, which she must've gotten from the flying glass, but didn't notice until now.

With her heart thundering in her chest, Tatiana crept toward the waiting area of her office. She nudged the swinging door open a crack, peered into the innocuous-looking room, and to her relief, found it empty. Tatiana slipped through the door, opening it only enough so she could sneak through. She padded silently to the front doors. She pressed her body against the wall next to the door, avoiding the windows.

Shaking with fear and adrenaline, she shut her eyes and focused on the area around the building. Her gut instinct was to send her energy signature in search of the others, but she worried that might be like sending a fucking bat-signal to Eric, alerting him to her location. Tears stung her eyes, but she pressed the heels of her hands against them, refusing to cry.

Tatiana didn't know what to do.

The woods were quiet. Unnaturally quiet—even the animals seemed to be holding their breath, waiting to see what would come next. Her hand lingered on the doorknob as she debated about what the hell she should do. She had to do something because sitting in here waiting had to be worse than dealing with whoever was out there head-on.

Tatiana's hands were sticky with blood and slick with sweat as her fingers slid on the knob, but her heart skipped a beat when she felt it move. Someone was trying to come inside, and based on the energy, it was a human man. Caedo?

Tatiana scrambled across the room and hid under the receptionist's desk. She pulled her knees to her chest and held her breath, praying that whoever it was would find the room empty and leave.

With heart pounding in her chest and sweat covering her quivering body, she waited. She covered her mouth with one hand to keep from crying out as the distinct sound of the door opening broke the silence. Tatiana held her breath, worrying that even that small sound would alert her hunter. The footsteps of someone creeping slowly across the room echoed, and she thought she would go crazy as she waited, praying for the man to leave.

"Come out, come out, wherever you are," he sang.

The squeak of the exam room door opening and closing gave her hope. As quietly as possible, she crawled out and peered around the desk. Whoever it was had gone into the exam room and left the front door open.

Finding her courage, Tatiana rushed to her feet and ran out the door.

"There she is," he shouted.

Tatiana leapt from the steps, and as her bare feet hit the pine-needle-covered ground, her eyes flickered to their clan form. A growl erupted as she pictured her clan form, and in an explosion of static, Tatiana erupted into her timber wolf.

With a lower center of gravity and the power of four legs instead of two, she raced into the tree line with gunshots ringing out behind her. The heat of a bullet whizzed by her head as she ducked behind a massive tree. As her paws skidded on the thick bed of needles, the bone-shattering roar of a big cat filled the air.

Tatiana spun around to see Richard in his lion form as he leaped onto the man and tackled him to the ground. The gun went off as it skittered out of his hands and across the ground. Richard's massive tawny body stood over the man as he sank his teeth into the man's neck, crushing his windpipe and silencing him forever.

Relief flooded Tatiana, and she ran out of the woods toward the prince. His large, muscular feline body was covered in splattered blood, and he was breathing heavily.

Got you, you son of a bitch. Richard stalked toward her but stumbled and fell onto his side. *Caedo assassins. Eric was working with them.*

Dominic? Her mind reached out to his, but he didn't

answer or couldn't. She wasn't entirely sure which. Tatiana trotted up to Richard and whined as she nuzzled his massive head with hers. *Where's Dominic?*

Tatiana pictured her human form, and seconds later she shifted. She knelt next to the prince and inspected the two gunshot wounds, one at his shoulder and the other had grazed his head.

"How touching." Eric's voice chilled her to the bone. "Decided to play on Team Amoveo, after all?"

Richard growled, but he was clearly in no shape to go anywhere or do any more fighting. Tatiana squatted on her heels and turned to face Eric with her hands in the air, a clear sign of surrender.

"Where's Dominic?" she asked in a surprisingly steady voice.

"Dead." Eric's voice was void of emotion, but it hit Tatiana the same as if he'd punched her in the stomach. "William too. Well, I think he is. I pinged his sorry ass mid-flight, so I'll go find him to be sure."

"No," Tatiana whispered. Her eyes filled with tears, and nausea swamped her as her body shook uncontrollably. "He—he can't be dead. I don't believe you."

"Believe what you want." Eric shrugged. "It's all the same to me. I get paid based on the body count, and as of now, I'm up to three. Well, four, once I kill you, but the prince over here—he counts as two. That's the big payday right there."

"Payday?" she asked with confusion. "The Purists are paying you?"

"Purists?" he scoffed. "Those assholes don't have money. Shit, they're all pretty much gone now, and thanks to them so is my mate." His features darkened, and he stalked toward her, his yellow clan eyes glowing brightly as he grabbed Tatiana's arm and yanked her to her feet. "My mate died in that fucking breeding program because Richard didn't get there in time to get her out."

"So it's about revenge?" She licked her lower lip and glanced to the woods, praying by some miracle Dominic would appear. "Not Purists or Loyalists?"

Keep him talking, she thought. Just keep him talking, and buy time until Pete or the others get here. Kerry said she'd send help, but if they didn't get here soon, it would all be over. She kept her eyes locked with his, but the cold, flat look on his face chilled her to the bone. He was emotionless, barren of empathy, and locked solely on his mission.

"I'm not a Purist, baby. I'm an opportunist."

"But—these are your people?" she said in disbelief. "Your friends."

"Oh please. They don't give a holy shit about anything but their women. I've got no mate. I'm fucked, lady. In about a year, I'm gonna be without my powers, so I figured if I have to live my life as a human, I may as well be rich."

"Money? You did this for money?"

"When I cornered that Caedo assassin at the ranch, he offered me a big payday to let him go. I took the offer. We made it look good though. I let him shoot me and everything." Eric's grin broadened, and he pulled her up against him, dropping his voice low. "Then, they offered me *ten times* that to kill the prince and any others I could get," he murmured. "Well, why the fuck not. I screwed with the horses to mess with

Richard's head, and it worked. Your boy Matt overheard me talking on my cell phone with the Caedo. Couldn't very well let him go blathering back to you, now could I?"

"Let her go, Eric."

Dominic's voice washed over her like a soothing balm, and as ridiculous as it could be, she laughed with relief. Eric growled as his eyes glowed brighter. He spun around, his fingers digging into Tatiana's arm as he held her in front of him. She stilled as he pressed the cool steel of the gun against her temple.

"I thought you were dead." Eric let out a curt laugh. "I should've known you were too fucking stubborn to die."

Wounded and bleeding from the chest and his left leg, Dominic limped toward them with his arms out to his side. He kept his glowing amber eyes on Eric as he stepped closer. Tatiana had no idea how he could be on his feet given the amount of blood that covered him. She hoped it wasn't all Dominic's.

"This must be your worst nightmare, brother," Eric barked. "I've got your mate, and the prince is passed out—practically dead, actually. I shot the other two, and now, it's your turn. So much for doing your duty. Look where it fuckin' got you."

Eric pointed the gun at Dominic, but the sound of Casanova barking from inside the bullet-ridden house momentarily distracted Eric. Tatiana screamed and fought to free herself as Richard reared to life and latched his massive jaws around Eric's ankle. Eric bellowed in rage, knocking Tatiana to the ground as his gun fired. She looked up just in time to see Dominic throw the dagger he always kept tucked in his belt. It sliced through the air and landed squarely in Eric's chest.

Eric dropped like a stone as a gurgling noise escaped his lips, and the light faded from his eyes. Lying in an awkward position with a knife protruding from his chest, it was abundantly clear he was dead.

Shaking and crying, Tatiana scrambled to her feet and ran to Dominic as he dropped to his knees. She wrapped her arms around his neck and held him, breathing him in. Blood, sweat, and tears covered them both. He linked one arm around her, but the other hung limply at his side, stained red with blood. She pulled back to look at him but could barely see through the tears.

"Sorry I was late," Dominic said through heavy, shaking breaths. "I got held up."

"Uh-huh." She laughed and leaned her forehead against his. "You're not going to use that old I-was-killing-a-Caedo-assassin excuse, are you?"

Tatiana rained kisses over his face and hugged him again, but he winced as she put too much pressure on his wounds.

"Sorry." She helped him into a sitting position and looked over at Richard, who had shifted to his human form, but had passed out again. "We have to get you two help. Kerry was sending some, but—"

The sound of branches cracking and gravel being displaced set Dominic rigid in her embrace, but a moment later, Pete stepped out of the woods carrying William over his shoulder like a sack of potatoes.

"This guy keeps getting shot." Pete jutted a thumb at William's limp body, but his eyebrows flew up when he set eyes on Richard and Dominic and the dead bodies.

"Shit. You guys really need to develop an Amoveo power that makes you bulletproof."

To her surprise, Dominic started laughing and shook his head but stopped as pain shot through his body. "Fuck me, that hurts."

"William is gonna be so pissed I saved him again," Pete said. His eyes glowed red, and Tatiana got a glimpse of his fangs when he smiled. "He really hates to say thank you."

"Yeah," Dominic said through a deep breath as Tatiana helped him to his feet, "but at least it's over, and everyone can go back to their lives." He sliced a glance in her direction. "You can have your life back, Tatiana. Whatever makes you happy."

Tatiana's heart sank as Dominic limped away from her and out of her grasp. She watched as he went to Richard's side, but she turned her back on them, struggling to get herself together. As her teary gaze skimmed over her bullet-ridden house, she knew her old life was gone. Nothing would be the same ever again.

A moment later, Casanova came barreling out through the ramshackle door and ran down the steps. Like any good therapy dog, he went directly to the most banged up guy in the group and sniffed the prince. The dog had more sense than she did. Through it all, he knew where to go and what to do, he knew not to fight his nature.

"No." Tatiana spun on her heels with her hands on her hips and glared at Dominic through the glowing eyes of her wolf. "I don't want it."

Dominic helped Richard to a sitting position while looking at her as though she'd lost her mind. Pete, with William still flung over his shoulder, looked between them but said nothing. Dominic grunted and rose to his feet as he held her challenging gaze.

"Pete," Dominic ground out. "Take William and Richard to the Presidium. Tatiana and I have things to take care of. I'll be along after I clean this up."

"Are you sure, man?" Pete gave him a doubtful look. "You got your ass kicked."

"I'm fine," Dominic growled over his shoulder. He held one hand over the wound on his chest and fought to get the words out. "Just get them some help."

Pete nodded and mouthed *good luck* to Tatiana as he, Richard, and William vanished into the night.

"What the hell do you want, Tatiana?" Dominic ground out once they were alone. "Do you know? I sure as hell don't. Shit. I could spend the rest of my days trying to figure that out."

Dominic took another step but paused and ran a hand over his chiseled features, his eyes fierce and glowing in the dark night. Covered in blood, sweat, and dirt, he was still the most desirable, sexy man she'd ever met.

"All *I know* is that I love you, Tatiana. I love when you nibble on your thumbnail when you're nervous, or when you talk to animals like Dr. Fucking Dolittle, or when you look at me like I'm a macho dickhead. But you know what? Through all of the shit that went down today, the *only* thing I could think of was getting to you and keeping you safe. I want you to be happy, and if that means you staying here without me, then fine."

His jaw twitched and he squared his shoulders through the pain. He looked as though he was ready for her to rip his heart out of his chest.

"I don't know what happened with Steven and

Courtney," he sighed. "Or how their wires got crossed, but I do know my feelings for you are real. My body might be genetically programmed to respond to yours, but no one can tell my soul what to feel."

Tatiana's heart hammered in her chest as she glanced over her shoulder at the disaster that was her house. She surveyed the debris and chaos around her until her gaze finally landed on Dominic.

As she studied him and took in the bloody, wounded sight, she remembered how she felt in that moment when she couldn't reach him and had no idea if he was dead or alive. Tatiana recalled the aching void, the one that pulsed deep in her chest when his comforting, soothing energy was absent. In that instant, like fog dissipating from a mirror… everything was clear.

Tatiana moved toward him, taking each step with purpose until she stood inches from him.

"I'm sorry," she murmured. Tatiana popped up on her toes, and his eyes widened with surprise as she linked her arms around his neck and brushed her lips over his. "It was foolish and insulting to imply that what we feel for one another isn't true." She peered up at him as her fingers fluttered along the base of his neck. "I do love you, Dominic, and I promise I will spend the rest of my life proving exactly how real that is."

Dominic growled and pressed his warm lips to her forehead. "Tatiana, you do realize what this means, don't you?"

Tatiana pulled back to look him in the face and found him giving her that mischievous smirk. "What?"

"Make-up sex," he whispered against her lips. "Lots and lots of make-up sex."

Tatiana laughed as his mouth covered hers. Dominic's energy signature curled around her like a blanket, wrapping her up with desire and protection. She knew that she was home.

Whether it was a bullet-ridden house in Oregon or a cabin on a ranch in Montana, as long as Dominic was by her side… she was home, and she was safe.

Read on and escape to the sizzling paranormal world of Sara Humphreys's Amoveo Legend series

UNLEASHED
UNTOUCHED
UNDENIED (NOVELLA)
UNTAMED
UNDONE

Available now from
Sourcebooks Casablanca

From *Unleashed*

"SAMANTHA," HE WHISPERED IN HIS DARK SILKY VOICE. *Sam's skin tingled deliciously with just one word from him. A smile played at her lips as she waited for him to call her again. Her silent prayer was answered as he murmured her name. "Samantha." That same delightful rush washed over her like the warm waves that rippled by her feet. She stretched languidly on the sandy beach, and her eyes fluttered open. She was home.*

She sat up and glanced at the familiar seashore of her childhood home. Sam knew it was only a dream. It had become a familiar one. The ocean glowed with unnatural shades of blue as if it was lit from beneath. The sky swirled with clouds of lilac and lavender. She stood up and relished the way the soft, pebble-free sand felt on her bare feet. A gentle breeze blew Sam's golden hair off her naked shoulders, and her long white nightgown fluttered lightly over her legs.

She closed her eyes and breathed in the salty air. He was near. She could feel it. Her blood hummed, and the air around her thickened. She'd come so close to seeing him many times, but she always woke up just before she found him.

Not this time.

This time she would stay on the beach and call him to her. It was her dream after all, and she was getting tired of coming up empty-handed. Eyes closed, she tilted her face to the watercolor sky and waited. Her heartbeat thundered in her ears in perfect time with the pounding waves.

"Samantha," he whispered into her ear. She stilled, and her mouth went dry. He was standing right behind her. How the hell did he get there? Where did he come from? Why couldn't he stand right in front of her where she could actually see him? This was supposed to be her dream, her fantasy. Jeez. Can you say intimacy issues?

Sam jumped slightly and sucked in a sharp breath as large hands gently cupped her shoulders. She should open her eyes. She wanted to open her eyes, but the onslaught of sensations to her body and mind had her on overload. Samantha shuddered as he brushed his fingers lightly down her arms leaving bright trails of fire in their wake. He tangled his fingers in hers and pulled her back gently. Sam swallowed hard as his long muscular body pressed up against hers. He was tall, really tall. She sighed. If he looked half as good as he felt, she was in big trouble.

"It would seem that you've finally found me," he murmured into her ear.

Sam nodded, unable to find her voice amid the rush of his. She licked her dry lips and mustered up some courage. It was a dream after all. Nothing to be afraid of. She could always wake up. But that's what she was afraid of.

"Why don't you ever let me see you?" she said in a much huskier tone than she'd intended. She pressed her body harder against his and relished the way his fingers felt entwined with hers.

He nuzzled her hair away from her neck and placed

a warm kiss on the edge of her ear. "Come home," he whispered. His tantalizing voice washed over her and he seemed to surround her completely. Body. Mind. Soul. Every single inch of her lit up like the Fourth of July.

"Please," she said in a rush of air. Sam wrapped his arms around her waist and relished the feel of him. It was like being cradled in cashmere covered steel. Leaning into him, she rubbed her head gently against his arm. He moaned softly and held her tighter. The muscles in his chest rippled behind her, and his bicep flexed deliciously against her cheek. "I need to see you."

Eyes still closed, she turned in his arms as he said softly "Samantha."

Sam tumbled out of bed and landed on the floor with a thud. Breathing heavily and lying amid her tangled bedclothes, Sam stared at the bland white ceiling of her soon-to-be former apartment.

"Talk about a buzz kill," she said to the empty room. "Typical. I can't even get good sex in my dreams." She puffed the hair from her face and pushed herself up to a sitting position. Sam grabbed her cell phone off the nightstand and swore softly when she saw the time. She was going to be late. Crap.

From *Untouched*

"YOU ARE ONE SEXY BITCH." KERRY GRINNED BROADLY and shut the door to Samantha's bedroom. She leaned back and folded her arms to get a better look at the bride. "Seriously, does Malcolm know how freaking lucky he is?" she asked skeptically. Kerry bent down and smoothed out the train of Samantha's simple ivory gown.

"Oh he does, and so do I." Samantha smiled serenely and adjusted the bodice of her strapless silk wedding dress. Kerry stood behind her best friend and removed the one or two kinks in the delicate veil. She smiled at their contrasting reflections in the oval antique mirror. Kerry was a good head taller than Sam. Sam's hair, swept off her neck, was as blonde as Kerry's was black. Samantha had always been beautiful, but today she was truly radiant.

Tears stung at the back of Kerry's eyes. Her best friend, her only friend, was getting married. She took a deep breath, wrapped her arms around Sam's waist, and braced herself. It was always a gamble touching another human being. Samantha was the only person Kerry could bear to touch. Everyone, including Sam, thought it was a germ phobia. The truth was much more complicated.

It was far more frightening.

She embraced Sam and saw the one image that

always burst into her mind, an enormous gray wolf. As odd as it was, that unique image gave her comfort. Since they were children that was the only thing Kerry saw when she touched Sam. Unfortunately, that wasn't the case when she touched other people. Kerry let out a heavy sigh, a mixture of relief and comfort as Sam gave her arms a squeeze.

"I'm not going to Mars, you know. I'm just getting married." Sam laughed. "Now I'll be two houses down the beach instead of one. At the very most I'm a phone call away."

"That's what they all say." Kerry sniffled and released Sam from the embrace. She turned quickly and wiped the tears away, feeling foolish for such a display.

"Besides, you're the famous model," Sam said with a teasing lilt in her voice. "You know… always jet-setting around the world on photo shoots. We only get to see each other a couple of times a year anyway. Who knows? We may see each other more now."

Sam took Kerry's hand and gave it a reassuring squeeze. The wolf image burst into Kerry's head, but at least there was no pain. She could almost tolerate the visions. It was the crippling pain that terrified her. Kerry's body stilled, and she prayed her friend wouldn't notice.

"I promise nothing will change! Look at it this way, every time you come to your parents place for a break at the beach, you can count on me being here."

"He better not be one of those Neanderthal types that won't let you have a girls' night out. I mean I don't even know this guy. Are you sure this is it? You've only known him for a month."

Even as the words escaped her lips she knew what

the answer was. In truth, she'd never seen her friend this happy. Ever since Samantha met Malcolm, she glowed. Kerry had heard about that but hadn't witnessed it until now. Her lips curved. She had always been envious of Sam because she'd been raised in a household with real love and affection. Sam's family was a far cry from the icy environment of her own childhood.

Sometimes she wondered if her parents' cool behavior was a reaction to her unusual… sensitivity. They hadn't tried to embrace her or touch her in years. They had tried a few times when she was a child, but whenever they did she screamed bloody murder and wouldn't speak for days. Soon they just stopped trying. It saddened her to know that they never would've adopted her if they'd known how different she was.

To top it all off, she didn't exactly fit the preppy, upper-crusty mold that the Smithsons were cut from. She towered over everyone in the family and was built more like an Amazon than a delicate WASP. In every picture she stuck out like a sore thumb. Tall, big-boned, dark-haired, dark-eyed… loner. They didn't know human contact brought not only horrifying images, but excruciating pain.

Except for when she touched Samantha. There was something special about Sam. Thank God.

"Hey!" Sam snapped her fingers and brought Kerry out of her trance. "Hello in there? You okay?" Sam knitted her brow worriedly at Kerry. "Maybe we should've postponed the wedding? I don't think you're quite yourself since…"

Kerry put her hand up in protest before Samantha could finish her thought. "Don't even think about bringing up that ugliness, especially today! I'm fine. I don't even remember any of it. I mean it!" She clapped her hands and quickly changed the subject. "Hey, why are we standing around here? You've got a big hunk of man waiting to marry you underneath that beautiful tent on the beach."

Sam smiled and gave a quick nod, knowing her friend well enough to know the subject was closed. She picked up her bouquet of red roses and headed out the door toward her new life. Kerry held Sam's train off of the floor, a traditional maid of honor duty, and followed her down the stairs. She tried to concentrate on the smooth fabric between her fingers, instead of the fact that she'd just lied to her best friend.

She did remember.

She had a vivid memory of one thing from the day she was attacked. A pair of eyes had been fixed on her, eyes that glowed like embers in a fire, accompanied by a deep guttural growl. Every night since the attack, her dreams were haunted by that memory. As she walked into the bright September sunlight, she couldn't help but wonder if she would ever sleep soundly again.

The music from the lively band flowed lightly around Kerry and the rest of the wedding guests. She sipped the cool, crisp champagne as she watched Samantha dance with her new husband and could practically feel their happiness mixed with the late summer breeze. Her gaze drifted over the intimate group of guests gathered around the bride and groom. They all had that same serene look while they watched Malcolm and Samantha share their first dance as husband and wife. He towered over her as he twirled her around the dance floor, and the sound of her laughter peppered the air.

The two of them hadn't taken their eyes off each other for one second. If Kerry didn't know any better, she'd swear they were reading each other's minds. She chuckled quietly and sipped her champagne from the delicate crystal flute. The guests were limited to only thirty or so close friends and family members. Her own parents had sent their regrets from Europe, which was something of a relief. Kerry could only handle them in limited doses and didn't want their chilly demeanor ruining such a beautiful day for Sam.

"May I have this dance?"

The deep voice rolled over her like sudden thunder in the distance. She jumped with a yelp and splashed champagne onto her red satin gown. "Shit," she hissed under her breath. Kerry brushed at the droplets, which were now making dark stains on her dress, and shot an irritated glance at Malcolm's best man, Dante. "I don't dance." Something about this guy threw her off balance. Kerry prided herself on her ability to stay in control, and this guy rattled her.

"I'm sorry. I didn't realize I'd have that effect on you."

The amusement in his voice made her want to punch him square in the mouth.

Or kiss him. Shit, she was in trouble.

She glared at him through narrowed eyes and put on her most stuck-up and obnoxious tone, hoping she could frighten him away. "Don't flatter yourself, Tarzan. I got startled. That's all."

He had moved in next to her without a sound. How

long had he been standing there? He didn't go away, but instead, he moved in closer, just a breath away from her. The warmth of his body whispered along her bare arm and all the little hairs stood on end. She was terrified he'd touch her and at the same time worried he wouldn't. She quickly turned her attention back to Malcolm and Sam, trying to ignore him, but failing miserably.

He was a difficult man to ignore. At five foot ten, she was usually taller than most men, and this guy towered over her, even in her Jimmy Choos. He was massive, well over six feet tall—a solid wall of muscle. He had a handsome, masculine face with the most enormous amber eyes she'd ever seen. His thick auburn hair was almost the exact same color as his eyes.

Not that she'd noticed him or anything.

Kerry scolded herself. There was absolutely no point in getting all hot and bothered over some guy she'd never be able to touch. *I must be the oldest living virgin that isn't officially a nun.* She drained what was left of her drink.

Her goal was to be as horrible to him as possible and get him to go away. Dante smiled as though he knew she was doing her best to upset him, and she could feel his gaze wander down the length of her body.

"You'll dance with me. Maybe not today," he whispered seductively into her ear. "But eventually… you and I will dance."

From *Undenied*

"WHAT DO YOU MEAN YOU RENTED THE ROOM TO someone else?"

Lillian attempted to keep her voice calm, but her temper was getting the better of her. She glanced around the shabby apartment house and found it difficult to believe that it was booked solid. With all the gorgeous rentals in New Orleans, how on earth could this dump have no vacancies—especially since she had booked a room here for the next six months?

"Sorry." The old woman took a long drag off her cigarette and blew the smoke into Lillian's face. Her pale blue-gray eyes stared back unapologetically as she shifted her rotund frame in the chair behind her desk. "I sent you an email, but you never responded, so I figured you were just pissed."

"Well, I am now." She ran her hands over her face and let out a sound of frustration. The row of silver bangles on her wrist jingled their familiar tune and instantly calmed her. Something about that tinkling sound always brought her a certain level of serenity.

"Here's your deposit back." The woman shoved the envelope into Lillian's hands.

"Thanks… I guess." She sucked in another cleansing breath and braced both hands on the desk, hoping to appeal to whatever human decency this woman may have. "Gladys, I've been on the road for almost ten days, and my computer died right after I left Washington, so I haven't had Internet access. That's why I didn't answer you—because I never got the email. What am I supposed to do now? I gotta tell ya, Gladys... you're asking for some bad juju. How can you do this to someone?"

"Aren't you a fortune-teller?" Gladys looked at her suspiciously and pursed her lips. "Must not be very good at it if you didn't see this coming."

"I'm a palm reader." Lillian adjusted the leather satchel slung over her shoulder. "I read palms—not minds."

And she did. She could run her finger along the deep-seated lines in a person's palm and see their past, present, and future. She tried to read people in other ways, but it never worked. It wasn't just a touch of flesh. Touching someone on the arm or anywhere else didn't tell her squat.

It was the connection to those creases in the hands... the ones created in the womb that stay with us until the grave... those held a multitude of secrets and truths.

"Yeah?" She stuck her meaty hand out to Lillian. "Prove it," she sneered.

Lillian bit back the urge to tell the old bag off and took the woman's plump hand. She turned it over and sucked in a deep breath before trailing her finger along the deep lifeline.

Her eyes rolled back in her head and her lids fluttered closed. Images flashed through her mind as she moved her finger slowly along the crease in her palm—like a slide show of Gladys's entire life.

Playing in the bayou as a child. Sitting on Santa's knee at Christmas. Fooling around with a boy behind the bleachers of her high school football field. Stumbling drunk out of bars on Bourbon Street. Coughing up blood, and finally, lying in a casket—not long from now.

Gladys tugged her hand away. "I said, let go." She rubbed her hand and looked at Lillian with a scowl. "Well? What'd you see?"

"Been to the doctor lately?" Lillian flicked her gaze to the still-burning cigarette dangling from her lips. "They call those coffin nails for a reason."

"Whatever." She shrugged and took another drag off her cigarette. "The holidays are just a few weeks away, and the tourists have already invaded the Quarter, so I doubt you'll find anything around here."

The cell phone on the desk rang, and the horrible creature picked it up without sparing a glance at Lillian. She started yelling at the caller. It was someone named Bob, and from the way she was screaming—Bob was in deep shit.

Looking around the beat-up old place and listening to Gladys berate poor Bob, Lillian decided that perhaps it was better this way. The old bat was not someone she wanted to deal with on a daily basis. She had bad karma.

Resigned to her fate, she stuffed the envelope in her bag and turned to leave.

"Hang on," Gladys barked into the phone, before holding it to her ample bosom. "The only place you might actually find a room is over at The Den. It's a bar just down the ways on the corner of Ursulines and Dauphine. Word has it that Boris has a room for rent, but since that thing happened with his sister, no one wants to rent the place. That's your best shot."

Lillian nodded absently as she pushed the screen door open. It creaked in protest and slammed shut behind her with a nerve-shattering crack. She stepped onto the sidewalk and made her way to her old VW bus as she fought the tears threatening to spill down her face.

Great. Her only chance of renting a room was with some guy who had a shady story involving his sister. Boris? He was probably some fat, crusty Russian dude who barked at everyone. Could this day get any worse?

Standing on the corner, she wondered what in the hell she was supposed to do now. The truth was that she had limited options and even more limited funds. She rolled into town on fumes and had only fifty dollars in cash in her pocket. She had no credit cards, and the banks were closed, so she couldn't deposit the check.

She shielded her eyes from the bright afternoon sun and looked up and down the quiet street. This place was nothing like the wild stories she'd heard about New Orleans, but she was on the edge of the French Quarter, not on Bourbon Street—perhaps that's where all the action really was. She had planned to check into her room and then go have a look around Jackson Square, where she'd be working for the next six months—so much for her bloody plans.

Lillian checked the locks on her van to see that they were secure and decided to take a walk up Ursulines to see if she could find the place that Gladys mentioned. She figured she had nothing to lose by trying. Everything she owned was locked in her flower-and-peace-symbol-covered van. She'd already spent the past week and a half sleeping in it—a streak she was looking forward to breaking once she reached New Orleans.

Sleeping in her van was uncomfortable, but she hadn't been sleeping well in general for the past few weeks anyway—van or no van. Her dreams had been bright, loud, and persistent. It was the dreams that got her to change her plans and come to New Orleans instead of San Francisco.

She'd always considered the tiger her spirit animal or personal totem. She'd dreamt of tigers her entire life, and the dreams were strongest when she was at a crossroads or needing comfort. When she turned eighteen she even got a tattoo of a tiger on her lower back. It lay along the top of her ass and looked at the world through glowing yellow eyes—just like it often did in her dream.

Her mother, of course, freaked out, and that was the last straw before she was kicked out. She'd been on her own ever since, living like a gypsy, roaming from city to city, and reading palms along the way to earn her keep.

A few weeks before her scheduled move to San Francisco, she dreamt of her tiger, but for the first time—he spoke. He told her to come to New Orleans. The animal never actually moved his lips and spoke—but she heard him—his deep, smooth baritone whispered, calling her here.

Lillian tied her wavy blond hair back with an elastic band from the pocket of her jean jacket as a cool gust of wind whipped her ankle-length skirt around her legs. She tripped, almost falling in the middle of the street. Her face heated with embarrassment as she looked around to see if anyone noticed because the activity increased as she moved closer to the French Quarter.

Satisfied that nobody saw her typical clumsy move, she let out a sigh of relief. Stranded and homeless was bad enough, but falling on her face in public would add insult to injury. As she unfurled the batik skirt from her legs, the treacherous voice of self-doubt nibbled away.

Why had she listened to that voice in her dream? Why didn't she go to college and settle down like her mother always wanted her to? Why did she always follow her gut instinct and listen to talking tigers in her dream?

Look where it got her. Alone and essentially homeless.

"What a dope." She hugged her jacket closed against the surprisingly brisk wind and wondered if she was doing the right thing.

From *Untamed*

Why wouldn't her legs go any faster? Her lungs burned with effort, and sweat dripped down her back as she stumbled blindly through the fog-laden woods. He was right behind her. Always. His energy signature, the spiritual fingerprint that was so distinctly his, rolled around her in the mists. Behind her. Above her. In front of her.

He was everywhere.

His energy enveloped her, but still—she couldn't see him.

Layla's breath came in heavy, labored gasps, and a bare branch caught in her long, curly red hair as she tripped over a log. She pulled the tangled strands away, swore softly, and ducked behind the trunk of a giant old elm tree. Layla pressed herself up against it, praying he wouldn't see her. In response to her silent plea, the fog in the dream realm thickened and provided additional shelter from her relentless hunter.

She'd been able to avoid him so far, but tonight it felt as if he was dreadfully close to finding her—and claiming her. His powerful energy swamped her and stole from her lungs what little breath she had left. She squeezed her eyes shut and prayed that the tree and the fog would swallow her up. Could she do that? Could she control the environment of the dream that much? Just as she was about to try, an unfamiliar voice tumbled around her.

Why do you run from me? *The smooth, deep baritone*

flooded her mind and filled every ounce of her being in a shockingly intimate way. The sharp pang of desire zipped through her and made her breasts tingle. The sudden onslaught caught her off guard and had her head spinning.

Layla froze.

He'd never spoken to her before. She could barely hear him above the rapid pounding of her heart and wondered for a moment if she'd imagined it.

You did not imagine it. *His voice had become irritatingly calm.* Please answer my question. Why do you run away from me? *That distinctly male voice rumbled through her. It reverberated in her chest just like the deep bass beat of one of her favorite songs.* Why are you afraid of me? *Amusement laced his voice and floated around her in the fog.*

That did it. Now she was pissed. He was laughing at her? First he haunts her sleep every night for the past two weeks, and now he's making fun of her? Oh, hell no! Layla's eyes snapped open, and she expected to find him—whoever he was—standing right in front of her. However, she was met only with the thick fog she'd created.

I'm not afraid of you. *She placed her hands on her hips and looked around at the swirling mist. Layla tilted her chin defiantly.* I just don't want anything to do with you. So why don't you piss off!

Rich, deep laughter floated softly around her. You make it sound as if there is a choice in the matter.

You bet your bossy ass there is. *Layla shouted boldly into the gray abyss.* I decide my fate. Me. Layla Nickelsen. *She pointed at her chest with her thumb.* Me. Not you or anybody else.

She waited. The beautiful sound of silence encircled her. Was he gone? She sharpened her focus and found him quickly. No. His energy still permeated the dream but had lessened. He had backed off? Interesting.

Layla stepped away from the tree, and the fog retreated in response. She steadied her breathing as her heartbeat slowed to a normal pace. A victorious look came over her face as she found herself gaining control. She pushed her hair off her face and watched the familiar woods where she had grown up come slowly into focus. A satisfied smile curved her lips; she nodded and made a hoot of triumph. Fate can kiss my ass.

The words had barely left her mouth when two strong arms slipped around her waist and pulled her against a very tall, hard, and most definitely male body. Stunned and uncertain of what else he might do, Layla stayed completely still and glanced down to discover that her hands rested on two much larger ones. She could feel his heartbeat against her back as it thundered in his chest and thumped in perfect time with hers.

He dipped his head, and warm, firm lips pressed an unexpectedly tender kiss along the edge of her ear. Luminous heat flashed through her with astonishing speed, making her breasts feel heavy, and sending a rush of heat between her legs. It took every ounce of self-control to keep from sinking back into his strong, seductive embrace. Her body's swift reaction was positively mortifying. She shivered, bit her lower lip, and fought the urge to turn around and kiss him. Why, and how, could she be turned on like this? Layla stiffened with disgust at her lack of self-control and her body's obvious attraction to his.

You cannot outrun your destiny. *His surprisingly seductive voice dipped low, and his breath puffed tantalizingly along the exposed skin of her neck. She closed her eyes and tried to fight the erotic sensations, but it was like trying to stop the tide as it throbbed through her relentlessly.* And for future reference, Firefly, the only one kissing your ass—or anything else on your beautiful body—will be me. *He released her from the confines of his embrace and disappeared with the mist.*

The shrill ring of the motel's wake-up call tore her from sleep. Without even looking, Layla picked up the receiver and slammed it down harder than necessary. For the first time in a long time, she hadn't wanted her dream to end. That was a switch. She pushed herself up onto her elbows and blew the bed-head hair out of her face. She looked around the cheap motel room and squinted at the sun that streamed so rudely into her room.

"Why can't the damn curtains ever close all the way in these places?" Her sleepy mumble echoed through the empty room. The memory of last night's dream was still fresh and raw, which was painfully evident by the heat that continued to blaze over her skin. Layla flopped back down and threw her arm over her eyes. It looked like her bossy stalker was right.

There was no escaping fate.

"Shit."

From *Undone*

White light pulsed and flickered through the club in time with the gritty dance music. The crowd of writhing bodies throbbed with the unmistakable energy of lust as they clamored for a connection—any connection. Hands wandered, looks were cast, and figures melded together, almost becoming one.

Maybe living like a human wouldn't be that bad.

Marianna leaned back in the horseshoe-shaped VIP booth and watched the humans as they danced. The scene before her flickered rapidly between darkness to blinding, artificial light as the strobes flared. She observed couples as they disappeared into the crowd, losing themselves in the music, the sex in the air, and in the moment.

No conversations. Eyes closed.

No past. Bodies touching.

No future. Hips swaying.

No consequences.

Just now.

She sipped her champagne and crossed her bare legs as she witnessed the mating rituals that they participated in with relentless energy. They spent their lives looking for someone to ease the loneliness, with no idea who or what they were looking for. No predestined mate. No clan. No telepathy. No shapeshifting. No powers of visualization. Aging and eventually dying.

On second thought, living like a human was going to suck.

Marianna shuddered and took a swig of her champagne. As a pure-blooded Amoveo female from the Bear Clan, she should have found her mate by now, or he should've found her, but he hadn't. Having past her thirtieth birthday, she could already feel her Amoveo abilities waning, and if she didn't find her mate soon, they would disappear altogether, and she would have to live, for all intents and purposes, as a human.

Mateless. Powerless. Alone.

Yup, she thought, sighing heavily, it was going to suck.

The bass beat vibrated the tabletop beneath her fingers. Hayden sat next to her with his arm draped behind her, wearing his usual air of irritating arrogance. She wanted to tell him where he could stick it, but instead, opted for ignoring him as much as possible.

He hated this place—most Amoveo did because it was owned and operated by vampires—but of course, that's exactly why she came here. Up until tonight, hanging out at The Coven had been a surefire way to keep Hayden and the rest of the Amoveo out of her hair. Apparently, his desire to try and get her to mate with him overrode his innate disgust of vampires.

"I have to admit, Hayden," she said over the music. "I'm more than a little surprised that you came to The Coven tonight."

Marianna glanced at him over the rim of her glass and offered him a tight smile. She could still connect with any Amoveo telepathically, but didn't necessarily want to. She didn't care for being next to him in the booth, so the last thing she wanted to do was invite him into her head.

"You practically live here now." He drained the rest of his scotch. "Although I can't fathom why."

He didn't look at her, but leveled his dark eyes at the humans who passed by their table. Marianna noticed how hard and unforgiving his features were. Hatred and contempt oozed off him like bad cologne and stuck in her throat. She knew most women found him handsome, but she thought he was far too much of an asshole to be attractive.

Hayden was a self-entitled tool who rode his father's coattails with obnoxious ease and made no secret that he wanted her for himself. He wasn't her predestined mate, and he knew it as well as she did, but that didn't stop him from trying. Unfortunately.

"Olivia is my friend, Hayden. If I'm going to go clubbing in the city, then I may as well go someplace where I'm friends with the owner." She narrowed her eyes and struggled to keep her voice even. She didn't want to fight with him. She just wanted him to go away. "I like sitting at the VIP booth and doing a bit of people-watching."

"Your *friend*? She's a vampire," he said with contempt. "Vampires are dirty, disgusting creatures. They drink the blood of humans, which makes them no better than humans. In fact, it makes them worse and puts them far below us on the evolutionary chain. If it weren't for you, I would never step foot in a place like this."

At that moment, a young human girl with dark, heavy eye makeup sauntered by the table and gave Hayden what was surely her most seductive look. Clad in a tiny black dress, fishnets, and several tattoos, she looked like a regular here at The Coven. She ran one hand through her long dark hair and winked at Hayden as she swayed to the music.

Hayden promptly looked away and inched closer to Marianna. The girl shot him a dirty look and turned her attentions to another clubgoer who had almost as many tattoos as she did. Moments later, they were absorbed into the dancing mob.

"As for your *people-watching*," he sneered, "I could do without it. I may as well be at a farm watching pigs wallow in mud."

Your friend looks a tad uncomfortable. Olivia's voice touched her mind gently, and Marianna suppressed a grin. She scanned the club and found Olivia behind the bar with her two bartenders—both vamps. Her bright red hair made her easy to spot in the sea of black. Olivia was the owner of the club, the head of this all-female vampire coven, and one of Marianna's best friends.

He's not my friend, and you know it, but I'm thrilled that he's squirming, Marianna thought back with a smirk. *You have to come over here soon. It will annoy him and hopefully get him to leave.*

He's not bad looking, but you obviously loathe him, and you already told me he's not your mate, so why even bother? Olivia continued to make drinks and tend customers without missing a beat. *Tell him to fuck off.*

Let's just say it's politics. She gripped her champagne flute and gave a slanted glance toward Hayden. *I have no interest in picking sides in this stupid civil war that my people started. However, I'm getting tired of playing nice. Now be a good friend. Get your ass over here, and flash him your fangs.*

Tall, Dark, and Vampire

by Sara Humphreys

She always knew Fate was cruel...

The last person Olivia expected to turn up at her club was her one true love. It would normally be great to see him, *except he's been dead for centuries*. Olivia really thought she had moved on with her immortal life, but as soon as she sees Doug Paxton, she knows she'd rather die than lose him again. And that's a real problem...

But this is beyond the pale...

Doug is a no-nonsense cop by day, but his nights are tormented by dreams of a gorgeous redhead who's so much a part of him, she seems to be in his blood. When he meets Olivia face-to-face, long-buried memories begin to surface. She might be the answer to his prayers...or she might be the death of him.

Praise for* Untamed*:

"The characters are well-developed, the twists and turns of the plot are well-crafted, and the situations are alternately funny, action-packed, and sensual." —*Fresh Fiction*

"An excellent paranormal romance with awesome world-building and strong leads." —*The Romance Reviews*

Acknowledgments

As always, a big shout-out to my editor, Deb Werksman! Thank you for your support, patience, and understanding. Most of all, I thank you for giving me my first book contract. Many thanks to the rest of the editorial team: Susie, Eliza, Skye, and Cat!

Thank you to Danielle J. for her publicity efforts and the amazing art department at Sourcebooks. I love my covers!!

Big hugs to my agent, Jeanne Dube! As a working mom with four children, you definitely "get me." Thanks for everything!

Thanks to the various community relations managers at Barnes & Noble who are always willing to have me in for book signings.

I, of course, have to thank my awesome street team gals and guys—Sara's Angels. You are awesome, and I'm so blessed to have you in my corner.

Last, but certainly not least, my biggest shout-out goes to my husband and our four sons. What on earth would I do without all of you? I love you madly.

About the Author

Sara Humphreys graduated from Marist College with a degree in English literature and theater. She started her career as an actress. Her credits include *Guiding Light*, *As the World Turns*, and *Rescue Me*. She specializes in public speaking, presentation development, and communication skills training. But she has loved romance novels and sci-fi/fantasy for years, beginning with *Star Trek* (she had a huge crush on Captain Kirk). She is now married to her college sweetheart, with whom she has four boys and two "insanely loud" dogs. They live just outside of New York City, a perfect inspiration for things that go bump in the night.

Sara's fascination with sci-fi/fantasy eventually grew into a love for all paranormal creatures, including ghosts, shapeshifters, and the undead. She considers herself a hopeless romantic and a sucker for happy endings.

Sara's first manuscript caught the eye of a major national bookseller, who championed her publishing career. Sara utilizes her acting skills during her writing, using sense-memory recall and creating backgrounds for her characters so they have a history. Even for shapeshifters, she researches the animals and utilizes their natural traits in her characters as they take on their forms.

You can find information about upcoming books on her website: www.sarahumphreys.com.